R.A.W. Hitman

S. Hussain Zaidi is a veteran investigative, crime and terror reporter with a career spanning decades. His previous books include *Mafia Queens of Mumbai, Dongri to Dubai, Byculla to Bangkok, Mumbai Avengers* and *Eleventh Hour,* some of which have been adapted into popular Bollywood films. Hussain Zaidi lives with his family in Mumbai.

R.A.W. Hitman

The Real Story of Agent Lima

S. HUSSAIN ZAIDI

SIMON & SCHUSTER

London · New York · Sydney · Toronto · New Delhi

PARAMOUNT

First published in India by Simon & Schuster India, 2023

7 9 10 8 6

Simon & Schuster India
818, Indraprakash Building,
21, Barakhamba Road,
New Delhi 110001.

www.simonandschuster.co.in

Paperback ISBN: 978-93-92099-64-9
eBook ISBN: 978-93-92099-63-2

Typeset in India by SÜRYA, New Delhi
Printed and bound in India by Replika Press Pvt. Ltd.

For
Dr Shabeeb Rizvi,
My Friend and Mentor

CONTENTS

Foreword

S. Hussain Zaidi towers over the world of true crime writing in India. He is widely recognized for his seminal works on the Mumbai underworld and is considered a moving encyclopedia on the commercial capital's mafia. His books *Dongri to Dubai, Byculla to Bangkok, My Name is Abu Salem,* etc. are reference books on the Mumbai underworld and are grist for the Bollywood mill. He is equally drawn to the genre of espionage and spy thrillers. *Mumbai Avengers* written by him has been adapted into a popular Hindi movie called *Phantom*. He has written the screenplay for the web series *London Confidential,* a spy thriller, currently showing on Zee5. It is, therefore, not surprising that the story of commando Lakshman Bisht, who claims to have been a hitman for one of India's secret service agencies, has drawn his attention and interest. This book, *R.A.W. Hitman: The Real Story of Agent Lima,* is based on extensive interviews that the author has conducted of the self-professed assassin.

Besides being a hugely successful author, Mr Zaidi has encouraged and promoted many other aspiring writers to get published. One of them is me. I met him at the launch of his book *Byculla to Bangkok* in 2013 where I was invited to be the chief guest and was in conversation with him. Since I had dealt with many members of the *dramatis personae* of the book, I did not hesitate in pointing out factual errors. I was rather blunt and held no punches back. I thought that I had annoyed him sufficiently. But it is his greatness that the following day he met with Chiki Sarkar, the then editor-in-chief of Penguin Books and convinced her that I had many stories to tell from my long career as a police officer. A writing contract from Chiki was on my table the following day. I had been served with a fait accompli and thus commenced my dalliance with crime writing. *Dial D for Don* and *Khaki Files*, published by Penguin, are fruits of this relationship.

I feel that it is in the same spirit to promote others, particularly from government agencies who are privy to personal tales of crime and criminals, that he is drawn to the story of commando Lakshman Bisht, as narrated to him by the self-proclaimed hitman. The story is rather intriguing. A youngster from the hills of Uttarakhand is recruited by one of the central intelligence agencies, given specialized commando training in India and in Israel and deployed in various locations in the strife-torn northeast, and then as personal security officer of VVIPs, including our now prime minister. Around the same time, an agent by the name of Agent Lima is deployed to execute a local arms dealer in Uttarakhand. He carries out the hit job successfully. But Lakshman Bisht is caught by the police and has to spend several years in jail as an accused in the case. Eventually he is acquitted and has now brought his story to the world.

As a career policeman, I have several issues with this narrative. Firstly, no operative of an intelligence agency worth his salt would come out in the open to reveal the details of such operations in public. Secondly, it is equally hard to believe that the agency, whose task is to collect external intelligence, would ask its hitman to conduct such an operation where the target is a local arms dealer. Lastly, even if we give credence to the story of Lakshman Bisht, his chest-beating in public is difficult to fathom.

Irrespective of the incredulity of Bisht's story, the master craftsman that S. Hussain Zaidi is, he has narrated the tale in his inimitable style and with his customary panache. His fans, who number millions, would find it hard to put down. The narrative unfolds and builds up gradually evoking the reader's interest and then gripping it intractably. It then proceeds at a rapid pace, leaving the reader breathless. The book is engaging and unputdownable and is bound to find its way to the silver screen giving commando Lakshman Bisht immortality and fame, and the author's legion of fans another gem to savour.

Neeraj Kumar
(Ex-Delhi Police Chief)

PROLOGUE

The Man in the Backseat

6th September 2011, Nainital, Uttarakhand

Half an hour past midnight, raindrops pelted the roof of the Ford which was speeding past the jungles of Bhowali. The car was being driven by Rajendra Pargai aka Raju Pargai—the most dreaded criminal of Uttarakhand. Pargai's love for speed was at its peak as the speedometer flickered around the seventy kmph mark. It was as fast as one could drive on these mountainous roads.

Amit Arya, seated beside Pargai, gulped down a mouthful of beer directly from a glass bottle. Arya was Pargai's confidante and partner in crime. At just thirty-three years of age, Pargai's dossier of crime was filled with cases of outrageous audacity. Most recently, Pargai had smashed the skull of a man named Dangwal under the wheel of his SUV. He had also been accused in the murder of one Yogesh Sunehri of Haldwani which had taken place six months ago.

Arya passed the bottle of beer to another man who was seated in the backseat of the car. This man had recently befriended Pargai and Arya (or so they thought). But Pargai and Arya had no clue that the man in the back was not just the messenger of death but the incarnation of death itself; a trained assassin par excellence.

The car strode a few miles further. The man in the backseat took the last swig from the bottle and threw it away. Glass shattered as the bottle hit the tar. The man put his clammy hand on Pargai's shoulder and raised his pinkie finger to indicate that he wanted to pee. Arya chuckled.

Pargai swerved the car to the side of the road and put his foot on the brake. They had stopped near an area known as Shyamkhet. The man opened the rear side door and made his way to the bushes in the distance. As he lowered his track pants, he checked the pistol which he had concealed in his track pants. The weapon was already cocked. The man had taken a great risk by carrying a cocked weapon. He couldn't afford to cock the weapon in the midst of the night as the sound would have echoed greatly in the silence of the jungle. The man took his time to empty his bladder. In the distance, there was the constant chirp of crickets.

"Hey," Arya shouted from the car. "Are you going to piss all night?!"

Pargai laughed at the joke. It was the last time anyone would see him smiling. The man said nothing and started walking back towards the car. Seeing that they were almost ready to go again, Pargai turned on the ignition of the car. Soon enough, the man reached the car. But instead of opening the door to the back seat, he knocked on the dark, tinted window of the front seat.

Arya rolled the windows down. "What the fuck are you waiting for now?"

Boom. The man aimed his 7.65 mm pistol and fired a single bullet which entered Arya's skull and exited through Pargai's temple. A loud noise pierced through the ubiquitous silence of the night. Dead. Both criminals were dead. The shooter felt Arya's warm blood on his face and wiped it off with the sleeve of his shirt. The windscreen of the car was also smeared with blood.

The shooter checked Pargai's and Arya's bodies for signs of life. No pulse. No breath.

A headlight appeared in the distance. It was a random biker who happened to be passing through the area. The biker was wearing a helmet and he happened to glance at the car as he passed. And then, perhaps the biker realized what had occurred. He halted his bike a few metres ahead. The biker turned his neck and found that the shooter had now pointed the gun in his direction. The shooter gestured with his gun, signaling to the biker that he wanted him gone as quickly as he had arrived. The biker, for the love of his life, turned his wrist on the accelerator. He sped away like he'd seen a ghost.

The shooter pulled out his mobile phone and switched on the flashlight. Pointing the light on the ground, he desperately began searching for something. A few seconds later, he spotted what he was looking for; the casing of the bullet which had ejected out of the pistol in the aftermath of the shot. The casing was resting in the vicinity of the crime site from where it could be recovered easily by the cops who would arrive at the site in due time. Surprisingly, this is exactly what the mystery man wanted. He made no effort to hide the casing.

Then the shooter took a bag filled with notes which was placed on the backseat and carried it four hundred metres away from the site. He flung the bag in the bushes, hoping that the cops would find it when they swept through the area. If he left the bag in the car, it was likely that the witness who would find the body and report it to the cops would also find the money and keep it for themselves. If the cops would find the money, it would be evident that the murder was not a supari (contract) killing.

The shooter now checked his wristwatch, waiting for the second half of his plan to come to fruition. As if on cue, two more cars arrived at the scene. One of the cars was an Alto while the other was a Scorpio. Four men alighted from the cars. They were carrying swords, choppers and guptis (a traditional Indian blade shaped like a walking stick which can be carried in a concealed case) in their hands. The men darted towards the shooter with hasty steps. The darkness grew grimmer by the moment. Incremental rain had washed off the blood from the shooter's face and hands. The four men stared at the shooter. They were his companions.

"Are you fools waiting for the police to arrive as guests in your baraat?" the shooter shouted at the men. He looked towards the Ford. "Those two are still breathing. Kill them!"

The men rushed towards the car and began attacking the two dead bodies with all their might. The shooter stood at a distance and heard the sounds of sharp metal cutting through human flesh. This went on for a minute or two. The four men came back to him, panting for breath.

"They are minced meat now," one of the four men said.

The shooter walked back towards the car. The four men followed him. The shooter now pretended to check the vitals of the victims he had killed only a few moments ago.

"Useless bastards," the man shouted at his associates again. "You can't even handle a sword properly. What am I paying you for?"

The four men were confused. "Why?" one of them asked. "What happened?"

"These two are still alive," the shooter said. "Finish the job!"

The shooter ordered them to pick up the boulders which were lying nearby and smash the skulls of the victims. The men obeyed. They picked the heavy boulders, hoisted them above their shoulders and threw them on the bodies of the slain with full force. Cracking sounds were heard.

The shooter now smiled. An important part of his job was done. The state of Uttarakhand had got rid of two menacing criminals that night. All it took in the end was one bullet. But not many knew that the firing of this bullet was the result of months and months of planning.

The shooter ordered his men to get back into the cars while he lingered around the crime scene for a few more seconds. He looked around. Wind rustled through the trees. With deft hands, the shooter undid the holster of his weapon from his waist and dropped it in the footrest of the Ford where the two criminals lay dead.

Then the shooter got inside the Scorpio. The vehicles turned around and left a trail of smoke and dust as they sped away. They drove for a good thirty-five kilometres before the shooter asked them to stop at a certain point. He shook hands with his associates and jumped out of the car and bid them goodbye. "Go underground," he advised them.

Then the shooter kept walking till he disappeared from their sight and into the forest. He reached his hideout on foot where he disassembled his pistol, part by part. He put each part of the pistol in the pressure cooker. Then he put the pressure cooker on the flame of the stove and allowed the steam to cleanse the weapon. The steam began clearing the stains of chromite which had gathered inside after the weapon had been fired. Then he used a certain oil, known as ox-52, to clean each part of the pistol. After assembling the weapon again, the shooter hovered his hands above the flame. The oil which he had used began to drip off his hands. Now his hands were clean.

As the clock struck three, the shooter began planning his next move. The men he had killed were two of the most dreaded criminals of the state. If there was retribution, it would be ruthless. He had to escape; and perhaps disappear into the darkness of the night forever.

one

Arrested

6th September, 2011, 8:00 am

Twenty-three-year-old Laxman Bisht aka Lucky Bisht, a commando from the formidable National Security Guards of India, was sleeping at his family home in Haldwani. He had arrived from Delhi nine days ago after taking a leave from duty as the personal security officer of Shri L.K. Advani, a prominent politician of the country. Days ago, Lucky was informed that his mother was suffering from an unusually high bout of fever which had not receded despite medication. So the young commando had traveled back home to take care of his mother.

Lucky's home in Haldwani, Uttarakhand was located in the defense colony where other defense personnel and their families lived. His father had served with the army and his grandfather was also a martyr of the 1971 Indo-Pakistan war which had resulted in the creation of Bangladesh.

Around 8:00 am, Lucky's sleep was disturbed by loud and incessant rapping on the door. When Lucky's father answered the door, he was surprised to find a huge contingent of policemen at the doorstep. Eight police vehicles had surrounded the house. Haldwani was a relatively small village where nearly everyone knew everyone. Lucky's father recognised some of the officers who had now barged into the home—Vijay Choudhary, Pramod Shah and Senior Superintendent of Police K.S. Chauhan were present among many others.

Lucky woke up after his father prodded him in the back. With sleepy eyes, he appeared in front of the police officers. His mother, sister and grandmother were standing by the walls of the house with worried looks on their faces.

"Where are your personal weapons and ammunition?" SSP Chauhan asked. The question was evidence of the SSP's knowledge of the high position Lucky occupied in the Defence Agency and the kind of weapons the position permitted him to carry around.

The SSP had conducted his research well. Being a commando, Lucky had two personal weapons—a 7.65 mm pistol and a shotgun—both of which were licensed by the government for use across all of India. Besides these two, Lucky also had a Glock pistol which was issued to him by the government as a part of standard equipment. Lucky had duly deposited the Glock back at the weapons unit in Delhi before proceeding on his leave. The licensed personal weapons he owned, however, were at his home.

As part of his training, Lucky was adept at using weapons. His outstanding tactics included ambidextrous firing. He could fire a carbon machine gun without pulling the trigger. He could cock an AK-47 using the barrel alone without using the cocking handle which is the standard method of usage.

"Where are the weapons?" the SSP said.

Lucky had only taken a step towards the almirah when the cops immediately stopped him. Clearly, they did not want him anywhere near a gun. The SSP asked a constable to open the almirah.

"Do you have a search warrant?" Lucky said.

"No," the SSP said. "But if you don't cooperate, I'll put a danda inside your ass so that a warrant can come out with it."

The news of cops being present at Lucky's home had spread like wildfire. Residents of the area had assembled outside with animated curiosity. The media had also reached the location and were trying to get inside the house but the police were blocking them with force and a volley of verbal abuses. On orders from the SSP, a constable retrieved the pistol from the almirah along with a set of rounds. The SSP glanced at the weapons and smiled. He patted Lucky on the back.

"Chal," he said. "Come with us."

"Why?" Lucky said.

"Nothing much," Chauhan shrugged. "Routine enquiry."

"I want to make a phone call."

Lucky knew this was anything but a routine enquiry. No sooner had he asked for the phone call, the policemen confiscated the two phones which Lucky owned. They insisted on taking him to the station. The cops had been respectful towards his family members and Lucky had no choice but to comply if he wanted to keep it that way. His mother was in tears now. Not bothering to change the blue jeans and white shirt that he was wearing, he slipped his feet into his regular flip flops and made his way to the door.

"I'll be back in a few hours," Lucky said to placate his mother.

He was led outside, where it appeared that all of Haldwani had gathered. The media rushed towards him but the cops bundled him into the waiting Bolero. The rearmost section of the Bolero was occupied by three policemen. Pramod Shah moved into the front passenger seat. In the middle section, Lucky was flanked by two policemen who had their hands on their loaded weapons, ready to shoot if the situation arose. The car began making its way to the local police station.

A few moments into the journey, Pramod Shah turned his neck around. "Where were you last night?"

"Why are you asking me this?"

Shah grinned. "You'll come to know soon."

As soon as the Bolero reached the police station, Lucky was made to get out of the car. Two policemen were still guarding him from both sides. SSP Chauhan had already reached the station, followed by the procession of media personnel, and had been waiting for Lucky to arrive. He flew into a rage when he noticed that his men had not handcuffed Lucky yet.

"Fools!" he thundered at his men. "I'll suspend your asses."

The next moment, the cops forced Lucky's hand behind his back and clamped them together by the tight grip of the handcuffs.

The posse of cops at the station included two of Lucky's close friends—Virendra Chauhan and Jeetu Arya. Additional Superintendent of Police, P. Renuka, IPS was also present. Lucky remembered her vividly as he had conducted an explosive detection training for Uttarakhand Police about six months earlier where P. Renuka was also present along with two hundred other personnel.

A handcuffed Lucky was lugged into a huge conference room. A large round table was placed in the centre with a number of chairs encircling it. A number of senior officers took their seats on the chairs. Lucky was made to sit on a bench. He was seething with rage on account of being handcuffed. The cops hadn't even told him why they had brought him here. Nor had they officially arrested him. Lucky tried to calm his anger by filling his stomach with a mouthful of air.

But nothing could have prepared him for the question which the SSP was about to throw at him.

"Laxman Singh Bisht," said SSP Chauhan. "Let's talk."

"About what?" Lucky asked. "The weather?"

"No." SSP Chauhan spoke after a pause. "Tell us why you killed Raju Pargai and Amit Arya?"

Lucky took a moment to play the question in his mind again. Had he heard it correctly? Yes, he had. The gravity of the situation hit him like a slap in the face. He had promised his mother that he'd return home in a few hours. But if he was being accused of a double murder, he was in for a long haul. He blanked out and felt that the earth was slipping from underneath his feet. To add to his woes, the men he was being accused of murdering were not only two of the most dreaded criminals in all of Uttarakhand but also the favourites of some powerful politicians of the state for carrying out their dirty jobs. Now he was scared for his own life.

two

Blind Man's Bluff

All eyes were on Lucky in the conference room where he was being interrogated. Beads of sweat dripped down the side of his neck. He felt that the walls of the room were closing in on him. Lucky did not provide a clear response to any questions about his official role in the Indian Army. He did not want to indicate that he was working for the *Agency*.

"Why did you kill Pargai and Arya?" SSP Chauhan asked.

"I did not kill them."

"You knew Pargai, didn't you?"

"Is that a crime, huh? He was a naamcheen gangster," Lucky said. "All of Uttarakhand knew him. But he'd never have become so famous if *some* people took their jobs seriously."

Lucky's curt responses drilled a hole in SSP Chauhan's ego. Other officers were surprised that a suspect had shown the gall to speak to the senior officer in such a manner. Lucky was implying that the cops had allowed Pargai to blossom under their noses owing to his connections with powerful politicians of the state.

"We have other ways to make you speak," SSP Chauhan said.

"Try using the best one."

"You think we are chutiyas?" SSP Chauhan said. "You fired your weapon. Then you cleaned it. You think we'd not figure that out?"

The SSP barked for Lucky's confiscated pistol to be produced. A sub-inspector obeyed the command. The SSP then directed the sub-inspector to load three rounds into the weapon. The sub-inspector put on a pair of gloves and wrapped the handle to the pistol with his handkerchief to ensure his fingerprints weren't imprinted on the weapon. The three rounds were loaded into the pistol.

On further orders from the SSP, the sub-inspector dashed out of the conference room and headed towards the open garden. A few moments later, Lucky heard his weapon being fired thrice by the sub-inspector. With each shot, Lucky felt that the policemen were hammering a nail in his coffin. Such fake evidence would be used in court to prove that the weapon had been fired recently. The sub-inspector then entered the conference room again. The barrel of Lucky's pistol was still emanating whiffs of fresh gunpowder.

The holster recovered from the scene of the crime was brought in front of Lucky. It was secured inside a sealed pack. The rounds which were fired by the sub-inspector were sealed in another pouch of plastic. The sub-inspector announced to the SSP that the holster was fitting the pistol perfectly.

The SSP and a forensic scientist, who was dressed in civil clothes, signed on the package. This exercise was conducted to intimidate Lucky into pleading guilty. Though Lucky was worried, he put on a poker face to prevent the cops from getting a whiff of his fear.

"So you want our best shot?" SSP Chauhan said.

Lucky nodded.

"Let's see if you can take it."

The SSP had a word with his juniors and ordered them to take

Lucky to a different place. Two sub-inspectors escorted Lucky out of the conference room and tugged him towards the exit gate where a police vehicle was waiting for them.

Again, Lucky was made to sit in the passenger seat. Two sub-inspectors flanked him. Other police vehicles started following them to an undisclosed location. Lucky had not eaten a morsel since morning. Though he was offered food and water a number of times during the transit, he simply refused. He was afraid that the cops would spike his food or drink and force a fake confession out of him. Moreover, he hadn't been able to make contact with the Agency or any of his family members yet.

As Lucky was being taken to the undisclosed location, his father was running from pillar to post to obtain information on his son. The Kotwal at the police station informed him that Lucky had been taken into custody for a routine interrogation and will be back home by the next morning. His father did not know what else to do. He was calling his contacts but help was not forthcoming.

Meanwhile, the police vehicle drove for nearly forty kilometres before stopping outside a five-star hotel near Bhowali. Lucky was worried that the cops were taking him to such a luxurious hotel. Surely, they hadn't booked a suite for him there, Lucky thought. *What were they up to, then?*

Around 5 pm, Lucky was taken to a room on the top floor. Inside, Vikas Chaudhary who was in-charge of Uttarakhand's Special Operations Group (SOG) was gazing into the screen of a laptop and tapping on the keyboard earnestly. The SOG is a crack team of cops which conducts operations across the state and also conducts encounters of criminals when the need arises.

Chaudhary had an imposing personality. The man was a Randeep Hooda lookalike, clean shaven and well built. Of the three pistols he carried, only one was licensed. Cold gusts from the air conditioner sent shivers down Lucky's spine. Chaudhary closed the lid of the laptop and turned his steely gaze towards Lucky.

"You called someone at 11 pm last night," Chaudhary said. "Who is that person?"

"A friend," Lucky said. "I talk to him regularly."

"Why?"

"Just to say hi and hello."

"Why did you call him again at 4 am?"

"Just to say hi and hello," Lucky repeated blandly.

Chaudhary smiled at Lucky's impunity. He turned on the television in the room and switched from one channel to another. The media was having a field day, running amok with breaking news based on conjectures and hearsay. One news anchor asserted that Laxman Bisht was the man behind the "dohra hatyakand" (double murder). Another anchor claimed that Lucky was the personal security officer of Mayawati. Some reporters were suggesting that he was the security officer of then Gujarat CM Narendra Modi. However, the news which disturbed Lucky the most was the allegation that he was working for an organized criminal syndicate.

Chaudhary offered food and water to Lucky, which he refused. However, Lucky asked to use the washroom which Chaudhary allowed on the condition that Lucky would not shut the door and that one of his officers would stand guard outside. Chaudhary's magnanimity stemmed from the fact that he knew Lucky personally from their earlier interactions.

But late into the night, Chaudhary and his four men bundled a handcuffed Lucky into an unmarked police vehicle. This time, Chaudhary also put a black mask over Lucky's face. Lucky felt like the prisoner who was being masked before being hanged in the gallows.

Lucky could not see a thing as the vehicle rumbled to life.

Soon, the car was swerving from one side to another at high speed. Lucky tried to conjure a path in his mind, trying to use his knowledge of the roads to figure out if Chaudhary was taking him towards the jungles where the SOG had conducted encounters of notorious criminals in the past. His heart started thumping. As it was 1:30 am, the date had moved to 7th September. Lucky wondered if his death anniversary would fall on this day each year.

When the car stopped, Chaudhary's men dragged Lucky out of the vehicle. The forest was as silent as a dead man's grave. Not even a bird flapped its wings. One of Chaudhary's men pulled the black mask off Lucky's face. To his horror, Lucky found himself staring at the business end of Chaudhary's pistol!

"It was a high precision shot." Chaudhary, standing at a distance, eased into his shooting stance. He was referring to the single shot which had killed Raju Pargai and Amit Arya. "Only a trained man could have fired it."

"I didn't fire that high precision shot," Lucky said.

Chaudhary cocked his weapon. "Don't test my patience," he said. "Tell me. Why did you kill Pargai and Arya?"

To scare Lucky further, Chaudhary cocked his weapon for the second time. But this turned out to be a mistake. Now Lucky began smiling as he realized that Chaudhary was trying to bluff him. If Chaudhary's pistol was truly loaded, a round would have moved into the chamber when he cocked it for the first time. And if a round had moved into the chamber, it should have fallen to the ground when Chaudhary cocked his weapon for the second time; while another bullet would have moved into the chamber in place of the first round. However, no round was ejected from the pistol which meant that it wasn't loaded!

Lucky rolled his eyes and called Chaudhary over, gesturing as if he wanted to tell him a secret. Chaudhary grinned. He felt that Lucky was about to confess his crime and moved closer. Lucky leaned over Chaudhary's soldier and whispered a question into the cop's ear.

"Do you feel brave when encountering handcuffed men?" he said. "Have you ever done a real encounter on a real battleground?"

Chaudhary had a puzzled look on his face.

"My score is 139," Lucky said, "All genuine. No handcuffs. So if you are done with your games, let's get moving."

Chaudhary realized that Lucky had called his bluff. He did not want to be embarrassed any further in front of his men. So Lucky was bundled back into the police vehicle by the SOG team who drove him to Bhowali Police Station and threw him into the lockup. Now Lucky awaited the next move of the cops, even as he began planning his own.

three

Haldwani to Tel Aviv

Laxman Singh Bisht aka Lucky was born in 1985 in a village called Boongli located in Pithoragarh district, Uttarakhand. The village is so far behind the times that it awaits pukka roads to this day. Young men from these regions have an inherent inclination to serve the armed forces of the country. Families in the village take great pride in sending their children to protect the borders of this great nation.

Lucky's family was no different. His father had worked with the Ministry of Defence. His grandfather was a Subedar with the Indian Army and laid down his life to pave the way for the Indian army's victory against Pakistan during the 1971 war. Lucky's father was also adamant that his son would serve the armed forces and groomed him for the same from an early age. Lucky and his two sisters were enrolled in schools and his father paid equal attention to the educational needs of all his children.

Lucky studied in a local school up to the fifth standard and then shifted to his aunt's place in Jaipur to continue further studies in an urban school. As soon as Lucky passed the tenth standard examinations, his father sent him a form to fill for an entrance test into an “Agency” which was running under the aegis of the Ministry of Defence.

On 12th December 2003, Lucky was sent a call letter from the Ministry asking him to report to Dimapur, Nagaland for the initial round of testing. His father promised to pay him three thousand rupees to cover his expenses for the trip. Lucky readily agreed to visit the north-eastern state of Nagaland. He had heard much about the beauty of the region and wanted to experience it firsthand. He packed his bags and boarded a train to reach Dimapur on the stipulated date.

Many aspirants had come for the tests from different nooks and corners of the country. Initial enthusiasm amongst the aspirants, however, started to wane as the nature of testing was very tough. Dearth of space and lack of general comfort added to their woes. The testing centre was surrounded by many shops, all in dilapidated condition. The aspirants had no choice but to take refuge in the shops to sleep during the night.

The aspirants formed groups of twelve students and paid hundred rupees each for sleeping in those shops for a night. One bed sheet was provided to each student by the shopkeepers but there was no bed. Lucky vividly remembers being crammed with eleven other students inside the small shop with a single bathroom and an unyielding floor. But even then, he felt a sense of camaraderie and brotherhood which he had never experienced before.

The testing was not child’s play by any measure. The army men who were conducting the tests were real taskmasters. A mistake as small as a slacking posture when standing was punished with severe beatings on the backside.

The first physical test was to run 1600 metres in less than five-and-a-half minutes. Lucky passed the test as he completed it in five-and-a-half minutes. This was followed by a 100-metre sprint to be finished in less than eleven seconds. Lucky passed this one too with flying colours. He was an expert runner and had been practicing sprints and long distance running for months. The training which his father had been providing to him was finally bearing fruit.

Lucky then completed sixteen pull-ups as ordered by the army men. He followed this up with sixty push-ups in less than a minute. Now it was time for leaping across a nine feet ditch. To this day, Lucky remembers the exhilarating feeling of flying through the air and landing on the other side. "I felt that I'd grown wings," he said.

Written tests were also conducted where the aspirants were asked basic questions from the elementary school curriculum. The last examination was the medical examination. The aspirants were made to strip and were subjected to several physical examinations. After spending a fortnight in Dimapur, Lucky was finally going to return home.

He returned to his normal life of playing cricket and wandering on the streets of the village with his friends. After a month-and-a-half, Lucky had forgotten about the tests and its impending results. But one fine morning, he got a call informing him that he was required to report at the Bangalore Training Centre. He had passed all the tests in Nagaland for which nearly one lakh and forty-two thousand students had appeared. His father was overjoyed on hearing this news!

In Bangalore, Lucky was subjected to another medical test along with the others who had cleared the tests in Nagaland. Psychological tests were scheduled to begin soon.

When his roll number was called, Lucky entered the room which had a table on one side. Four men and a woman in civil clothes were seated behind the table. To put Lucky at ease, the interviewers started with basic questions. This test was tricky because the psychological consistency of the aspirant was put under considerable scrutiny. The psychological test is a game of nerves between the aspirant and the psychologist. Sometimes, aspirants get asked bizarre questions to test their reactions to certain situations. A psychologist may also raise their voice and express anger just to see how the aspirant deals with the stress.

As the conversation progressed, Lucky expressed that he would like to join the army. The lady on the interviewing panel countered him by asking what he would do if he was not posted as a soldier on active duty but deployed as the Personal Security Officer of the Prime Minister of the country instead.

"Will you fulfill the given responsibility with honesty?" the psychologist asked.

"Of course," Lucky said. "To the best of my abilities."

"Between your mother and sisters, whom do you admire more?"

"My mother," Lucky said.

An interviewer interjected. "Does that mean you don't admire your sisters?"

Lucky was caught off guard but he regained his composure quickly. "I do admire my sisters, but I admire my mother the most."

"You appear to be short tempered," another psychologist said.

"No," Lucky said. "I am calm under most situations."

"What would you do if you were visiting the market with your sisters and a man teased them?"

"I will break the bones of that man."

The psychologist smiled. "Didn't you say that you keep calm in most situations?!"

Lucky was puzzled. But later he realized that the psychologists were only assessing his personality by his responses. The next three months were spent as "zero week" in Bangalore. Basic training in discipline and drills was provided. Sometimes, the cadets would march to the tune of left-right-left all day at the training ground. They were also given tasks such as sweeping the floor, dusting the room, polishing shoes, etc.

On 19th April 2004, the cadets were taken to the Delhi International Airport. An IL-76 aircraft, a four-winged airlifter introduced in India by Indira Gandhi and subsequently christened as IL-76 Gajraj was waiting at the airport. Lucky did not have any clue as to where they were being taken. He had never applied for a passport but the government had arranged a temporary one for his travel.

About one hundred cadets boarded the aircraft. After flying for two-and-a-half hours, the plane halted at a location. The cadets were not allowed to disembark from the plane. No one knew the location of this stopover. To this day, Lucky does not know where the plane had halted. Then the aircraft took off again and landed at Tel Aviv, Israel.

A military truck was waiting to pick up the cadets. Lucky now understood that he was in Israel for his commando training. At that time, he had no clue that the training would test him beyond the limits of physical and mental endurance.

four

Snake Pit

Tel Aviv, 2004

Lucky and his batchmates sat encircling the snake pit which was covered with short mounds dotting across its entire surface. Each mound had burrows filled with snakes. Zora Singh, a course instructor at the commando training centre in Israel, stood fearlessly in the midst of the pit. He was an imposing figure, deputed here by the Indian military in collabouration with their Israeli counterparts. His broad shoulders and booming voice were enough to make a mortal shiver in absolute fear. For a man who was fifty-four years of age, Zora Singh was spectacularly fit.

Zora Singh thrust his hand in one of the burrows. Moments later, like a magician pulling a rabbit out of his hat, he pulled out a slithering cobra from its hold. The reptile hissed, wriggled and twisted but there was no escaping Zora Singh's strong vise.

He shifted the snake in his left hand nimbly and let it coil around the forearm. Reaching for his pocket with his right hand, he pulled out a sharp knife that reflected the afternoon's sun off its dazzling surface. Then the veins in his wrist popped as he slid the knife under the snake's head. The head of the cobra was ripped from its torso in a mere blink of an eye. Blood gushed forth from its headless body.

Zora Singh's sonorous voice filled the air. "Commandos!" he said. "The one who can eat a snake will never die hungry."

He skinned the dead reptile with his bare hands. His assistants lit a fire in the ground and Zora Singh roasted his lunch over the flame. Lucky watched in utmost fascination. His admiration and respect for Zora Singh would multiply with each turn of the dead snake being heated on the fire.

Zora Singh carried a grim air about him. He demanded the best from his cadets. Even the smallest of mistakes incurred the greatest of punishments in Zora Singh's books. He was amongst the senior-most veterans in the academy. Many soorma cadets had passed under his hand and he had crushed them at first and then reformed them into the finest of officers and soldiers. He was a recipient of various accolades from the Ministry of Defense in India.

At the end of the day, whenever the trainees would be drained out to the last breath of their lives, Zora Singh would resort to an antic which became a nightly ritual for the rest of Lucky's training.

"Commandos," he would say. "My house is five kilometres away. My wife has been waiting for me to return all day. On my last order, you must shout so loud that my wife should know that her husband is on his way home."

Then Zora Singh would shout: "Commando, line *tod*!"

The commandos would scream so loud that it appeared that they would wake up all of Tel Aviv at this unearthly hour. Lucky would feel the strength return to his lungs and shout along with young men of different nationalities. Zora Singh would allow the cadets to stop only once he was assured that they were back in a state of complete wakefulness.

Lucky and his buddy pair, Hencho, a fellow trainee from Portugal, had been at the receiving end of Zora Singh's severe lashes on their backsides as punishment for minor lapses. Lucky's buttocks had blackened with the beatings. And if he turned around and looked closely in the mirror, he could see the imprint of Zora Singh's boot on his ass. Lucky wore these scars with pride. It was a rite of passage to ... toughness.

Lucky and Hencho did not even speak a common language. Both of them knew bits of English. Yet, they were expected to work together. The first week also saw rigorous training in the slithering section where the trainees had to master the skills of slithering down the rope from a helicopter.

"Commandos, I want you back on the training ground in fifteen minutes," Zora Singh would command sternly before giving them a meal break.

All cadets would disperse and scramble for their bicycles and for the purpose of transit from one training ground to another. And in those fifteen minutes, they were also expected to finish their lunch. Many times, Lucky did his drills on an empty stomach for hours on end as the time allowed for eating simply wasn't enough for everyone to be able to eat.

Hencho was shorter than Lucky but he was fitter. He would beat Lucky to the bicycle race to and fro from their rooms. The two would come to share an invaluable bond during their two-and-a-half years of training. Lucky, on the other hand, was already manifesting a knack for extraordinary skills with the handling of the weapons.

The initial days also consisted of psychological training once trainees were done with the exhausting physical exercises for the day. The trainees would be ordered by Zora Singh in his intimidating voice. "Go back to your rooms, change into army clothes. And report to the classroom in thirty minutes."

This would be followed by the usual rush of the worn-out trainees hurrying back to their rooms on their bicycles and pedaling all the way by summoning whatever energy was left in their bodies. The instructors in the classroom would read from books of philosophy and psychology. Zora Singh would go around the class carrying a long stick in his hands to keep a vigil on students who tried to steal even a few winks of sleep.

Lucky would not even let his backside rest on the chair because he feared that he would doze off and then Zora Singh's stick would sting his back with such force that his flesh would burn for the next thirty minutes. He would just half-sit on the chair such that his hips would be hanging in mid-air. Hencho once gave in to fatigue and sat properly in his chair. Eventually his eyes closed. It was like a slow death. Lucky noticed and tried to wake him up before he attracted Zora Singh's attention.

"Hencho, no sleep." Lucky whispered in broken English. "No sleep."

Alas, he was too late. The sharp rap from Zora Singh's stick on Hencho's ear sent him flying at least a couple of inches in the air before he landed back on the chair. As night fell, Lucky and Hencho were back in their rooms, laughing about the incident and looking forward to a few precious hours of sleep. But Lucky could remember Zora Singh munching on the snake as if he were eating a chicken lollypop. Lucky knew that soon enough, he would be standing in the snake pit and be expected to eat one too. He began preparing his mind for that moment by repeating Zora Singh's words in his head: *The one who can eat a snake will never die hungry.*

five

Third Degree

September 2011

The room in the police station was devoid of light and windows. Lucky was sitting on a chair. His hands were still handcuffed on his back which forced him to sit somewhat slouched. He gazed at the team of policemen who had encircled him. A solitary bulb hanging from the lofty ceiling only added to the grim atmosphere. The soles of Lucky's feet brushed against the jagged floor. The bathroom, which was situated in a corner, was indistinguishable from the rest of the room. The air reeked of insufferable stench and sludge.

The SSP stepped forward. "Why did you kill Pargai?"

Lucky felt something snap in his head. Until this moment, he had never abused the cops. But now he couldn't bear it anymore. They were asking him the same question and expecting a different answer.

"Bhenchod," Lucky said to the SSP. "Am I a tape recorder that will keep playing the same song again and again?"

The SSP fumed. On his signal, the constables pulled out thick ropes and chained Lucky's hands to the chair. And just as quickly, a few cops crouched and tied Lucky's legs to the chair. They pulled his jaw apart and stuffed a bandage into his mouth.

"I warned you Lucky," the SSP said. "We have other ways of making people talk."

The SSP kicked the chair, and the force of his kick coupled with Lucky's weight threw the chair to the ground. Now the chair lay horizontally on the floor which hoisted Lucky's feet in the air. The SSP jerked his head. A couple of policemen produced a long, solid sugarcane stick from a corner of the room. Before Lucky could get a grip of the situation, the cops began smacking the sole of his feet with the cane, employing ruthless force.

Lucky screamed with each strike. But no sound emerged from his throat. The bandage shoved in his mouth denied him even the least outlet of relief. He could only hear a solid rapping sound on one foot which would be followed by a more powerful rap on the other. Each hit sent a sharp sensation of pain from his legs to his brain.

The SSP interjected his questions between the whacking. "Tell me," he said. "What was your motive for the murder?"

Lucky's soles swelled. The veins in his feet throbbed. He bobbed his head from left to right and produced stifled sounds from his gagged mouth. Then Lucky nodded his head as if he wanted to confess.

The SSP gestured to one of the policemen to pull out the bandage. "Couldn't stand a little caning, could he?" the SSP sniggered. "Some commando he is."

However, as soon as the constable pulled out the bandage, Lucky went on a rant which left the policemen even angrier than before. "Motherfuckers!" Lucky screamed. "Untie my hands. I'll cut all of you to pieces."

The policeman quickly replaced the bandage in Lucky's mouth.

The beating continued until Lucky had no strength left to scream. Many whips later, the cops were also tired and decided to take a break. The SSP got up from his chair and left the room. Two policemen lifted Lucky's chair up and set it upright on the floor. His handcuffed hands were brought forward and they left him with a policeman pointing his AK-47 at him.

A constable walked in with a plate of food. He tread cautiously and placed the plate next to Lucky's chair and retreated at lightning speed. The plate contained dal, chapati and some rice. Lucky mustered all the power in his bound legs and kicked the plate in the air. The plate went wobbling and hit the wall opposite to the chair, causing all its contents to spill onto the wall and the floor.

The constable jumped in response to the clattering sound. He looked from the spilled food to the upturned plate and then stared at Lucky. Then he ran out of the room.

An hour or so passed. Lucky anticipated that the policemen would return any moment. He closed his eyes and rested his head on the chair while wondering what his parents must be going through. He had promised his mother that he wouldn't be away for long. And as he sat there wondering, minutes changed into hours with no sign of the SSP and his band of torturers.

Around what Lucky estimated to be around 5 pm, a man clad in civil clothes entered the room. Appearing to be in his late forties, the man approached Lucky with sheafs of papers clipped onto a writing pad while assuming the air of a high-ranked professional. Lucky knew that he must be one of the forensic experts. A constable waddled into the room as well. He undid the shackles from Lucky's legs and took leave.

"I am Dayal Sharan," the official said while shuffling through the papers. "Fingerprint expert." He paused. "Laxmant Bisht, I've learnt about the offense for which you have been arrested."

"Can I tell you something?" Lucky said.

"Go ahead."

"There's no way I am going to cooperate with you," Lucky said. "You can fingerprint my ass if you want."

Dayal was shocked at Lucky's petulance. Still, his greed was overpowering as he suggested that Lucky had murdered Raju Pargai for a huge bounty. There could be no other reason. "I mean," he said, "an elite commando will commit such an offense only if the return is exorbitant." He paused. "The papers in my hands are going to prove crucial once the trial begins."

Lucky understood the doctor's hint. The doctor was seeking some monetary benefit for going easy on him. He took a moment to process the information. A plan took shape in his head. He made some mental calculations. He did not want to let this golden opportunity go to waste. It was an opening he wanted to capitalize on.

"I will give you a phone number," Lucky said. "Dial the number. Tell them I asked you to call. And quote a figure of your choice. They'll pay you the amount you want."

"Any amount of my choice? Are you sure?"

Lucky nodded.

"Give me the phone number," the doctor said eagerly.

"Not so fast," Lucky said. "You have to promise me something in return."

"What do you want?"

Lucky demanded that the doctor should take his fingerprints. And then the doctor should sign the papers on which the fingerprints are taken with the current date. The doctor agreed without skipping a heartbeat. He took Lucky's fingerprints from all fingers of both hands and the ten digits of the feet. For a man who was greedy, the doctor kept his end of the bargain and signed the papers with the current date, 7th September, 17:00 hours.

"Now give me the phone number," Dayal said. "Quick."

Lucky rattled a ten-digit phone number which the doctor noted in his personal diary.

"Make sure that you tell them the code: 19420," Lucky said, "it will make them recognise you and treat you accordingly."

Tucking the spectacles in his shirt's pocket, Dayal glanced gleefully at Lucky before trudging towards the door. As Dayal exited the room, Lucky could not help but let a silent smile spread across his face. The number which he had dictated to the doctor was a phony one. In reality, the phone and the code number were both fake and useless. But the papers on which the doctor had signed and dated would go on to benefit Lucky tremendously when the trial would begin. For now, Lucky decided to hold his cards close to his chest.

He recounted what had just happened. His smile had begun to turn into a maniacal laughter. But then the door was kicked open. The SSP and his men had returned. Their faces looked as angry as ever. And they were carrying more ingenious tools of torture.

six

Red Chillies

A constable came forward with a coil of rope in his arms. The rope was flung through a hook nailed to the ceiling while Lucky's legs were wrapped with a bedsheet before binding them with another length of rope. The bedsheet layer was a precautionary measure taken to prevent any external injuries on the accused before he was produced in the court.

Lucky was heaved with his legs up and hitched to the rope such that he hung upside down from the ceiling. A mound of red chillies was placed right under his face. The SSP lit a matchstick and put the chillies on fire. The burning pile began to exude billows of smoke which wafted straight into Lucky's nostrils. It first induced an interminable coughing which was followed by inflammation in the eyes and a scorching visage. Lucky turned and twisted from the rope tied to his legs but it did little to mitigate the suffering. His senses started to give way. The room, it appeared, was rotating around him.

The suffering grew unbearable. Still the SSP seemed in no mood to stop the torture. Lucky decided to feign unconsciousness and play possum. Gathering enough resilience to withstand the malignant smoke entering the orifices of his nose, he dropped his handcuffed hands, shut his eyes close and let his body hang limp. A couple of minutes of complete inactivity on Lucky's part had the SSP concerned. He did not want to be responsible for the custodial killing of the prime suspect of a high-profile murder.

"Get him down," the SSP said. "Quick!"

The cops obeyed the command. After ten minutes of dabbing and nudging by the policemen, Lucky acted as though he was coming out of his fake unconsciousness. The next ten minutes saw the SSP yelling, screaming and thumping and stamping his feet in an effort to elicit a confession from Lucky.

"This motherfucker won't speak easily," the SSP said. "Let's take him on a virtual tour of Shimla."

Four to five policemen swung into action and stripped Lucky's clothes. He was stark naked. Another reverberating command from the SSP caused two orderlies to haul a bed-sized slab of ice, mounted on an iron rack with two sling belts into the room. Lucky was hurled prone on top of the slab and was secured against it with the sling belts. A searing sensation that seemed to originate in his guts went shooting up into his head and hit him like the blow of a hammer.

A policeman made sure that Lucky remained tightly bound to the ice by driving a roller up and down on the back of his naked body. His body started losing temperature rapidly. His brain was next in line to succumb to the punishment. Hallucinations. For a moment, he really felt that he was in Shimla and enjoying the snowfall. Breathing became harder by the second. Everything began to fade. He felt the last round of roller going up and down his body. Then he faded into darkness.

Hours later, Lucky had no idea where he was when he heard his name being called out by a woman. "Lucky," a feminine voice whispered. "Lucky?"

He toiled hard to lift his eyelids to look at the source of the voice while regaining consciousness. The effects of hypothermia caused by the ice slab were slowly starting to withdraw and he was getting back to his senses. Bit by bit. With a blurred vision, he saw that a pretty woman was beckoning him through the caged door of the room. Lucky then realized that the cops had pulled him down from the ice slab, put his underwear back around his groin and left him on the floor. As his vision cleared, he figured that the woman was a three-star police officer. The jail gong went three times, the time was three in the morning. He shuffled towards the door to attend to her call.

She spoke in a dulcet voice. "Lucky," she said. "Your loved ones are worried about you. Do you want to speak to them?"

Lucky nodded.

She pulled out a brand new Blackberry from her pocket and held it out for him. "Call the person who is most important to you at this time."

Lucky was still in a daze. He didn't know what to do. He simply began walking away from her. She called out to him again. "Call the person you love the most."

Lucky stopped in his tracks and turned back. There was indeed someone whom he wanted to speak with. At that time, he was in love with a girl. He wanted to let her know that he was alive and she shouldn't worry about her as he hoped to get out of there soon. But then he saw that handcuffs were clasped around his wrists. He raised both hands to show that to the officer.

"I'll get them removed," she said.

The officer ordered the constable who stood guard near the door to get the keys. The constable hesitated and cast an apprehensive look.

"Get the keys," she said firmly, "He's an innocent man."

The constable ran to another room and returned with the

keys. After trying herself and failing, she asked the same constable to unlock the handcuffs. Lucky snarked, thinking that a three-star officer didn't know how to unlock a handcuff. The constable completed the task and removed the handcuff from Lucky's left hand. He let the other remain such that it was hung loose from his right hand.

Lucky took the phone and started pressing the keypad wearily. Beep. Blaap. Beep. He was about to press the fourth digit when his brain recovered fully from the ice slab trauma. He realized the gravity of the blunder he was just about to commit. The officer was apparently sent to take undue advantage of his drowsy state and beguile him into sharing the contact number of his beloved one so that they could get hold of that person and put Lucky under psychological duress.

Again, something snapped inside Lucky's brain. Letting out a dreadful howl, he hurled the phone towards the wall. The phone blazed through the air and smashed hard against the wall, causing it to burst open. The body of the device was scattered to one side and the battery, which got expelled from the phone to another.

The lady officer gasped. "Bhenchod. Mera naya phone tod diya!?"

Lucky went mad with rage. He stamped upon whatever remained of the phone several times until he was certain that he had rendered it completely useless. But he was not done yet. He picked up the mangled piece and tried to wrench the SIM card out, bleeding his fingernail in the process. He bit the sim card several times. The lady officer kept abusing him while more constables gathered.

But none of them dared to venture inside the cell because Lucky's handcuffs had been removed. He was slinging the handcuff as a weapon now, warning anyone who came close to the cell to keep away. "Step back," he screamed. "Or I'll burst your head open in such a manner that no doctor will be able to stitch it together again."

Then as the lady officer watched in complete horror, Lucky put this SIM inside his mouth, crunched it under his teeth like a piece of meat and spat it out towards her. He had unleashed his beast mode.

The constables started convincing Lucky to calm down. The SSP arrived. He ordered Lucky to stop.

Lucky stormed to the door full speed, swung his right hand. *Bang*. The handcuff landed on the iron door and produced a mortifying noise that rang through the air for a few seconds before slowly dying down.

"The cop who enters my cell is a dead man walking," Lucky said.

The SSP's face lost colour. He looked in the direction of the policemen, each one of whom looked equally terrified. As a last resort, the cops brought a massive flood light and threw its intense light directly over Lucky's face. The beast now retreated to a corner of the room. His rage seemed to have gradually subsided. Lucky slumped in a corner and dozed off with nothing but the underwear to cover himself.

He spent the night dozing on and off to make sure no one sneaked into the room and put him back into handcuffs while he fell asleep. Meanwhile his mind kept wandering towards an idea which he hadn't been able to conceive in its complete form. But out of the blue, the idea struck him like a bolt and he snapped his eyes wide open. It was the morning of 8th August.

He strolled to the door and told the guard that he wanted to meet the SSP.

"Why?" the guard asked

"So that he can screw your ass." Lucky dismissed the question. "Go call him!"

The guard scurried away. The SSP got the entire team along with him. All the cops entered the room with their weapons drawn, including the three-star lady officer who was still mourning the loss of her new Blackberry. They all stood forming a circle around Lucky.

"I did *it*," Lucky said. "I won't be able to take more torture."

The SSP smiled. He was convinced that he had broken down the suspect. "Where is the murder weapon then?" He asked, oblivious to the far-sighted scheme playing in Lucky's mind.

"It's hidden in a forest," Lucky said.

The SSP heaved a sigh of relief. Once they recovered the swords, knives and guptis which were used to slash Raju Pargai and Amit Arya, the case would turn heavily in favour of the prosecution. "Okay," the SSP said. "Take us to the place where you have hidden the weapons."

Lucky simply nodded. In his mind, he had conceived a game plan to save his life and he was doing his best to stick to that plan.

seven

Hidden Weapon

Lucky swayed side to side with the two policemen who flanked him in the Bolero which was bound towards the location where Lucky claimed to have hidden the weapons. The cops, occupying three Boleros in all, were looking forward to finding the swords, choppers and guptis which were used in the murder. The journey was due to last nearly six hours.

Jeetu, an acquaintance of Lucky from earlier times, from the Special Operations Group (SOG) was amongst the police party accompanying Lucky in the vehicle. Sub-Inspector Daanu, seated in the front passenger seat, was part of the expedition. He turned around and smiled at Lucky. With the supposed confession, things between Lucky and the cops had eased a lot.

Lucky returned an expression which was between a smirk and a smile. He was waiting for the Agency to get wind of the situation and make an intervention. The Commanding Officer (CO), Subhash Arya, struck an avuncular conversation with Lucky, wanting to know about his family and village.

Subhash Arya, a man wizened by old age, was high in spirit and amiable in disposition. The hardship of the long journey was lessened to some extent as they both chatted, laughed and cheered before Lucky noticed a dhaba at the side of the road.

"Wait," Lucky said. "Stop the vehicle."

"Why Lucky beta?" Subhash Arya said.

Lucky pointed his finger outside the window, towards a roadside dhaba where tandoori chicken was being cooked. Pangs of hunger clinched his stomach. His mouth watered. *When will I ever eat a chicken tandoori again?*

Lucky told the cops he would lead them to the weapons only if they let him eat a tandoori. It had been two days since his unofficial arrest on 6th September, two days since he allowed a morsel of food to go down his throat. Grudgingly, SI Daanu ordered the policeman behind the wheel to turn around and park beside the dhaba. The Bolero pulled in next to the dhaba. Lucky had barely stepped out when SI Daanu stood in front and waved a couple of pieces of papers in his face.

"Sign these papers," Daanu said.

Lucky examined the papers. It was blank, with no government marks or emblems upon it. Lucky fully understood that Daanu would take his signature on the paper and then write that Lucky had confessed to his crime and taken them for recovery of the weapons. But Lucky was also aware that such a confession would not hold even a drop of water in a court of law. He readily signed the blank paper.

"Oye," Lucky shouted at the waiter as he headed towards the dhaba. "Get some extra masala ready for my tandoori!"

The cuffs were taken off from Lucky's left hand while he ate. He relished this meal to the fullest and licked his fingers clean at the end. The handcuffs were put back on as the cops and Lucky resumed their journey towards the jungles of Champawat. They reached the spot at 5 pm and headed into the forest.

"Lucky beta," Subhash Arya said. "Where are the weapons?"

Lucky scratched his head. He looked around and pointed to a spot. Quickly, the constables began digging. They dug a few feet before things came to a grinding halt.

"Stop!" Lucky said. "That's not the place."

The cops looked at him with disgruntled faces. Lucky led them to another spot and asked them to start digging again. But the cops were flabbergasted when Lucky stopped them again after they'd dug for another twenty minutes. He kept taking them from one spot to another on the pretext that he was confused about the location of the weapons.

"It's too dark," Lucky said. "I can't remember"

"We have to find the weapons, beta," CO Arya said.

But by then dusk had settled in and the place turned into a dark and forbidden territory to foray into any further.

"I am sure I'll be able to remember the place tomorrow morning in ample light," Lucky said.

Daanu and Arya had no choice but to grin and bear it. The entourage checked themselves in a lodge for the night. Daanu ordered tea and biscuits for all. The cops and the accused were eating at a table together. Subhash mentioned to Lucky that there was tremendous pressure on the police to crack the case. Raju Pargai was close to a powerful politician of the state who was pressuring the department. Lucky told the cops that he understood their plight.

Night fell. The cops were a little relaxed after dinner. The conversation took many turns and drifted from hidden weapons to politics. Each policeman was also guessing the true nature of Lucky's work. Whom did he work for? Was he serving with the Indian Army? Or the SPG? Or the NSG? What was his exact position? No one seemed to have definite answers and Lucky wasn't providing them with anything either.

Lucky, who had kept his distance from Jeetu so far, signaled to him to pass his phone. Jeetu was currently working with the Special Operations Group of Uttarakhand but had known Lucky for a long time. When no one was looking, Jeetu passed his phone to Lucky at great personal risk.

Lucky then tried to download the TOR browser so that he could establish a connection with the Agency over the Dark Web. TOR is an acronym for The Onion Router and is a special type of browser which allows for anonymous surfing on the internet and prevents traffic analysis of the websites that one may have visited. It is the browser used to connect to the Dark Web which is a subset of the regular internet. A number of legal and illegal things happen over the Dark Web. Many private and public organizations use the Dark Web to do their dirty work and use it as a medium of communication between its members.

However, the internet connection was terribly slow. Lucky would not have been able to make more progress without attracting the attention of the cops. After several failed attempts, Lucky gave up and returned the phone to Jeetu whose anxiety was quelled after the device was back in his pocket.

At the break of dawn, Lucky was handcuffed and huddled into the van. They went back to the jungles again. It was quite a pleasant sight now. At night, the forests appeared dark and sinister, but they appeared lush and green during the day. On Lucky's directions, the cops began digging again. Dawn turned into forenoon and yet there was no sign of getting any closer to the hidden weapons. Lucky remained elusive and vague about the exact spot. He kept asking Subhash Arya about the time.

"Lucky beta," Subhash Arya said, though he was sounding irritated now. "Where have you hidden the weapons?"

SI Daanu joined the conversation. "Speak up, you idiot!"

There wasn't much time remaining for completing forty-eight hours from the time the forensic expert had taken his fingerprints on the official papers. It meant that the scheme he had in his mind wasn't very far from becoming successful and there wasn't any need to put up a display of unnecessary courtesy.

"*Arre madarchods,*" Lucky dropped the act with a bang. "If you can't find the weapons yourselves, at least find a monkey in this jungle and jack him off."

The SI was taken aback. Subhash Arya's fatherly sentiments also came crashing down. They realized that the person they were dealing with wasn't one to be bullied or intimidated into submission. Lucky just refused to cooperate with the cops now. Daanu and Arya tried hard to convince Lucky to lead them to the weapons but Lucky was having none of it.

Finally, Lucky asked Subhash Arya. "What's the time?"

"It's 3 pm. Why do you keep asking?"

"Because I haven't seen a more inefficient and stupid bunch of cops than the ones in this forest right now."

"What? What do you mean?"

"The journey from Bhowali to Champawat and back is twelve hours at least. Assume I committed the murder at midnight. Then I came all the way to Champawat to hide the weapons. But then how the heck did you all find me sleeping in my house, next morning, at 8 am?"

Daanu's face turned pale. He closed his eyes, heaved a deep sigh of sorrow mixed with anguish and instructed the driver to take them back to the police station. Lucky had played them through and through.

In reality, Lucky knew that law mandates the cops to produce an accused in their custody in front of a judicial authority in twenty-four hours. The cops had held him for days without showing an arrest up to this point. He only wanted to go past the twenty-four-hour mark from the time the fingerprint expert had taken his fingerprints officially so that it would weaken the case of the prosecution. The cops would have to acknowledge, whether they liked it or not, that he was in their custody when the fingerprints were taken.

Daanu was sulking. He couldn't believe he got played into Lucky's hands. He made a last attempt to regain the dignity he had lost in the whole process. "So, where did you actually hide the weapons?" He was trying hard not to appear wounded.

"I immersed them in the Ganga as a mark of respect," Lucky said and let out a laugh. "Let's go to Haridwar then?"

Daanu looked away and was morose for the rest of their journey to Bhowali Police Station. Lucky was in the know of a hidden weapon, but it wasn't the one that Raju Pargai was killed with. Rather it was this move which he had played against the cops, who had run out of time. They had no option but to break the news of his arrest to the whole world now.

eight

A History of Violence

Two men, with their hands bound and mouths gagged, looked up at their captors with teary eyes. A group of three to four goons stared down at them. The goons had swords and scythes in their hands.

"We made a mistake," one of the captives pleaded.

"Please let us go," the other added.

Just then, a heavyset man entered and all the voices in the room were hushed in a reverence that was born more out of fear than respect. Clad in a white kurta, the man's flamboyant gait demonstrated the awe and dread he commanded in Haldwani. During the mid-80s, this region was still a part of Uttar Pradesh. The state of Uttarakhand was yet to be formed as part of reorganization of certain states which were eventually done by the NDA government during 1998-2000.

The population of the town was not even in lakhs but it was considered to be the crime capital of Uttar Pradesh. The only other prominence for the region was that it was one of the largest commercial markets in the state and a town connecting tourists to various hill stations. The laid-back town had rivers flowing by as streams adjacent to rows of houses and limited connectivity in the form of road and railways to other parts of the country. One could hardly imagine that such a picturesque town could be the underbelly of crime.

The man who had entered the room was named Bhopal Singh Rawat and he was quite the terror in Haldwani. Starting his criminal career in the early 80s, Rawat had become a force in the state's underworld to reckon with. Out of the various illegal trades that he commanded dominance over, the Gaula River mining trade was the most precious to him. The route was used for smuggling wood, forest extract and medicinal herbs which were in high demand in the black market. And it went without saying that whoever tried to mess with something that Rawat held dear would meet the same fate as the two men kneeling down in front of him right now.

Rawat sat down in the chair set out for him, leaned close to the two men and stared at them menacingly. The men looked at him like goats being led to a slaughterhouse. One of them brought his hands forward and uttered whatever words of apologies he could manage through his gagged mouth.

"I am a soft-hearted man," Rawat said. "But if I don't make an example out of you, others will dare to finish what you had started."

The men fell on his feet instantly and began to sob and moan incessantly. They were two upstarts who had dared to venture into the territory of the Gaula river and tried to get their hands into the smuggling trade happening on that route. Rawat nodded to one of his goons. The goon pulled out a pistol and shot the two men in the head and they fell dead on the ground instantaneously.

The dead bodies of the two men were discovered the next day at the railway station. They turned into mere statistics, two numbers added to the increasing pile of the deaths caused for control of the illegal mining trade carried out in Gaula river of which Bhopal Singh Rawat was the indisputable king.

Starting as a small trader of wood from illegal cutting of trees from the forest, Rawat's differences with one of the police personnel over the unlawful cutting became the event of his entry into the crime world. The cop was found dead a few days after the dispute. These were border regions of a massive state like Uttar Pradesh and the law-and-order situation was quite out of control. The murder went unchecked and Rawat wasn't held to account for his action. This inaction on the law's part to bring the murderer to book emboldened Rawat and he felled men who came in the way of his business with the same cruelty and regularity that he felled the trees to illegally trade them.

There were reports of several men from the Forest Authority Department turning up dead in the forest and with Rawat's increasing clout and power in the trade, all the fingers of suspicion pointed in his direction. But no one dared to question his authority or speak out against him. He even started exporting wood illegally to Nepal and to other Indian states. Soon, he had gathered a large group of men around him on the strength of which he ventured into other illegal trades such as lisa which is extracted from Pine trees and used to make oil of turquoise and turpentine. He also monopolized the smuggling of Keeda Jadi, a type of fungus extracted from caterpillars and traditionally used in treating various diseases as well as boosting sexual drive. Its trade has been declared as illegal by the Indian government. But the exorbitant returns from the sale of this particular fungus which now go as high as 10 lakhs per kg make it a lucrative business. He also reigned over the illegal mining of khadia, a highly demanded white talc chalk mineral in the cosmetic industry. He illegally traded the mineral and eliminated all possible competition by employing brute force and, oftentimes, inhumane means. He would kill his detractors by flinging them under the blade of the chainsaw machine and ripping them apart as if they were logs of wood. Dead bodies washing up at the shore of Gaula River or roasted to bones in a brick kiln became commonplace.

Two men, Bharat Shah and Ramesh Bambaiya, became Rawat's trusted lieutenants. Bambaiya had worked in the Mumbai underworld and had invited the ire of don Chhota Rajan. To escape Rajan's wrath, Bambaiya returned to his home state and began working for Rawat. By the early 90s, Bhopal Singh Rawat was considered the biggest mafia of the region. Rival gangs and police authorities alike shuddered at the mention of his name. From controlling the mines to overseeing the smuggling of goods from Nepal, Rawat had become a demigod of sorts in the state.

Endless power can make a lot of acquaintances. But it also makes even more enemies. In the case of Rawat, his enemies were none other than those he wined and dined with, i.e., close aides, Shah and Bambaiya. Themselves aspiring to make it big in the crime and political world, Shah and Bambaiya were squirming in jealousy at the sight of Rawat's undisputed rule in the state.

But by virtue of being mere sidekicks of a big-time criminal and possessing little contacts, Shah and Bambaiya exercised restraint when it came to acting upon their jealousy. They waited patiently, hoping for the day their master, in his hubris, would make one awful mistake which would turn the tides against him and set him up for an eventual downfall. In the early 1990s, Rawat announced that he would enter politics and it proved to be that one awful mistake Shah and Bambaiya were eagerly waiting for their master to make. The state's white-collared politicians of the time could not tolerate the sight of a ruthless criminal such as Rawat entering politics and they decided to finally bring an end to his ever expanding reign of terror. They started looking for a henchman to do away with Rawat, and Shah and Bambaiya were only happy to oblige. Within a few months of Rawat's ominous announcement, Shah and Bambaiya, with the backing of high-profile politicians, hacked him to death and the two subsequently became the natural successors to Rawat's unimaginably large empire. Soon the duo rose to power and became the face of terror in the regions formerly controlled by Rawat. Time passed and the same old jealousy that compelled them to kill Rawat raised its head again and Bambaiya got Shah killed in a police encounter to become the sole owner of the large empire of illegal trading and businesses.

Bambaiya was said to be a ruthless man who was once reported to have carried out the murder of 10 people en masse and buried them in a single grave. In his bid to gain a monopoly over the state, he went on a killing spree, murdering key members of his rival gangs, one of whom was Harish Palariya. According to some, the number of murders committed by Bambaiya reached beyond hundred.

Bambaiya was also known to give the slip to the cops by deliberately keeping the railway crossing near his house closed when they would come to chase him. This would give him enough time to escape.

When the state of Uttaranchal was formed (it was renamed Uttarkahand in 2006), Bambaiya was eventually brought to book in early 2000 and was put behind bars in Haldwani. There was emphasis by the newly formed state government to straighten the law-and-order situation. According to some, his imprisonment came a little too late as it was said that Bambaiya was behind the murder of Abdul Rabb.

Abdul Rabb started his public career in Haldwani along with his close friend Middu Khan. Haldwani had more than 30 per cent of Muslim population and this fact helped Abdul Rabb and Middu Khan to quickly rise to prominence during the year 1995. But

Abdul Rabb's friend had different plans in mind and Middu Khan resorted to crime to establish his influence in the state. Abdul Rabb, however, carved out a respectable image for himself through his social work. Whereas his friend, Middu Khan, was gaining notoriety in oppressing and terrorizing the citizens, be it Hindus or Muslims, Abdul Rabb's impartial nature gained him a messiah image in the eyes of the people from both the communities. His increasing influence was envied by many, especially the leaders from the Muslim community that saw Abdul Rabb as a big threat to their power and influence.

One day, Abdul Rabb was sitting in a salon for a shave when bike borne assailants shot him dead and fled. Abdul Rabb died on the spot. With his death, the prospect of Uttar Pradesh seeing a politician with an unprecedented influence and authority over the state as well as the hearts of the people came to an end.

Bambaiya's imprisonment had created a vacuum in the mafia space during the early 2000s and many small-time criminals vied to occupy the throne. One such small-time criminal was Rajendra Bisht aka Raju Pargai. Starting as a small-time rookie in the scene of the crime, Pargai ascended towards the throne of the underworld by leaps and bounds. Pargai had started to dabble in illegal trades that extended up to Nepal.

Over a period of time, Pargai was handling the D-Company's business from Haldwani. The gang would send packages containing arms or narcotics to Nepal through Pargai. The smuggling would take place through Sharda river, also called Mahakali river, which flows along Indo-Nepal's western border. The river covering more than 14,000 sq. kms of area, originates from the Himalayas and connects Nepal and India at Pithoragarh district.

One such instance of arms being smuggled via this route was when Deepak Sisodia, belonging to the Chotta Rajan gang, had gotten a gun delivered to kill Bambaiya, to end the rivalry between his gang and Bambaiya.

The plan was to kill Bambaiya when he was on his way to the hospital, while he was being transported from jail. However, he was unable to accomplish that task and the weapon was lying with him.

He used the same gun when Rajan had assigned him the responsibility of gunning down Mumbai-based journalist Jyotirmoy Dey. Dey was killed by motorcycle-borne sharpshooters on June 11th 2011, near his residence at Powai by Chhota Rajan's men. He had nine exit wounds in his body.

Sisodia was mentioned as an accused in the murder. He was lodged in Amravati jail after he was sentenced to life imprisonment by MCOCA court on May 2nd 2018. But he has allegedly fled to Nepal while out on parole in February 2022.

The rise of Pargai soon started to look like the second coming of Bhopal Singh Rawat. He was even successful in establishing ties with certain powerful figures of the then ruling party. He went on killing, extorting, terrorizing and illegally trading without restraint and without anyone daring to cross his way, that is, up until he made his first visit to the Tihar Jail to meet Prakash Pandey. He started making regular visits to Tihar in the hopes of becoming Pandey's second-in-command and thus gain an unprecedented dominance over the entire state. But little did he know that his meetings with Pandey would eventually land him on the radar of the agencies.

nine

The Rise of Raju Pargai

Around 2004, Pargai had committed a brutal murder which marked the beginning of his reign of terror. He was sitting behind the steering of the car, the engine roaring. His face was red with fury and his hands were stained with the blood of the person who was lying prone on the kaccha road. Pargai had already beaten this man, whose name was Dangwal, to an inch of his life after a heated argument inside a desi bar. Pargai had thrown a punch on Dangwal's face which sent him flying before he crashed to the ground. Then mounting him, he kept punching Dangwal till his face was smeared with blood.

Dangwal's crime was that he had refused to lend his car to Pargai, an SUV which had caught Pargai's fancy. Since the SUV was registered in his name, Dangwal did not want to take a chance by lending it to a reckless Pargai. But little did he know that the refusal would cost him his life. Pargai dragged him outside the bar, all the way up to the car over which the deal had gone wrong. He heaved him and threw him on the road such that his face lay exactly in the path of the front wheel of the car. Then he pulled the car keys out of Dangwal's pocket, got into the driver's seat and turned on the ignition. Pagari drove full throttle, crushing Dangwal's head under the wheels.

This incident had marked the inception of one of the most menacing criminals in the hills of Uttarakhand. Dangwal was survived by a two-year-old son and his geriatric parents, none of them in a position to hold Pargai to the law. In yet another bar, in 2006, where he had a brief quarrel with one of the patrons, Pargai had smashed a bottle and drove it in his opponent's guts countless number of times.

Pargai became synonymous with murder, loot, extortion and bribery. Small-time traders and shopkeepers wouldn't dare cross him and would submit obsequiously to his demands. The people in his neighbourhood despised the fact that he had two wives, but nobody had the guts to say anything to his face. He was also believed to have been in a relationship with a schoolteacher prior to his marriage. And therefore, there wasn't much room for speculations about the perpetrator when one day her dead body was found in the locality. He began to spread his tentacles and widen his dominance. He extorted ten per cent from each player who was making money from mining in the state.

Killing and extortion in Uttarakhand continued at regular intervals and eventually the reins of organized crime was firmly in Pargai's hands. This attracted attention from some politicians and Pargai ultimately ended up striking a covert politico-mafia liaison with a powerful lady politician of that time. The alliance with the higher ups gave him the courage to violate the law of the state that mandated that liquor shops be closed after ten in the night. He would grant protection to liquor shops running after ten in exchange for a hefty sum from the owner. He also put himself in control of who would get the ticket to contest the college elections. The college boys were awestruck at the sight of "Raju bhai" wielding incredible power and authority and began to revere and idolize him.

He, together with his henchman, Amit Arya, would run amok in the entire town. The duo needed little provocation to kill. They soon began a feud with Yogesh Sunehri, who was also a small-time gangster albeit one with the testicular fortitude to challenge Pargai's hegemony.

Pargai made many attempts to eliminate Sunehri but each time the latter would manage to give him the slip. Sunehri could only postpone his impending doom and not repel it. One day, Sunehri was on his way to a court hearing in his car. His eyes fell upon a girl who was seated in an autorickshaw. The exchange of glances escalated quickly, and soon Sunehri leapt out of his car and hopped inside the autorickshaw in the hopes of striking an acquaintance with the girl.

However, one of Pargai's informers noticed that Sunehri had abandoned his car and let his guard down. The informant called Pargai and provided him with Sunehri's location. Pargai and his gang were nearby and began racing towards Sunehri. Amit Arya, who was as good as Pargai's shadow, joined the chase. The duo were riding their motorcycle recklessly and searching for the rickshaw in which Sunehri was seated.

Pargai had kept the pistol loaded and ready. On the backseat, Arya began recording the murder live so that he could use it to threaten his subjects into submitting far more easily in his future exploits. Pargai zoomed past several vehicles before he came across Sunehri's auto rickshaw. Driving parallel to the autorickshaw, he screamed Sunehri's name.

Sunehri craned his neck. Before he could comprehend anything, Pargai stopped the rickshaw and emptied his loaded pistol into Sunehri. And then, Pargai and Arya vanished from the scene, swerving the bike and maneuvering a full u-turn. This had taken place around the year 2009.

Though the murder took place at one in the afternoon in

broad daylight and that too on the spot very close to a police station, Pargai was acquitted within six months by the court as nobody had the courage to testify against him. While he spent the majority of these six months in an opulent hospital by feigning illness, he used the one month he spent in the jail to cement his ties with Prashant Rai, a prominent Maoist leader and an outstanding orator who could brainwash the brightest of minds. Pargai had met Prashant Rai during his brief stint in jail. Not having picked up a single weapon in his life, Rai was capable enough to stir his supporters to rise in arms simply by his oratory. Pargai foresaw himself dabbling in the cross-border dealings and jumped at this opportunity to forge a strong bond with the movement's foremost leader.

Getting away with a high-profile murder committed openly had motivated Pargai endlessly. He became the only person in the town to wander the streets while tucking an unlicensed pistol in his pants such that it lay exposed.

Now that his tentacles had spread wider in the underworld, he began to sink them deeper. And he couldn't have desired it at a better time. Prakash Pandey, one of the most notorious criminals of the underworld was nabbed by Interpol in 2010 in Vietnam and was put behind bars in Mumbai on charges of several murder cases. A few days later, Pandey wrote a plea to the jail authorities to transfer him to a different place as he believed that his life was in danger in Mumbai.

Prakash Pandey was believed to have had a fall out with Chhota Rajan. He was also said to have played a pivotal role in spilling the beans on politician Dilshad Baigh's hideout in Nepal which helped the Intelligence to zero in on Dilshad Baigh and put an end to him and his increasing illegal cross border activities from Nepal. Baigh was believed to have links with Dawood Ibrahim's D-Company.

Pandey's transfer request was eventually granted and he was

transferred to Tihar Jail in Delhi. The well had come seeking the thirsty. Pargai wasted no time in gaining an audience with Prakash Pandey and would pay regular visits to Tihar to placate the gangster and win his confidence.

Prakash Pandey eventually passed the mantle of managing his illegal dealings, that spanned from UP to Nepal, to Pargai. The backing of a powerful politician and a prominent gangster made Pargai even more reckless in his disregard for the law.

With his newfound association with bahubali Prakash Pandey, Pargai carved out a place for himself and made illegal cross border dealings through Nepal. He started smuggling stolen luxury cars from Nepal which would later be used by the Maoists in carrying out terrorist activities in India. Further, he became the intermediary through whom illegal weapons from Nepal would get unlawfully imported into India. The boy who was a new jack on the block of crime in 2006 had become an icon of crime by 2010. He had gained popularity amongst the youth of Uttarakhand owing to his glamorous lifestyle.

Pargai also began aiding the safe passage of shooters from Nepal to India. After providing them shelter in Uttarakhand, he would disseminate these shooters to vital cities such as Mumbai and Delhi for contract killings.

But this meteoric rise of Raju Pargai was not going unnoticed. Soon, he blipped on the radar of Indian intelligence agencies. Noting that Pargai's influence was growing by the day, they took due note. A few weeks later, the agencies also learnt that Pargai had political ambitions and was poised to run for the upcoming elections. The agencies feared that Pargai was on course to become the Dilshad Baigh of India. That proved to be his death warrant.

Around August 2011, an immediate meeting was called by a secret government agency to seal the fate of Raju Pargai. A highly trained assassin was chosen to eliminate Pargai. And the code name of this secret assassin was: *Agent Lima.*

ten

Shoot to Kill

23rd August, 2011. Secret Facility, Manipur

Agent Lima was sitting on his haunches in the shooting range with his left leg folded and propped up; and the right one knelt on the ground. He peered through the scope of his 7.62 mm DSR Sniper Rifle whilst his left palm firmly curled around its barrel. The solidness of his weapon was firm against the slow gusts of wind drifting from the east. Four bags of rubble in the distance of 1300 metres were set as the targets. An earthen pot was placed as the equivalent for a human head on top of each bag. He steadied his breath and calmed his nerves. The imposing frame of the rifle was augmented by the spectacularly austere arms that were wielding it.

He pulled the trigger. The first pot blew into splinters in all directions, grinding to the dust in microseconds. The rest of the earthen pots followed suit as bullets ripped through air, spurred by his incredibly nimble hand-eye coordination and hit their targets.

Agent Lima's training drill—Shoot to Kill—was complete. This was one of the most important drills that an Agency personnel was required to be thoroughly skilled in. It was designed to train the personnel to eliminate their target even in the midst of a large crowd of people. An agent was as good as his last bullet. But Lima had gained mastery in his marksmanship. His ability to fire precise shots without bringing about any collateral damage was unmatched.

Lima removed the shooting muffs from his ears and stood up. Behind him, the company sergeant (havildar) had been waiting for him to finish the drill.

"Agent Lima," the sergeant said. "Report to Colonel Veerabadran's office. Immediately."

He dusted off his military gear and headed towards the colonel's office. The colonel was sitting behind a table, his fists under his chin, glaring at his laptop intensely. Major Kamat was also seated in the same room. Agent Lima marched in and saluted the seniormost officer smartly.

"*At ease,*" Colonel Veerabadran said.

Lima allowed his limbs to relax. Colonel Veerabadran nodded at Major Kamat. The young major laid down two photographs on the colonel's desk. The photos had been clicked from a distance with a zoom lens that clearly identified two men. Lima estimated that the men in the photos were about 28-30 years of age. But their fair faces also had something very insidious about them.

"Look at the chap on the left carefully, Lima," Major Kamat said gravely. "He is your next target."

Lima's eyes were fixed on the target. Major Kamat continued the brief. Rajendra Pargai's ascent into the orbit of crime had taken the security agencies by surprise. He seemed to have appeared out of nowhere. At one moment, it had seemed like he was just a small blip on their radar. But then in a relatively short period of time, he had turned into a behemoth who seemed intent on destroying anything in his path. He was now a threat to national security.

"The man to his right is Amit Arya," Major Kamat said.

Arya was Pargai's man-Friday. The two were inseparable. Arya was as good as Pargai's shadow. The brief to Lima was clear. Arya was not a target. But as collateral damage, if the situation demanded, Arya was fair game.

"Pargai's death will definitely create a political flutter," Major Kamat said. "We are preparing to deal with that."

Pargai was close to a leading politician of the state, and their party was in power at the centre too. Pargai had no allegiance or loyalty to any kind of political party or ideology. He was just a power-hungry criminal who would go to any extent to create his dominant streak and then maintain it at all costs.

It was also important that the Agency would use fair and foul means to eliminate their targets. Sometimes, these methods had also caused them much embarrassment. The Agency had hobnobbed with various members of the Chhota Rajan gang like Farid Tanasha and Vicky Malhotra in 2005 to plan an assassination attempt on Dawood Ibrahim at the wedding of his son with former cricketer Javed Miandad's daughter.

Tanasha and Malhotra were gangsters and wanted by the Mumbai Police in several cases. Mumbai Police tracked them to Delhi when they were in the midst of a meeting with a senior official of the Agency which led to a standoff between two arms of the establishment and created a furore in the media. Having learnt its lessons, the Agency was taking due care to ensure nothing went wrong and using its best man for a new job.

Major Kamat outlined further plans. Agent Lima was to proceed towards Haldwani in Uttarakhand, an area he was familiar with. A safehouse had already been readied for him. There was some local support for logistics but Lima would be working like a one-man stick for most parts of this mission. A new identity had also been prepared for Lima.

Major Kamat pulled open a drawer and fished out a ticket, a

couple of documents and a bundle of cash. "More funds will be made available if you need them," he said.

Colonel Veerabadran chuckled. "But don't overburden the exchequer."

Major Kamat handed over an identification card to Lima. His new identity was going to be of an employee at the Ordnance Factory, Chandigarh. Pargai had a love for sophisticated weapons and Lima was supposed to exploit this trait to draw him closer to his death. The modalities to be executed on the ground were left to Lima. He was a veteran of such missions, even across borders and continents. Haldwani, after all, was his own backyard.

Colonel Veerabadran stood up and ambled towards the window on the far side of the room. "Any questions?" he asked.

Agent Lima shook his head. He knew better than to ask questions of his superiors. The order had been given. He was to execute it. It was as simple as that. The mission had already started inside his head. He knew his objective, the elimination of Raju Pargai, and he was now planning backwards. He could see all of it, though it was a little hazy at first, he was sure that the path would eventually clear.

"Good luck, Agent Lima," Colonel Veerabadran said.

Lima saluted his senior and marched out. Back in his room, he pried open his handbag and stowed the documents in the side pocket. He grabbed his shotgun, disassembled it and placed it into the bag. Then he deposited his .9 mm semi-automatic rifle into it. He picked up two boxes of cartridges. He wouldn't need as many unless he had to take down all of Pargai's gang. That would create too much noise, but he had to be prepared for the worst. But if things went well, two bullets would do the trick for two men. And given his track record, even one bullet would be sufficient for both targets. Lima covered the weapons with his clothes and layered a woolen blanket over them.

He pulled out a little notebook from the drawer in his study table. Inside, there were contact details of some local operatives in the region. The names and numbers were written in codes which only he understood. The local operatives would serve as his clean-up crew.

Setting the alarm clock to five in the morning, he sat upright on his bed and meditated on the seriousness of the task that lay ahead. Implications of his success or failure would go a long way. Like in each mission, there was an element of risk to his life. That was a given in his line of work. But the apprehensions of a new mission were also a given, no matter how many times he had executed something similar. So now he was full of nervous energy and he needed to expend it.

Throwing away the covers, he plunged onto the floor and began a string of push-ups. An hour of vigorous exercise later, the storm in his mind started to ebb and paved the way for calmness. He had only three-and-a-half hours to sleep. Eight hours of sleep were requisites of lesser mortals. He had been through enough sleep deprivation exercises. For Lima, three point five hours was the gold standard.

He clambered back into the bed and drifted quickly into a peaceful sleep. The next morning, before the sun could rise, Agent Lima turned off the buzzing alarm bell, took a shower and dressed up in civil clothes. He picked up the handbag and slung it across his shoulder. Then he headed for the railway station from where he would chart his way towards Haldwani, through rail and road. Now there was just one objective in his sight: to eliminate *his* target. From that moment, Raju Pargai was a dead man walking. The operation was codenamed *Nimloch* which meant sunset in Hindi. Ironically, the sun was about to set on Pargai's life.

eleven

Arraignment

September 2011

The cops called a hurried press conference to declare that they had cracked the brutal double murder case which had rocked Uttarakhand. Lucky was presented before the media by SSP Anant Ram Chauhan who was accompanied by IPS P. Renuka, The CO and Kotwal of Haldwani, Inspector from Bhawali and several other similarly ranked officials. The media came in full attendance. Lucky was standing behind the SSP while the cameras rained flashes on them. Enthusiastic reporters spoke over each other to get their questions answered first while Lucky tried to shield his eyes from the flash of the lights.

"Laxman Bisht, on whose orders did you commit these murders?" One of the reporters asked.

Lucky strained to spot the reporter amidst the continuous camera flashes and a huge crowd of media personnel. Then, looking at the reporter, he said, "Why don't you suggest some names?"

The entire congregation of journalists was stunned and all at once the intolerable commotion came down to silent murmurings. "Tell me the names of your liking," Lucky said, "and print them in all of tomorrow's newspapers on my behalf."

SSP Anant Ram Chauhan quickly weighed in and told the reporter that the investigation was underway and they will be kept informed about the latest developments in the case. He took upon himself to answer the questions from thereon. Lucky listened to the back and forth between the cops and the journalists with utmost disbelief. The cops had prepared a story that they had arrested Lucky on 8th September 2011 at 3 pm from the Bhakra forest on the basis of a tip-off received from an informer.

"Tell them (the media) the motive behind the murders," the SSP told Lucky.

Lucky looked the other way and did not speak a word. The cops tried to bask in their glory for the rest of the press conference. As the media got their masala and dispersed, Lucky leaned over to the SSP and spoke in a muffled voice. "Sir," he said. "You are sending me to jail. I can bear this. Keep my friends and family out of this." He paused. "Please."

The SSP turned his face to look at Lucky and nodded. Lucky was led into the police van handcuffed while an array of at least four police vehicles trailed behind. He was being taken to the Nainital District Court to be presented before the judicial authority.

The vehicle reached the court premises. Lucky peered through the meshed window. The court premises were swarming with media reporters, onlookers, and a crowd of around two hundred and fifty people which mostly consisted of his friends, relatives and other curious people. There was also a group that stood in a separate corner which consisted of prominent lawyers, businessmen and local politicians. All of them wanted to have a glimpse of the man who had supposedly killed two of the most dreaded criminals of the state. The air was as tense as an electric pole.

Lucky stepped out of the vehicle and was greeted by his father. A stout man dressed in a black coat was standing next to Lucky's father. This man's name was Balwant Singh, a reputed criminal lawyer whose clientele included high profile criminals such as bahubali Prakash Pandey. Lucky's father had sought Balwant Singh's counsel to fight the case on behalf of Lucky.

Lucky's eyes moistened upon seeing his father. He was handcuffed and surrounded by so many policemen. The father-son reunion however was short-lived as Lucky was soon tugged away by the policemen and led to the court.

A steady stream of lawyers, clients, convicts and policemen was moving in and out of the court. Lucky's name was called out. He was taken to the witness box. Three policemen stood guard around him.

The judge perused the documents before casting a sweeping glance towards Lucky. On the judge's approval, the public prosecutor rose from his seat and read the statement drafted by the police. It ran thus: "Based on the evidence collected from the crime scene as well as the circumstantial evidence, the police department was sure that the murder is the handiwork of a highly skilled individual who is adept at handling and using firearms. Our first suspicion in such a scenario came upon Laxmant Bisht on account of his presence in the town at the time of the murder as well as the fact that he is a trained operator who is capable of pulling off such an extraordinary assassination.

"We were tipped off by one of our sources that Laxman was reported absconding and had been sighted heading towards the Bhakra forest. The police department planned an ambush and was able to nab Laxman Bisht from the forest on 8th September around 3 pm. A pistol and shotgun which he had on his person at the time were also confiscated."

The public prosecutor took his seat. The judge addressed Lucky by asking, "Do you have anything to say in defense?"

Lucky and his lawyer asserted that the accusations leveled against him are false and are fabricated by the police to wrap the case hastily under political influence. He concluded his statement by pleading not guilty.

The court was adjourned on the note that Lucky will be sent to custody. He was hauled outside the court by the police and allowed a brief meeting with his father before being shoved into the van which was waiting to transport him to the Nainital District Jail.

Lucky's father gave a handbag to his son, which contained a few pairs of clothes and some essentials. Lucky sought his blessings by bowing down and touching his feet while the father pecked his son on the forehead.

"One more battle son," his father said in a resolute voice. "Fight with valour."

Resisting the tears welling up in his eyes, Lucky nodded and took leave. He was now being moved to Nainital District Jail, which was about two kilometres from the court.

On their way to the jail, some policemen expressed relief at the death of the two gory criminals. They also told Lucky that they had nothing personal against him, and all the torture they had put him through was a part of their job which they were obliged to do at the behest of their superiors. "On the contrary," they said, "we sympathize with you and pray for your speedy release."

The journey to the jail was full of roads cutting through the mountains which made the churn in Lucky's stomach even more excruciating. A short while into the journey, Lucky asked the cops to buy him a packet of popcorn from a roadside shop. He kept munching on the popcorn for the remainder of their journey to take his mind off the severity of the travel.

The SSP looked at him in amazement and thought that he'd never seen a man like him in his career of thirty years. Some 200 metres from the jail, the cops and Lucky stepped out of their vehicles and took to walking the rest of the way. The road ahead, for Lucky, was going to be rocky in more ways than one.

Lucky was not surprised that his supposed infamy was preceding him. The inmates of the jail were eagerly awaiting his arrival with bated breath. The news of his arrest had spread throughout the entire state like a wildfire. Lucky was frisked as soon he stepped inside the jail premises. All this time, Lucky refused to let go of his popcorn.

Inmates from each cell huddled near the bars of their cell as Lucky walked past. The jailer, a grubby man in his mid-fifties, escorted Lucky to his cell but never asked him to put his popcorn away.

"This way Commander bhai," the jailer said, unable to pronounce *commando* correctly.

Lucky liked the sound of it. *Commander Bhai.* The jailer gestured towards the assigned barrack and Lucky stepped inside.

"Welcome Commander bhai," said a young inmate.

He came forward to shake hands. Lucky shook his hand and saw that unlike other barracks, which were crammed with prisoners, his was kept under-capacity and had only five prisoners in it. The five were in the perfect range of age, from as young as twenty-two to as old as fifty-five, as if someone had hand-picked them and admitted them inside.

The barrack was spacious with enormously high walls. The jail itself was a mighty relic from the era of British colonialism. A window overlooked the back side of the prison. The washroom was far less filthy than he had expected.

Lucky ambled to a corner, deposited his handbag and sat down. He sprawled his tense legs. A feeling of odd reassurance took over. It was only a matter of time before the Agency would intervene, Lucky thought. *They've surely heard about me from the news which has spread like wildfire in the entire country now.* Lucky looked at the window, which was near yet so far. Two weeks, he thought to himself. That's all it will take to be a free bird again. But he had no clue that he was wildly overestimating his chances. The ordeal had just begun.

twelve

Fourteen-Second Call

On his first night in jail, Lucky noticed that none of the inmates in his cell had slept until he had gone to sleep. This had raised his suspicions that the inmates were spying upon him on the directions of the jailer or worse, they could be Pargai's men lying in wait for him to sleep and then they would hack him to death. Despite his apprehensions, he had slept well. The idea of the Agency being his imminent saviour proved effective in bestowing upon him a good night's sleep.

"Commando bhai," an inmate nudged Lucky early in the morning. "Wake up."

Lucky turned around with half open eyes. The young lad, who walked with a limp, had brought him the morning tea in an old, squalid glass. Handing the glass to Lucky he said that a policeman had come to the cell to wake them up to go outside and line up for the attendance. But upon recognising Lucky, the cop had let him sleep rather than wake him up. The lad further informed Lucky to relax in the barrack and get the "room service" which meant that his food and tea would be delivered to him in the cell and he would not have to line up outside with the other prisoners. Lucky smiled on receiving such kind of hospitality. He was also offered medicine by the doctor during his procedural medical test post entering the jail which would soothe his nerves and offer him a good night's sleep. But Lucky refused. He didn't need any medication or sedatives at this time.

It was eleven in the morning when an orderly entered the cell. He informed Lucky that he should get ready to go back to Bhowali Police Station where Vijay Chaudhary was waiting for him for further interrogation. This time it was a legal order from the court to take Lucky into their remand again for interrogation. Lucky's smile faded and gave way to a grimace. He waved his hand and indicated that he'd be ready in a short while. Lucky was subjected to another medical test before being sent to the remand.

A short while later, he was sitting behind a table in the interrogation room at Bhowali. Vijay Choudhary entered and scurried to his chair and sat opposite him.

"Why am I here?!" Lucky said. "Let me guess." He paused. "Because the interrogation circus is back in town again."

Inspector Choudhary raised his eyebrows in amazement as he stood up and walked around the table. He put his hands on Lucky's shoulders. "We've been scanning through your phone records."

Lucky felt a jolt in his chest as his mind launched into a frenzy to guess what the cops were on to this time. Choudhary appeared to be knowing something which he felt could put Lucky into trouble.

He leaned forward. "Who is Sanjay Arya?"

"A real estate agent," Lucky said.

Sanjay used to stay in the same neighbourhood as Lucky. Their houses were barely two kilometres apart but Lucky had met him just thrice in his entire life. Choudhary strolled back to his chair and sat down. He tossed the follow-up question.

"Why did you call him on the night of the murder?"

"To inquire about a property."

"Your inquiry lasted only fourteen seconds?"

"I am that quick," Lucky said. Then he winked.

Choudhary knew that Lucky was taunting him, perhaps suggesting to the cop that he had committed the crime in a lightning quick fashion, just to get under Choudhary's skin. The cop picked up a file and appeared to go through some papers. Lucky recognised that Choudhary was playing the "file and dossier" trick on him. This is an interrogation technique used to make suspects believe that the cops have gathered a lot of evidence about the crime. But Lucky was aware that cops speak half-truths and whole lies all the time. They can claim to find DNA, physical evidence and witnesses of the crime when none of them exist. Besides, he had the presence of mind to notice that Chaudhary wouldn't have needed to scour through the file to obtain papers which supposedly held such crucial information relating to the case.

"As per the statement of Raju Pargai's wife," Choudhary said, "you took Raju Pargai and Amit Arya to Chandigarh on the pretext of buying sophisticated weapons at cheaper rates."

"Nonsense." Lucky guffawed. "The road on which their dead bodies were found does not even lead to Chandigarh."

Lucky also questioned that in the initial FIR which had been filed with the police, there was no mention of Lucky's name. If Pargai's wife knew that Pargai was in Lucky's company on the night of the murder, why did she not mention it to the cops when the FIR was being written? It was clear that the cops had tutored her into giving that statement.

Still, Choudhary didn't let go of Lucky easily. An hour passed. Choudhary kept throwing questions incessantly but each of them was swatted by Lucky with considerable ease. The cop briefly touched the topic of the fourteen-second call again before playing the last card in his arsenal.

"Does the name of Yogesh Sunehri sound familiar to you?"

Lucky nodded.

"Of course," Choudhary said. "He was your friend. And Sunehri was killed by Raju Pargai. That sounds like a reasonable motive to murder Pargai, doesn't it?"

Lucky got up and sneered. "A senior officer should not go around concocting ridiculous theories and expect a court of law to believe in them. Yogesh Sunehri was an acquaintance, not a friend. And for your information, Yogesh has got two brothers who have more reason to avenge his death than me."

Though Lucky had become slightly aggressive, he was aware that the cops were trying to use his links to Sunehri as a motive for the murder. Lucky also questioned why he would wait for two years after Yogesh's death to seek his revenge?

Finding the murder weapon, Lucky was aware, and the establishment of a motive could strengthen the prosecution's case against him. He had already led the cops on a wild goose chase for the weapons. So now they were trying to pin a motive upon him. But the conversation ended in a stalemate and Lucky returned to the barracks, completely forgetting about the fourteen-second call.

Back in the barrack, the inmates had set up the food for him in the plates and had arranged it neatly on the floor. Lucky was not too surprised to know that these inmates had procured access to the kitchen and the services of the cook by doling out one thousand five hundred rupees to those who managed the jail. Lucky sat and crossed his feet. He began eating with his hands. The daliya was watery so he crushed a bunch of Good-Day biscuits into it and rendered it swallowable.

After the meal, he went to the courtyard of the jail for a stroll. The inmates steered clear of areas where he was treading. He could see them from the corner of his eyes, huddled in the corners, watching him and speaking about him in hushed whispers. He could smell their fears. One inmate raised his hand to his forehead. "Salaam Commando bhai," he said.

The jailer, who looked like he had not slept all night, was watching Lucky from a distance. He arrived and tugged Lucky to a corner and advised him not to mingle with the inmates.

"Pargai was in this jail six months ago," the jailer said. "His cronies are still serving time. Be careful. They may try to ..."

Lucky nodded, knowing that the jailer wanted to say that Pargai's cronies may try to harm him. But he was capable of protecting himself. So he tried not giving any more attention to the jailer.

A rather surprising sight was awaiting Lucky when he returned to the barracks. A group of new prisoners entered the jail. One of them particularly caught Lucky's attention. He was the fourth person in the line. The man, who was as young as Lucky, appeared famished and had despair and dejection written all over him. Lucky rubbed his eyes, unable to believe them.

"Oh bhai!" Lucky shouted. "Sanjay Arya!? What the fuck are you doing here?"

Sanjay Arya, the person to whom Lucky had made the fourteen-second call, had been arrested and was now lodged in the same jail. Lucky rushed towards Sanjay, who instantly began weeping like a child who had been bullied. But why had the cops arrested Sanjay?

Sanjay was a close friend of Yogesh Sunehri. Secondly, Lucky had contacted him before the murder. This had led the cops to believe that Sanjay knew a thing or two about this murder. The cops had then picked up Sanjay for interrogation.

"They thrashed me for hours," Sanjay said. "They wanted me to implicate you."

He lowered his pajamas a little down the waist. Lucky could see that his hips had turned black due to the beating he had received. At first, Sanjay had refused to do the cops' bidding. But then they threatened to implicate his younger brother. He was left with no option. His younger brother had just landed a job with the forest department. A sarkari job in the region was a matter of great pride. People could sacrifice a limb or two for such privilege.

"That was the tipping point," Sanjay said. "I signed the papers and admitted under duress that you were the mastermind and chief perpetrator of the murder."

Lucky's head whirled. He thought that the entry of Sanjay in the scene and the coerced confession could possibly thwart the prospects of his early release from the jail. More so, Lucky would land in great trouble if the cops managed to convince the court that Lucky and Sanjay had collabourated to kill Pargai to avenge Sunehri's death. *Sazaa-e-maut,* the judge would pronounce. The fourteen-second call was starting to appear nothing short of a death warrant. For a moment … Lucky could already feel the hangman's noose being tightened around his neck.

thirteen

Accidental Death

Being in jail was mostly about staring at blank walls and thinking about an uncertain future. Lucky kept ruminating on the grim prospects that would result from Sanjay's arrest and the forged confession which the police had extracted from him. Lucky became extremely restive. Once again, he sought to confer with Sanjay to learn more on the matter and make better sense of his predicament.

Lucky's reputation in the jail afforded him with some special exceptions from the jail authorities. He was able to convince the guards to let him spend some time with Sanjay in the latter's cell when they were done with dinner.

Two bulbs fixed high on the ceiling illuminated the room. The rule in the jail was to *never* switch off the lights. This was done by the cops to ensure that no untoward incidents took place. Sanjay started the conversation by apologizing profusely to Lucky for whatever he did under pressure. Lucky tapped his shoulder and told him that he perfectly understood the situation he got stuck in. But one thing was certain, Lucky decided that very moment, that he would never confess to a crime he had never committed.

Still, he knew that he was in a dark ditch. He wanted to figure out the deepness of this ditch.

"So you were a part of Yogesh's gang?" Lucky asked.

"Not really," he said. "I only did odd jobs for him."

Sanjay admitted that he would perform some underhanded tasks for Yogesh. A few times, he had provided information on some of his rich clientele to Yogesh who had then gone on to extort huge sums from the rich men. But Sanjay himself was not directly involved in any kind of violent activities. He was abetting them.

"And you continued doing these jobs for him until the day he was shot?"

"No," Sanjay said. "I knew when to move away from a fight. Yogesh didn't."

Sanjay had noticed that Yogesh had refused to submit to Pargai's demands unlike the other gangs who had crawled when they were asked to bend. Perhaps, that was the right thing to do for most people when they found themselves facing a monster like Pargai. Some of the local gangs had folded and allowed Pargai to reign over the throne of the mafia king. But Yogesh was fighting like a guerilla, keeping low and bleeding Pargai's gang with small cuts. It was natural that Pargai was looking to make an example out of him.

Pargai first started taking down members of Yogesh's gang. Some shifted their loyalty to Pargai. A few who didn't were silenced forever. And finally, Pargai killed Yogesh too. However, the spilling of blood refused to stop even at that point. After Yogesh's murder, Pargai committed a much more brazen crime.

Pargai was arrested by the cops for the Yogesh Sunehri *hatyakand*. But Pargai took the much sought-after route of politicians when in police custody. He feigned an illness and got himself admitted to hospital for most of his jail term (before the chargesheet was filed). His eagerness to get himself out of jail also stemmed from the fact that he had received credible intelligence about a certain Naresh, one of the members of Yogesh's gang, wanting to testify in court about Pargai's involvement in the murder.

Pargai's sojourn to the hospital was arranged quickly by his politician patrons. The food served to him was lavish and sumptuous. Tandoori. Kebabs. He even got his drinks served in the hospital bed. Once, he even joked that the doctor should drip alcohol into his body through an IV.

His fully air-conditioned and television furnished private room was located in the Sushila Tiwari Hospital. Pargai's acolytes were posted at the door of the room with specific orders to keep vigil and act immediately against anyone or anything that was deemed suspicious. All visitors would be stopped, frisked and get asked several unintelligible questions before being allowed in. But when Pargai heard about the witness from Amit Arya, he was furious.

"What do we do now, Raju bhaiya?" Amit Arya had asked Pargai.

Pargai sprang up from the bed and strode towards his men. "Don't you watch Hindi movies?" he roared. "Finish him before he reaches the court."

Amit Arya had nodded and hastened towards the door with the others to put Pargai's plan into action. Pargai was enraged over the fact that one of Yogesh's men had shown the audacity to give his testimony to the police, despite knowing the fate of others who had dared to do such things. He made a couple of calls. And two days later, a headshot from point blank. He then *settled* the situation with the cops. A fake report citing accidental death was filed by the police. And the sole witness in the Yogesh murder case had vanished like a puff of thin air.

The fake police report cited that the man had died by the bullet of his own gun which he kept tucked beneath his pants, at his waist. It was *deemed* to be a case of accidental firing. Nobody bothered, or chose not to bother, to even think about the basic trajectory of a bullet. If a gun tucked in the waist had fired accidentally, it would cause damage waist down. Alas, the witness had been killed with a clean shot to the temple.

During those days, Paragi had also summoned Sanjay to his hospital room. When Sanjay made the visit, he saw that Pargai's wives were seated next to him. Apart from the police security outside his room, his men were present inside the room with guns in their hands.

Calling him closer to his bed, Pargai warned Sanjay. "You better not open your mouth against me in Sunheri's case."

"Why would I, bhai? I do not know anything about the case. You should watch out for Yogesh's brothers," said Sanjay and wriggled his way out of the room.

Now that his purpose was served, Pargai walked out of the hospital and perched himself in jail. For committing two murders while being charged with one, Pargai spent less than six months behind bars. The court acquitted him for the murder of Yogesh due to lack of evidence and witnesses.

Back in the cell, Lucky stared at the sullen face of Sanjay. The air turned gloomier as the night seemed to be ticking away, one second at a time. Sanjay now brought up the subject of his friends who had been arrested with him.

"The cops also picked up Virender, Prakash and Montu Arya," he said.

Lucky knew Virender Bora and Prakash Bora only by sight. The duo were friends of Sanjay and he had seen them together several times. But Lucky had no clue about the third person. "Who the hell is Montu Arya?"

"He's a rich dog who comes sniffing at the prospect of gobbling down free alcohol."

As it had occurred, Montu was passing by Sanjay's house when he saw Sanjay and his friends stowing away bottles of beer and whiskey in the trunk of the car in which they were going for a drive to Bhavali. Montu's eyes widened and mouth watered as he scurried towards his friends. He stood beside Sanjay like a mendicant who had not had a sip since years. Sanjay turned around and almost dashed into his puppy face.

"Bhai," he said meekly to Sanjay. "Please take me along!"

Sanjay tried to excuse him but Montu was adamant. He nearly forced himself into the car as it was driving away. And then he got picked up by the cops as he was spotted in the area where Pargai had been killed. Lucky and Sanjay let out a hearty laugh at how it began, and how it ended for Montu Arya. He landed behind bars for a few pints of beer. The joke had them in splits for a while before Lucky stood up, exchanged good night wishes and made his way back to his cell.

He staggered over the sleeping inmates to his place. One of them glanced at him by opening his eyes just enough to catch a look. This cemented Lucky's suspicion that the inmates were keeping a watch on his activities. He lay down, gazing at the grubby yellow light, hinged precariously on a single screw. Somehow, he managed to pass the night, whistling a Bollywood song to wash his blues away and eventually falling asleep.

The next morning, Lucky was called to the jailer's office. "Commander bhai," the jailer said. "Someone has come to meet you."

Lucky's heart jumped. He was sure that this visitor had come from the Agency. He was relieved that the organization had at long last stepped in. But this case had exploded to such an extent that it was going to be a hard nut to crack even for the *famed* Agency.

fourteen

First Attempt

August 2011

The bus stopped for a brief moment at Haldwani. Dressed in a t-shirt and jeans and sports shoes, Agent Lima stepped out of it before the vehicle sped away, blowing wisps of dust in the air. Appearing indistinct was a part of the mission. Lima had learnt the art of keeping low, remaining in the shadows and he was going to put it to full use.

After he reached and settled into his hideout, Lima began scouring for ways to establish contact with Raju Pargai. The season was just right as college elections were about to commence. Pargai had started getting involved in student politics. In fact, he was on a campaign trail to instill the fear of God in the candidates who were contesting against candidates of his choice.

During one of those days, Lima found himself in a crowd of onlookers who were thronging the gates of the college. One of their senior fellow students was getting thrashed by Pargai and his men ruthlessly. And not one person in the crowd dared to stop the brute. Agent Lima's blood boiled at this injustice but he was going to wait for his opportunity. His time would come.

Lima made more inquiries and found that a prominent contractor named Shival was particularly being troubled by Pargai and his gang. The shadow of Raju Pargai's criminal empire had spread all over Uttarakhand. Lima prepared to make use of an age-old adage. *The enemy of your enemy is your friend.*

Shival was the perfect catalyst to fast track the process of bringing an early death upon Pargai. The next step for Lima was to obtain Shival's phone number. Given the man's standing in the area, it wasn't all that difficult. Lima contacted Shival and requested to meet him on the pretext of some construction work. Shival sounded uninterested at first. He had bigger worries to take care of.

"But Pargai's dead body can save you a lot of money, yes?" Lima asked.

Shival paused for a second or two, probably to allow the message and the sudden change of voice to sink in. "Where do you want to meet?"

"You choose."

"My place," Shival said. "I will text you the time and address."

Lima had allowed Shival to choose the place to gain his trust. On the chosen date and time, Lima reached Shival's bungalow. Shival was a gaudy man who wore an immaculate white kurta which strained on his voluminous paunch. They sat in the verandah of his palatial house.

Lima cast a glance at the sprawling three-storey mansion which instantly made sense of Pargai's obsession for fleecing Shival. Lima had learnt that Shival had also been building another palace somewhere around which explained the bags of cement and mounds of gravel dotting the sidelines of the verandah. Shival was no saint and had used all means, fair or foul, in building his incredible fortune. Lima was also closely observing the labourers who were milling the verandah to fetch the bags of cement to the construction site. Although the Agency was constantly tapping the calls of each person involved in the secret operation directly or indirectly, Lima still wasn't ruling out the possibility of Shival snitching on him. He just wanted to make sure that there weren't any of Pargai's men lurking in the group of working men disguised as labourers.

Lima told Shival that he was a hitman hired by one of the rival gangs to eliminate Pargai. Shival was happy to hear this but he controlled his emotions well.

"What do you need from me, then?" Shival asked.

"Call Pargai to your house," he said. "Tell him you are paying the 50 lakhs he wants from you."

"Oye!" Shival said. "Are you out of your mind?"

"Just call him here." Lucky shaped his fingers like a gun and fired an imaginary bullet. "I will handle it."

"But I've only got fourteen lakhs in my vault."

Pargai had demanded 50 lakhs from Shival at the time and warned him to pay it in full if he held his life dear. But Lima convinced Shival that Pargai would be dead even before he'd counted a single note. Shival agreed to take the chance, knowing fully well that if Pargai got any inkling of this plan, he would kill not just him but also his entire family. Lima told Shival to speak with Pargai in the open area just outside the bungalow. From the other side, he would get a clean shot on the target. Shival called Pargai and fixed a date for the meeting.

On the agreed day, Raju Pargai arrived. Amit Arya had also, unsurprisingly, tagged along. Shival greeted them and engaged in small talk. Though the weather was pleasant, Shival kept wiping his forehead from time to time and wringed his fingers while speaking nervously to the two dreaded criminals.

Agent Lima was seated in a Wagon-R which was parked on the opposite side of the road, approximately seven hundred metres away. He had already assembled his DSR 7.62 mm gun. Now he rolled down the tinted windows just enough to let a part of the barrel peek into the other side. He set his eyes in the PSO1 scope. Raju's head was in the cross-hair. Lima wrapped his finger around the trigger. All of this was second nature to him. The shoot to kill drill had instilled muscle memory within his system that he was doing all the right things without even knowing he was doing it.

But just as Lima was about to press the trigger, the unthinkable happened. "Damn," he mumbled.

A group of small kids came frolicking upon the mound of sand right behind Pargai and Arya. If he fired, the bullet would take out his target but would also cause fatal collateral damage to the kids playing behind the two criminals. Lima was well aware that if not wielded by dexterous hands the gun he held in his hands could wreak havoc. A single shot could send the bullet piercing through 20 skulls at a time. He tried changing the angle of his shot but it just wasn't working out. Now Lima began to feel the pressure. A bead of sweat dripped down from the back of his ear. If he moved the car, he was sure to catch Pargai's attention which would throw the entire mission in jeopardy.

Agent Lima decided to wait till the kids would move away from the mound. Even Shival was sweating like a hog now. Lima could see that through the scope of his rifle.

Raju Pargai was getting impatient at being stalled for so long. He wanted the 50 lakhs which Shival had promised him. Shival ultimately rose from the chair and darted into the bungalow. Minutes later, he returned with a briefcase which contained the 14 lakhs which he had stored in his vault.

Pargai opened the briefcase and realized that the cash was too less to amount to half a crore rupees. Shival also threw in some jewelry which he had brought along to placate Pargai. But Pargai was having none of it. He started making menacing gestures towards Shival who was cowering under immense fear. Pargai and Arya warned Shival to pay up his dues as soon as he could. Then the deadly duo got back into their vehicle and left.

Agent Lima waited for their vehicle to disappear out of sight and rushed to catch up with Shival who was now sprawled in his chair with a pale countenance. When the blood began flowing through Shival's veins again, he berated and poured abuses on Lima for not keeping his promise.

When Lima recounted the reason behind not being able to fire, Shival plonked back into the chair and muttered a prayer to the Gods. "Pargai could have blown my brains out," he said. He threw his head back and closed his eyes in relief.

Agent Lima stood there and controlled the cold grin which was about to appear on his face. Lima had come fully prepared to eliminate not just his targets but also the sole witness of the shooting, had it occurred on that fateful day. In that manner, the kids had saved not just Raju Pargai and Amit Arya but they had also saved Shival whom Lima would have shot dead with zero regret. But the lifeline in Shival's palm was not going to be shortened now. Lima had already thought of another plan to draw Raju Pargai in his trap. And Shival was, again, going to be instrumental in it.

fifteen

The Gun Dealer from Hell

Days after the first attempt to assassinate Pargai failed, Lima established contact with Shival once again. It was a testimony to Lima's great persistence that Shival finally agreed to meet Lima. The world's most lethal assassins have this ingrained quality to keep taking shots at their targets even if an earlier attempt fails. Former President of France, Charles De Gualle, survived more than 30 assassination attempts including the one which inspired the Hollywood movie titled *Day of the Jackal*. Muammar Gaddafi, former ruler of Libya, was also the subject of several assassination attempts until he was killed by a coalition force on 20th October 2011.

Agent Lima belonged to the breed of assassins who wouldn't let their target get away so easily. During their tête-à-tête, Lima put forth another proposal. He asked Shival to set up a meeting with Pargai and introduce him (Lima) to Pargai as his nephew who was working in the ordnance factory in Chandigarh. Lima knew well that Pargai had a fascination for weapons and that he could use this as a bait for trapping Pargai.

But Shival was aghast at the idea. He stared at Lima with

absolute disbelief. Merely days after surviving a life-threatening situation, here was the man again—asking him to participate in another preposterous adventure with death. Shival's shoulders drooped.

He folded his palms together in an apologizing gesture. "I'd rather put my neck into a crocodile's maw," he pleaded.

Lima cajoled him further by giving him endless reassurances that his new plan was foolproof. Shival kept shaking his head, refusing to cooperate. Suddenly, Lima snapped into his grim reaper's voice and told Shival that he was not going to take no for an answer. He also tucked out his shirt and displayed the weapon he was carrying as a means to display his intentions. The trick seemed to work as Shival came down to the negotiating table.

"What's the plan now?" Shival squealed.

Lima told Shival that he should call Pargai to his bungalow on the pretext of giving away a Scorpio car to Pargai. Lima would be present at this meeting. And Shival should introduce Lima as his nephew who was working for an ordinance factory. "And I'll offer him a Kalashnikov," Lima said. "He won't refuse it for the world."

Lima also told Shival to give 10 lakh rupees to Pargai as down payment for the car. Shival wiped the sweat off his forehead. He had already given 14 lakh rupees to Pargai during the failed assassination attempt. But all this money was insignificant when compared to the cost of his life which was under threat from Raju Pargai. Shival agreed.

Soon after, Lima headed to the only car dealership in town which was authorized to sell the Scorpio car. The salesman at the dealership greeted Lima with a smile on his face and a striped tie around his neck. Lima asked him about various variants of the car, starting with the base version and going as high as the fully loaded model. Lima came to know that the dealership had run out of black colour models due to high demand.

"How long will it take to get the black variant?" Lima asked.

"Sir," the salesman said. "Waiting time is 30 days. I'll arrange a white one immediately."

"No," Lima said. "I'll wait for the black."

And just like that, Lima walked out of the store, leaving behind a flummoxed salesman. There was a method to Lima's madness though. On his way back from the store, Lima got a call from Shival who informed him that Pargai had instantly agreed to meet to discuss the new car. The meeting had been fixed at 11:00 am on the next day.

"He is a greedy, mad dog," Shival said.

"He'll be euthanized in a few days," Lima said.

On the day of the meeting, Raju Pargai arrived with his usual swagger and was accompanied, as expected, by Amit Arya. Shival greeted the two gangsters warmly and introduced them to his *nephew*. Lima smiled perfunctorily and shook their hands. His nerves were as steady as ever. Shival turned out to be a better actor than Lima had anticipated. He pointed his hands towards Lima.

"My nephew works for the ordnance factory in Chandigarh and is also a weapon enthusiast perhaps on a par with you," Shival said. "He has access to the best weapons in the country and even in Nepal."

Pargai's delight doubled at the prospect of access to the ordinance factory from where he could lay his hands on some exquisite weapons. Arya looked equally overjoyed. Lima made them drop their guard further by flexing his vast knowledge of sophisticated weapons. Pargai and Arya listened in awe while Shival kept tucking into the snacks placed on the table to conceal his nervousness.

"Which department do you work with in the factory?" Pargai asked.

Lima knew that Pargai was trying to test him. To gain his

confidence, Lima showed him the ID card which the Agency had prepared for him. His designation was marked as a "works manager". Even though Pargai was impressed, he wanted to test Lima's credentials further. He pulled out the 9 mm pistol which was tucked in the small of his back and flicked it on the table.

"What do you think about this piece?" Pargai asked.

Lima announced that it was a country-made pistol not worth more than eight thousand rupees. Pargai was visibly dismayed. Without any warning, he dismantled the gun so swiftly that Pargai had no time to register a protest. Several distinct parts of the gun, including the barrel, bushing, spring and extractor lay bare on the table. Lima pulled out the firing pin with equal deftness and held it between his fingers. The firing pin was an important component of the weapon. Without it, the gun was good as a piece of stone.

"Raju bhai," Lima said. "How much did you pay for this piece?"

"One lakh fifty thousand," Pargai said with a sense of pride.

"No way!"

"Why?" Pargai said. "Is something wrong?"

Lima pronounced his verdict. "This gun is a piece of crap. Made in Munger."

Pargai just slumped in his seat with his punctured pride. He was disappointed but Lima's display of weapon mastery and his dazzling talks had left him spellbound. Lima notched the spectacle further by offering to sell a Russian-made AK-47 to Pargai. Immediately, Pargai asked for an estimated cost for the weapon.

"Special price for the *bhai* of Uttarakhand," Lima said. "Thirty-five thousand only."

"What are you saying! An AK costs at least 80 thousand even in the black market."

Pargai was drooling, almost. Perhaps, he was imagining himself seated behind the wheel of a glamorous Scorpio with a

Russian made AK-47 by his side. He was probably shooting holes into bodies of various humans while driving at high speed. Lima barged into his daydream.

"Raju bhai, is it true that Shival Uncle is going to gift a Scorpio car to you?" he asked.

Pargai nodded in agreement.

"What colour have you chosen?" Lima said.

"White."

"Good choice," Lima said. "But I think that a black Scorpio will complement your macho personality, Raju bhai." Tactical pause. "Don't you agree, Amit bhai?"

Amit Arya gave an almost mechanical nod of approval.

"Done ji, done!" Pargai said. "The Scorpio *must* be black. Only black. Nothing but black."

On cue, Shival rang the automobile dealership which Lima had visited the previous day. He spoke with the salesman and ordered him to book a black Scorpio. Shival was informed by the salesman about the non-availability of the colour. He asked the salesman to hold for a moment and took the phone away from his ear to speak with Pargai.

"They're saying that the waiting period for a black Scorpio is one month," Shival said.

Pargai snatched the phone from Shival and unloaded himself on the salesman. "Raju Pargai bol raha hoon bhenchod," he said. "Has your *amma* died? No, tell me. Why else would you take a month to deliver a black Scorpio?"

The salesman was probably shitting bricks in his pants on hearing Pargai's name. A lingering silence prevailed before the salesman requested Pargai to hold the line for a moment while he checked with the owner of the dealership to see if a black scorpio could be arranged sooner. When the owner heard that it was Pargai who was asking for the car, he took personal responsibility of getting a car assembled and transported from the production factory in Pune to Uttarakhand in the next 10 days. The salesman also promised Pargai that the car would come with all the accessories pre-installed, free of cost. Pargai's ego was satiated now. He hung up the call.

Shival was still catching his breath. He handed over a briefcase containing 10 lakh rupees to Pargai and Arya. The duo then shook hands with their generous hosts and prepared to leave. Pargai tapped Lima on the shoulder and promised to keep in touch for purchasing the Kalashnikov.

As soon as Pargai and Arya were out of the house, Shival plonked back in his chair and pulled his hair with both hands. He just wanted this entire episode to reach its logical conclusion. But Agent Lima knew that things were now moving in the right direction. Pargai and Arya had booked the car. But if Lima has his way, they would not live long enough to drive it.

sixteen

Drinking Tea with the Cheetah

October 2011

Lucky strode out of his cell, came out of his barrack and stepped into the wide-open precincts. He went straight to the mulaqaat room where the visitor was waiting for him with his hands shoved inside the pockets. A whirlpool of thoughts swirled in Lucky's mind. Why had the Agency taken so long to get in touch with him? Did they really care for him or not?

But first he had to test the veracity of the man's claim of being sent by the Agency. The Agency had given various passcodes to its personnel which could be used to verify their credentials. The cops were guarding them from a distance. Lucky whispered a code just loud enough for the man to hear.

"One-eight-four-nine."

"Two-zero," the man replied.

The man had responded with the correct code. Lucky was now assured that he had indeed been sent by the Agency and gave a nod of approval. There could be no exchange of names. Lucky was sure that even if he asked, the Agency man would only give him a cover identity. The Agency man reassured Lucky that the Agency was trying its best to get him out of jail.

"Where is your ID card?" the Agency man asked.

The Agency had given Lucky an identification proof. It was necessary that the ID card did not land in the hands of the police as it would reveal a lot about Lucky's identity. Lucky had also taken due care to keep the card hidden. He told the Agency man to go to his home and ask his (Lucky's) father for the keys of his car. Lucky had purchased a Hyundai car only a few years ago. The ID card was hidden under the covers of the backseat of the Hyundai which was parked in the garage of his house.

The man gave a courteous smile and reassured Lucky that he would be out in no time. Lucky knew that the man was overpromising, but he wanted to believe him. Each second in jail was equivalent to a year and Lucky wanted to clutch at any straws of hope he could get. The duo shook hands before the Agency man left.

As directed, he reached Lucky's house, asked his father for the car keys, tore open the backseat cover, took out the ID card and left for Delhi. Lucky was left brooding. The road to his release began to appear blurry.

Late in the evening, Lucky ate dinner in an attempt to douse his hunger as well as his growing frustration. He was reclining against the wall, his eyes shut. An inmate from a different barrack came crashing in. He opened his eyes to see a person glancing across the entire length of the cell as if in search of something. The inmate's shifty eyes finally rested upon Lucky.

"Commando bhai," he said, "Zahid Cheetah from the ground floor barrack has invited you for tea."

Lucky arched an eyebrow. "When?"

"Tomorrow morning."

The news hit the other inmates like a thunderbolt. The

expressions on their faces turned from blank to baleful. They gathered around Lucky and warned him vehemently to turn down the invitation and stay away from Zahid Cheetah.

"Zahid is a loyalist of Raju Pargai," one inmate said.

"He is the one whom the jailer warned you not to mingle with," the oldest inmate said. "Shekhar Joshi is also in his gang and both are lodged in the same barrack."

Zahid Khan aka Zahid Cheetah's dossier of crimes was as tall as him. Cheetah was six feet tall and intensely dark in complexion. His mere sight could wet the pants of a lesser man. Zahid had everything about his personality that made him picture perfect as one of the goriest criminals of the country. But there was one exception—his stutter.

Zahid stammered when he spoke. Although the list of his crimes was inexhaustible, the one he was most (in)famous for was the murder of Middhu Khan who himself had twenty-two murders to his name. Middhu had cracked a nasty joke on Zahid's stuttering at a moment when the latter was already in a bad mood. Harmless banter soon turned into a scuffle which in turn gave rise to a rivalry between the two murderers. There were attempts on each one's life from either side. The contest of one upmanship went on for some time before Zahid was able to gain an upper hand. He got hold of Middhu and hacked him to death.

Shekhar Joshi, on the other hand, was serving a term on charges of a double murder. He had killed a man, was thrown inside the jail. Somehow, he managed to get bail. Once he went out, he murdered once again and was thrown back into the prison for good.

Zahid Cheetah and Shekar Joshi came under one roof with Raju Pargai when he was briefly lodged in jail for Yogesh Sunehri's murder case. Cheetah and Joshi persuaded Pargai to arrange for their release by invoking the influence he enjoyed within the higher circles of politics.

Cheetah's and Joshi's hopes of freedom came crashing down when Pargai got out of jail but was murdered before he could do anything for them. Possibilities of their release from the jail came to a disappointing end.

It was Lucky's natural thought that Cheetah and Joshi would be raging for his blood as he was being deemed responsible for Pargai's murder. Their invitation for tea might be a ruse for killing him. The duo was mighty capable of that. In front of the other inmates, Lucky acted indifferent to the invitation. At the same time, he processed the implications of accepting or turning down the offer.

Accepting the tea invitation meant that he could be walking into an ambush. He could end up as a member in the long list of Zahid Cheetah's murder victims. But not accepting the offer would create a perception in the entire jail that Lucky had chickened out. He would never be able to see eye-to-eye with Zahid Cheetah again. The other inmates would probably label him as *fattu*. This was something he would never be able to live with. He made a decision to accept the invitation—for a cup of tea with *the* Cheetah. But he would go prepared for any eventuality. After all, he had the whole night to prepare.

Lucky lay awake till the time the last of the inmates had drawn the sheets over their faces and slipped into a deep sleep. Flinging his cover aside, he trotted quietly across to the wall and pulled out a spoon from under his shoe. He had got the spoon as a part of his standard issue, along with a plate and glass, on the first day of his imprisonment.

He had then improvised this spoon into a weapon. The scooping part of the spoon was done away with, and the remaining handle ended with a pointed shape which was not fully sharpened. Grating the pointed end against the stone walls, Lucky began sharpening the weapon in preparation of a meeting that was going to bring him face to face with Zahid Cheetah. After a few hours, Lucky felt the sharpness of the blade against the meat of his palm. He was pleased with his work. He stopped grating and placed the weapon into the soles of his shoes carefully and went back to sleep.

Next morning, the jail authorities were in a state of tizzy. The news of the great tryst about to take place on the ground floor had apparently spread throughout the jail. The jailer did not know what to expect from the outcome of this meeting. The inmates were also buzzing with excitement.

Lucky ensured that the blade lay firmly tucked inside the cavity under his shoes before he ventured down to the ground floor. Some of the thickest mugs of Uttarakhand stared at him as he walked towards Zahid Cheetah's cell. He finally reached his destination and pushed the door to the cell. It opened with a metallic creak.

Cheetah and Joshi had the company of a couple of other men who rose from their seats on the ground to shake hands with Lucky. Cheetah followed suit. Lucky had to look all the way up while extending greetings to Cheetah. He beheld the towering figure of a man with certain awe but took great pains to not emote this.

Lucky cast a sweeping glance at the shabby and disorganized cell. The room was rumbling with the noise from the CRT television which was sitting on a small wooden stand fixed on the wall in front. No sooner did they take their seats, a young inmate shuffled in and placed a tray of biscuits and five cups of tea on the wobbly table.

Lucky grabbed the remote lying on the side of the table and tried to figure out the button on the decrepit piece of plastic to turn down the volume.

"C-c-commando bhai," stuttered Cheetah. He stretched out his hand for the remote.

"G-g-give it to me."

Lucky tried hard to control his laughter. He did not want to end up like Middhu Khan who had paid with his life for making fun of Cheetah's stammering. Lucky simply turned off the television to save himself from embarrassing or angering Cheetah.

The men soon got down to business. "P-p-pargai was probably our last hope of escaping the prison, Commando bhai," Cheetah said. "His killing also b-b-rought death to our hopes of an early release from the j-j-jail."

Lucky did not say anything in response. He was getting himself positioned so that he could reach for his hand-forged knife in time when Cheetah uttered, "But we are m-m-men, we do not wail over a dead person for long and we move on."

Cheetah proposed that all of them should put the past behind them and establish a new beginning. And he picked up a cup of tea and held it for Lucky who was astonished to hear the person who was supposed to be thirsty for his blood was now extending a hand of friendship. A twinge of suspicion ran through his body. He stopped Cheetah halfway in his motion of passing the cup of tea.

Lucky took the cup and poured the tea from his cup into each cup on the table, including those of Cheetah and Joshi. He just wanted to make sure if Cheetah had poisoned his (Lucky's) tea, then the same fate which would fall upon him would fall upon all others in this cell.

"I am not fond of tea," Lucky said and smiled innocently.

A conversation interspersed with occasional laughter and a friendly pat on the shoulder ensued. Lucky was careful not to take the first sip until each one of them had done so. He would bring the cup to his mouth and bring it down again on the pretext of speaking or grabbing a biscuit from the table. Cheetah finally downed his cup of tea all at once which, together with the soulful conversation, was successful in earning Lucky's trust and bringing about the formation of an unusual alliance. As a mark of his respect, Lucky also gulped his tea in one go.

The next few days saw the jail authorities getting tremendously incensed by the frequent visits Lucky paid to the ground floor. Food items began getting exchanged in the form of presents between Lucky and the Cheetah gang. During one such visit, Zahid and Shekhar also showed Lucky a mobile phone which they smuggled inside and were hiding in the loo of their cell, duly wrapped inside a ribbed condom. Lucky was blown away with their gall and ingenuity.

Lucky's newly formed alliance with the Cheetah gang earned him an even more respectable position in the eyes of inmates. The authorities became more wary of Lucky and feared coming close to him. One night, as the inmates of Lucky's cell were preparing to go to sleep, he ordered them to assemble near him. He directed the youngest among them to stand guard near the gate of the cell. Standing in the middle of the gathering, Lucky yanked out the spoon turned knife from under his shoes, brandished it before their horrified faces and spoke in a macabre tone.

"All of you, I know well, are the jailer's informants. But even if a word of my business reaches the jailer's ears, I will split your neck open with this blade."

The inmates shivered at the sight of the glazing blade. They pleaded with Lucky and tried to pacify him by saying that none of what he had heard was true and that if it pleased him, they would apply for a transfer from the cell. He hurled even more abuses at them at the suggestion and threatened them into giving up the idea of leaving the cell forever.

"Your destiny is now tied to mine," Lucky said. "If anything happens to me, you will also face dire consequences!"

The inmates began crying for mercy. They later shuffled to their designated spot for sleeping. Lucky basked in his newly acquired glory. He had forged an alliance with unlikely allies. He had put the jailer's spies in their place. He was now getting used to life in the jail and establishing his dominance. Life had come a long way—from being an NSG commando to feared prisoner in the jail of Uttarakhand. But unbeknownst to Lucky, his term at the current jail was about to end soon and he was going to be moved to a new jail where a different plethora of criminals were waiting for him.

seventeen

Phone in Talcum Powder

Lucky crouched in a corner of the cell. He was trying to cut open a bottle of talcum powder using his spoon knife. Sanjay was also trying to keep an eye on any approaching guards. Lucky traversed his knife meticulously around the top portion of the bottle while Sanjay provided him cover by trudging around purposefully and blocking all lines of vision. The sheared top finally came off. Lucky turned the bottle upside down for a chunk of powder to spill out. But Lucky did not need the powder to brighten his face. He was more interested in the mobile phone which was hidden in the bottle!

After Zahid Cheetah, Lucky had also developed the daring to get a cell phone inside the jail. Lucky and Sanjay had made the plans. The powder bottle, with the phone inside, was brought to them by one of Lucky's friends, Deepak, during the meeting hour. He handed the powder bottle with a shivering hand and, haunted by the thoughts of getting caught and having to spend some time in the jail himself, took flight from there as soon as he could.

Lucky was also given a bunch of fruits by his father during the meeting which he had later shared with the inmates of his cell when he got back from the meeting. Balwant Singh, the lawyer, had come along to meet Lucky and they spent a lot of time discussing the line of action to be taken against the fabricated narrative which the police department was going to put forward before the court.

After a long time, Lucky was able to relish the home-cooked food which was sent by his mother in a tiffin box. His eyes welled up when he put the first morsel in his mouth. Lucky was very attached to his mother, but he had specifically instructed his father to not bring his mother to this jail as she wouldn't be able to bear the sight of her son in such a terrible position. His mother had made her presence felt through the love and care she had put into cooking a special meal for Lucky.

Next few days, Lucky put the mobile phone to optimum use. He would use it stealthily when in the washroom, at the time of taking a stroll outside in the courtyard after his meals and under the blankets during the night. The phone had to be put to judicious use because even though Lucky had managed to smuggle the phone inside, there was no way he would ever be able to charge a phone inside the jail.

So, one of the last calls Lucky would make before the battery would die was to a friend in the neighbourhood. Lucky would ask this friend to stand at a certain spot behind the huge wall lining the perimeter of the jail premises in its backyard at a fixed time. At the designated hour, Lucky and Sanjay would walk up to the spot furtively, throw the phone to the other side of the jail wall which would be caught by their friend standing behind the wall. The friend would then recharge the phone and the credit balance and return it at the appointed time in the evening by flinging it back over the same wall!

The information of the daring adventures instigated by Lucky somehow trickled down to the jailer. The jailer's retirement was due in one-and-a-half years and he did not want to be placed under suspension on account of Lucky's misadventures. The suspension would disrupt his pension on which he was heavily dependent to get through his post retirement life.

The jailer rushed to the Chief Judicial Magistrate and pleaded with him to transfer Lucky from his jail to some other jail. The CJM spurned the plea at first. But the jailer immediately fell at the CJM's feet.

"Sir," the jailer said. "I'll have to beg for food on the road if this commando stays in my jail for a few more days."

The CJM eventually passed the transfer order when the inconsolable jailer wouldn't let go of his feet. Lucky was shocked to learn the news of his unceremonious transfer. To be lodged in a new jail and start everything from scratch just when everything was going in his favour in the current jail was immensely disheartening for him.

The new jail, situated in Haldwani, was 40 kilometres away from the current jail.

A band of six police personnel led him out of the jail and into the van waiting outside. The van took off and he kept staring at the jail station until it kept growing smaller and finally disappeared out of sight. He threw his head back on the meshed grill of the van behind him and closed his eyes. Flopping his (handcuffed) hands despairingly on his thighs, he fell into a tired sleep. Laxman Bisht was being transferred from his first jail 25 days after he was admitted into it.

The inmates of the new jail had already got the wind of Lucky's arrival. They were excited to see "Lucky Bisht" aka Commando Bhai—whom they had been reading about in the newspapers and watching on news channels for a while now—in person while also sharing the same space with him.

The Haldwani Jail building was larger than the Nainital Jail and a little cleaner too. The jailer, T.D. Joshi, was deferential towards Lucky and received him with a warm smile. He escorted him to his cell. "You don't need to worry about anything in my jail," he told Lucky. "*Waqt guzar jayega.*"

Waqt guzar jayega, i.e., this will pass, was the most common advice given to undertrials who had no control over their fate. This sagely advice would help them go through the motions. But Lucky was not someone who would resign to his destiny. He was someone who was trained to fight all odds. That was ingrained in him now.

"During those days, we faced a big problem of inmates keeping cell phones with them," said T.D. Joshi, jailer at Haldwani jail. "Firstly, we had limited space in jail and there was a staff crunch because the state was newly formed. These inmates would get SIM cards during mulaqat and then fix them in their shoe sole or on soaps. Even if we would check them, we would fall short on techniques used by them."

The jailer opened the gate of the mulahiza barrack allotted to Lucky. The mulahiza barrack was supposed to hold the persons who hadn't yet been convicted. So, Lucky's admission into this particular barrack was natural, unlike the three who were already inside this barrack: Waseem Kalia, Vimal Sharma and Javed.

The three were hardened criminals who were left to their own devices by the jail authorities and sequestered from other inmates by lodging them in the mulahiza barrack so that the range of their evil influence could be restricted.

Waseem Kalia, the most terrible among the three, was a huge beefy man who would pray his five daily prayers with as much fervour as he would gamble and snort drugs in the jail. Over six feet tall, his imposing frame would keep the constables from daring to even look him in the eyes. Vimal Sharma and Javed were partners in crime who would abduct their victims before killing if ransom money was not paid.

Lucky's supposed act of bumping off two of the deadliest criminals in the entire state had already gained him the respect (or fear) of the three criminals. The privileges of hot food, warm water for bath and exemption from lining up for attendance continued for Lucky in Haldwani Jail too. Not only the jailers and inmates, but some high-ranking officials in the police department would also line up to catch a glimpse of the alleged killer of Raju Pargai.

T.D. Joshi narrated one of the instances of Lucky's stay in Haldwani Jail: "Lucky was a good actor," he said. "Once, he threatened one of the cops inside the jail that he would smuggle a revolver inside and kill anyone who rubbed him the wrong way, cop or otherwise. This helped him maintain his threat in jail."

Great commotion prevailed in the jail a few days later. The inmates were ordered to report to the ground and line up as the Sub Divisional Magistrate (SDM) was on a visit to their jail. Half an hour later, the SDM called Lucky who scrambled away from the assembly of inmates.

Lucky walked alongside the officer in the yard of the jail. The SDM asked some routine questions to Lucky first. Few paces later, the SDM inquired about the Agency for which Lucky worked. He was interested in knowing his rank and role.

"Sir, I work for the government," Lucky said politely.

"But which division?"

"With due respect, sir, you have to get permission from the court to interrogate me on this matter."

Lucky had shown no signs of inhibitions while making this assertion. The SDM frowned but was visibly lost for a response. He summoned Jailer Joshi and spluttered furious orders to keep a close watch over Lucky. Then without casting another glance at Lucky, the SDM fumed and left.

"You leveled him with your response, commando bhai," said an amused Waseem Kalia as soon as Lucky finished narrating the incident to him. The duo was laughing over Lucky's retort to the SDM when a constable interrupted their conversation.

"Commando bhai," said the constable. "Someone sends their greetings to you."

"Who?" Lucky said.

"Someone who is not here now, but will be in a few days."

"Stop spinning riddles like some chutiya philosopher," said Lucky. "Get to the point."

"Underworld don Prakash Pandey sends his namaste to you, straight from Tihar Jail."

Lucky stared at Waseem Kalia, who was also taken by surprise by the peculiar tidings the constable had brought in. Prakash Pandey aka Bunty Pandey was a top gangster who had worked for Chhota Shakeel and Dawood Ibrahim. He had been arrested by the Interpol in Hanoi, Vietnam in 2010. The constable said that Pandey was scheduled to arrive in Nainital Jail in a few days. Lucky was apprehensive yet eager to know why the dangerous Prakash Pandey wanted to get in touch with him.

eighteen

Never-ending Sprint

10th July 2003, Training Camp, Tel Aviv

Lucky was twisting and turning in his bed, groaning in pain. He was also making sure that his hips did not touch the surface by adopting a prone position. His buttocks had turned black due to clotting of blood on account of a beating which he had received at the hands of Zora Singh. At the same time, he was trying hard to pull himself out of the bed and get ready for the *sprint* which was scheduled to start in the next few hours. Given his condition, Lucky doubted if he would be able to complete the sprint as it was one of the most daunting drills of the course which could put one's endurance under maximum strain.

Nearly a week had passed since Zora Singh had given him the danda treatment. The searing pain in his buttocks felt as fresh as it was on the day when a couple of doctors had come on a visit to the camp to check if any cadet was suffering from a severe illness or discomfort. The cadets were ordered to assemble at the combat training ground to attend the medical checkup session. They were seen a short while later scuttling towards the said ground with not a single one among them wearing the uniform that fit well on his person. The cadets never had the time to figure out which uniform belonged to whom as all the uniforms were thrown together carelessly in a heap once they came back from washing. A group of 50 commandos from different nationalities were made to stand in neat lines. They were facing the two doctors. Zora Singh, who had apparently returned from a game of golf as he was holding a golf stick in his muscular hands. Lucky could see the veins in his strong forearms.

The doctors began addressing the assembly of cadets. "Does any cadet here feel lethargic, weak or has any other problem in his body that requires medical attention?"

A short moment of silence followed before Lucky raised his hand. Immediately, Lucky felt that he had made a mistake as no other candidate raised their hand even though they were equally exhausted and in as much pain as him, if not more. Zora Singh's eyes narrowed which began to bother Lucky. But there was no going back now. He had raised his hand and crossed a certain point. He would have to deal with the consequences. Zora Singh asked Lucky to step forward.

Lucky had only limited pairs of shoes and socks which he used to wear during his training. The weather in the camp had been consistently rainy and it made it difficult to allow any pair of shoes or socks to dry completely before wearing it. He used to wear them soggy and the rains added to the peril. Thus, the soles of his feet had turned mangy and discoloured.

"What seems to be the problem, commando?!" Zora Singh asked.

"Skin infection on my soles, sir."

Zora Singh began tapping with his golf stick against his left palm as he saw Lucky ending his spiel and sinking back in an attempt to take his place. He did not bother to translate the whole thing to the doctors and simply asked the cadets to head to the next training ground. When Lucky tried to escape along with the other commandos, Zora Singh stopped him in his tracks.

"Stay where you are," he said.

Lucky nodded. Other commandos scampered in the direction of the training ground leaving a crestfallen Lucky behind in the company of Zora Singh who had a grave look on his face.

Lucky looked up at his instructor, applying all his might to not let the dread he was feeling spill into his eyes. Zora Singh ordered him to show them the affected areas of his body. Lucky removed his shoes and turned out his feet one at a time to show his soles which had turned hazy white. The doctors did not react at all. Strange, Lucky thought.

Zora Singh ordered Lucky to get in a "chair" position. Lucky extended his hands and half squatted. Although it sounded to him a curious manner of treating an ailment, Lucky complied with his instructor's orders.

Zora Singh stepped back to allow himself some room. Then he swung his golf stick with the kind of force required to smash the ball in a far away distance and landed a severe blow on Lucky's buttocks.

Lucky let out a deafening howl and sprang at least two feet up in the air before landing back on the ground! Screaming in pain, he kept on going in circles with his hands rubbing his posterior furiously. The doctors stood bemused.

"Commando," Zora Singh thundered. "An ailment contracted on the field will heal on the field. There's no need to bring such petty inconveniences to anybody's notice."

Lucky had learnt an important lesson that day. His mission and purpose was far greater than any pain or any infection. He was supposed to ignore them and move on. But the lesson had been delivered to him with a golf stick.

Now he had to brave the pain to get ready for one of the toughest drills of his training. The commandos had to carry their weapon and a bag stuffed with gravel weighing nearly 25 kilos for a full 16 kilometres and back. The bags were also sealed with the institute's stamp on it so that no commando would be able to shed his load.

The road was filled with panting commandos who were short on breath, trying to chart their way through the hills. Halfway into the drill, Lucky found himself amongst the remaining few who hadn't bailed out of this sprint. His eyes wandered every now and then towards the ambulance that was moving along with them. Commandos who had given up were supposed to check themselves into the ambulance. Lucky did not want to do that. For him, there was great shame in giving up.

Lucky was drenched in his sweat. Zora Singh fixed his eyes upon Lucky. The instructor was still running along—like a boss—showing the young commandos how things were supposed to be done. Lucky knew that Zora Singh always had higher expectations from him although he had never publicly lauded Lucky.

Lucky began to stagger. He was the only one left. All others had given up. But he could not find the strength to carry on. He felt his legs would snap under the unbearable pressure of ever mounting weight. He chucked the bag away and waved his hand in the direction of the ambulance. Lucky got into the vehicle and took his seat. No sooner had Lucky's butt rested upon the cushion, Zora Singh climbed into the ambulance and grabbed Lucky's collar.

Zora Singh fumed. "You are a fucking disgrace to the womb which gave birth to you."

Lucky felt as if someone had punched him in the face. Zora Singh's remark had pricked his ego and pride. He was also disappointed that he had let down Zora Singh, whom he had come to idolize during the span of their training. The van sped towards the training camp even as the day had started to decline.

At around 11 pm, Zora Singh observed that the cadets were once again showing signs of being lethargic. He ordered them to congregate and told them to perform the ritual of letting his wife know that he was on his way home.

"Commando. Line tod," he yelled into the pervading silence of the night.

"Commando-o-o-o!" shouted the cadets in chorus by mustering all the energy that was left in them after going through the insufferable drill. Lucky came back to his room with a bruised heart along with already bruised hips. He retired to the bed with a firm resolve that he would complete the sprint next time, no matter what, and regain Zora Singh's respect.

nineteen

Love Matters

February 2012

Inside Haldwani Jail, the mobile phone between Lucky's hands was reduced to a twisted wad of plastic. But the anger raging inside made him go beyond crushing the device. Taking matters further, he flushed the handset down the commode in the toilet. When he emerged out of the toilet, his anger had subsided but the emotional turmoil on his face was still visible.

Waseem Kalia was sitting on the ground, his back resting against the wall and smoking a beedi stuffed with charas. He asked Lucky for the reason behind his troubled state. Lucky told him what he had done with the cell phone. Kalia sprang up to his feet.

"Commando bhai," he said. "I spent a good one lakh rupees to smuggle that phone inside for you!"

Lucky shrugged. He just didn't care now. He had asked Waseem to arrange a mobile phone as he wanted to talk to the girl whom he loved. Like most others, this girl was unaware of Lucky's true identity as he had built another smoke screen to keep his identity a secret from her.

Waseem had not wasted any time in ordering his men outside to procure a phone and send it inside the jail. A high-end model was purchased. More money was spent to gain the cooperation of the constables who assured the safe passage of the phone down the line till it reached Waseem.

As soon as the phone was in his hands, Lucky called Ashmita Bhandari—the girl whom he loved—and waited earnestly for her to answer the call. She picked up the phone; not knowing that Lucky was calling. Lucky took a second to feel her voice in his heart. An uneasy silence prevailed between the two. Lucky knew that the girl had understood who was calling, despite him not speaking a word yet.

"It's me," he finally said.

Without wasting a second, she hung up. He rang her three more times but she did not pick up the call. Anger, snowballing into an unfettered rage, was starting to take hold of him. He opened the message application and sent her a message: Talk to me once. Just once!

The screen popped with a "sent" acknowledgement notification which remained the last activity for the next five impassable minutes. The phone beeped with "one message received". He opened the message.

Leave me alone.

One more beep.

Don't try to get in touch again. I have no interest in talking to a gangster and a liar.

Lucky sighed. His mind flashed back to March 2006, when he had first met the girl. He was back in his town for a short vacation after his training in Israel. He was going to the market on his bike to run an errand for his mother when he was besotted by the beauty of this girl who came riding on her scooter from the opposite direction and whisked past him. The moment was magical. He turned around his bike and followed her all the way up to a four-storey building. She parked her bike next to the side wall leading up to the stairs of the building. A board at the gate read: Sharma Coaching Classes, X to XII and Graduation.

It was four in the evening. He knew she wouldn't be back until her classes finished. There was a tea stall near the entrance. He ordered a cup of tea and sat there waiting for her. Seven cups of tea and two hours later, she stepped out of the building and walked into the parking area. She was accompanied by another girl, probably her classmate. The two girls stood next to the bike and chatted for a while. Meanwhile, Lucky hurriedly paid the tea vendor and scrambled towards the gate to catch a closer look at her.

He watched her giggling as she chatted with her friend. Her cheery laugh added to her mesmerizing beauty. Her hair was sleek black which was pulled back over her head that gave it a crown like shape. The dress she wore perfectly complemented her beautiful, brown complexion. She possessed fine features which had Lucky frozen in his place, simpering.

A young boy got down from the building, walked up to them, talked for a few minutes and made his way out of the gate. Lucky caught up with the boy from behind. The boy jumped but Lucky gave a reassuring smile and put his hand around his shoulder. He asked him how he knew the girls.

"They are my classmates in the coaching class," the boy said.

He was undoubtedly flustered as he mistook Lucky for a relative of one of the two girls who had misinterpreted his friendship with the girls.

"Which class are you in?" Lucky asked.

"BSc, first year."

Lucky pulled out a five-hundred-rupee note from his pocket just enough so that the boy caught a glimpse of it.

"This five-hundred-rupee note is itching my pocket," Lucky said, "I want to get rid of it. Can you tell me something more about the girl in the yellow dress?"

An expression of joy washed over the boy's face. The boy turned around, looked in the building's direction and nodded. The boy gave the information Lucky asked of him about the girl, including her contact number. The boy made Lucky promise that he would not snitch on him to the girl as the one who had leaked her number to Lucky. Lucky agreed and the boy grabbed the five-hundred-rupee note and sauntered away.

The girl's name was Ashmita Bhandari. Lucky called her as soon as he reached home that evening. She refused to take the conversation beyond the "hello" unless Lucky gave her the name of the person who shared her contact number with him. Lucky contemplated the option between snitching on the boy by divulging his name or losing the chance to establish a relationship with the girl forever. It was obvious that he would never have chosen the former. He reneged on his promise. But that was okay. All was fair in love and war.

The first call transpired into a first meeting appointment. And the first meeting led to many more meetings within the span of two months. Since Lucky couldn't disclose the work that he did, he told the girl that he worked in a call centre in Delhi and his name was Anuj Trivedi. The relationship blossomed and was just starting to mature into something more than a friendship when Lucky got a call that he had to report back to his duty.

Even throughout his duty, Lucky kept in touch with the girl using the cover of a call centre employee. But after Pargai's murder, Ashmita was horrified with the media coverage. News channels and anchors ran amok with wild theories about Lucky's actual role in the murder and his supposed links with the mafia syndicate. The sense of hurt she felt after knowing that she was lied to had torn apart every shred of her trust in Lucky aka Anuj Trivedi.

Back in Haldwani Jail, there was no end to Lucky's outpourings of frustration. Soon after returning from his court hearing, he announced that no policeman will take bribes or baksheesh from the visitors who came to visit the inmates.

The jailer thought that it was imperative to take some action before Lucky's actions gave rise to a more pernicious nuisance. The jailer felt that Lucky was instigating a rebellion by raising his voice against age-old customs of baksheesh. The jailer eventually passed an order that Lucky be lodged in solitary confinement. Other inmates were warned that they weren't supposed to be seen anywhere near him till the time he remained there. In solitary confinement, Lucky was flooded with thoughts and memories of Ashmita. The Agency also seemed to have forgotten about him. There seemed to be no end in sight to his enduring predicament.

twenty

The Final Destination

September 2011

Agent Lima, after successfully establishing an acquaintance with Pargai and Amit, wanted to make sure that his association with them remained discreet so that there would be few witnesses or whispers about him after bumping them off. In line with this thought, he began to make a plan to make sure that Pargai and Arya didn't reveal much about him to their families or companions.

Lima had mastered the art of employing psychological tactics to subjugate the target. He was as good with psyops as he was with firearms. He had learnt in the Agency that there always existed a chink in an opponent's armour. This chink could be exploited to bring about the opponent's downfall. Arya's armour, though, was suffering from a gaping hole.

Arya was completely fascinated by the glamour of movies and Bollywood. He harboured dreams of acting in films in the lead role. It had been quite a while since he had been recording himself reenacting famous scenes from Bollywood films and uploading it on his social media handles. He had garnered quite a following on account of this as well.

Lima called Amit over to a restaurant for a meeting to discuss something about a movie. The mere mention of a movie made Amit drop his guard and rush to the restaurant alone as Pargai had always held Amit's Bollywood fancies in ridicule. Pargai was smart enough to foresee Amit slipping out of his grip should he get a chance to enter the film industry.

"A famous film producer in Mumbai, whom I personally know, is looking for a fresh face to launch in his new film," Lima said. "Since the film is based in the mountains, he is looking for a good looking pahadi hero. Do you know anyone who'd be interested?"

Arya took a few seconds to process the information. Then he sat erect, fiddled with the button of his shirt and heaved his chest out.

"Why *someone*?" he said. "The hero is sitting right in front of you."

Lima feigned surprise and smiled. "Oh, why did I never think about it earlier?"

Lima told Arya that he had seen many of his videos and had in fact liked them a lot. Lima was enjoying the false flattering and the many unprecedented emotions that it evoked on Arya's face. He had to keep a straight face through his lies. Arya's videos, in reality, were full of cringe.

The swollen self-delusion of Arya was further inflated by Lima. To put the cherry on the cake, Lima told Arya that many actresses in Bollywood would eagerly want to work with someone as handsome and fresh as him.

"I think you will make a good pair with Kareena," Lima said. "Or Deepika, perhaps."

Arya's face went red with joy. He was on cloud nine. But

Lima warned him to keep this matter a secret between the two of them. If others came to know of his contacts in Bollywood, Lima explained, they would seek similar favours from him. The meeting ended on this mutually agreed note.

Amit left the restaurant, his gait demonstrating the immense joy he felt at the double prospect of landing a lead role in a high budget film while rubbing shoulders with some of the most beautiful women in the industry. Lima sat and wondered how a high-profile murderer could also be such a credulous buffoon.

Lima pulled at the last piece of chicken tangdi in his mouth, followed it up with a glass of water and came out of the restaurant with the intention of weaving a similar trap to ensnare the monster-in-chief, Raju Pargai. Lima then called Pargai to say that he had made arrangements for obtaining three AK-47 rifles at a mere one lakh ten thousand rupees. “Come and meet me if you want more details,” he said.

The meeting was fixed at a popular tea stall. Pargai came and a waiter brought two piping hot cups of tea without being asked. Lima rattled out the details of the supposed deal to Pargai. He told him that they would have to travel all the way to the outskirts of Uttarakhand-Chandigarh border to execute the deal. The payment was to be made in cash.

Raju winked. “There is no dearth of money for buying Kalashnikovs.”

He then reached out and clutched Lima’s hand in his and said grimly, “I would like to see the photos of the three Kalashnikovs first and it would be great if there is a piece of paper beside the rifles with my name and current date written on it.”

Raju was not a dumb man, far from it. He was well-known for his brains as much as his brawn. But being one of the topmost Agency personnel, Lima was not going to allow himself to be outsmarted by a street-smart gangster. He knew that something of this kind was going to happen, and he had already asked the Agency to send him the photos of three AK-47 rifles. Now he just had to ask them for the piece of paper with Pargai's name and current date inscribed on it.

"Not a big deal," Lima said, "you'll get the photos by tomorrow."

Lima then issued a similar warning to Pargai of maintaining secrecy over their excursion to the border of the state and their friendship, lest it fell into some unwanted ears. Pargai raised his thumb gesturing his assent and walked out of the shop without paying the bill. Nobody would have dared to present the bill to him anyway.

Lima got back to his room, flung the contents of the pockets of his pants on a table and threw himself on the bed. Duping two of the most gruesome criminals in the entire state while keeping a straight face the entire time took a lot of nerves. He stayed put for the next 10 minutes or so in his bed until his mind was clear. He became aware of his breath and the relaxed heaving of his chest once again. Then he began planning the next move in the ploy.

On the late evening of 5th September 2011, Agent Lima was standing near a coffee shop waiting for Pargai and Arya. Pargai was thunderstruck from the moment Lima had shown him the photos of three new and crisp-looking AK-47 rifles with a scrap of paper bearing his name and date kept next to them. He couldn't wait to get the weapons.

Lima had called him and Arya the day before and asked them to meet him at the coffee shop from where they would be commencing their journey for finalizing the deal on the AK-47s. He had already conducted a recce of the area to scan for CCTVs. There were none. The Agency was also tapping the phone of each person concerned, especially that of Shival. To add an extra layer of security, Lima had asked his band of men, whom even the Agency had never had any idea about, to keep track of all his movements till the time he had done the job. The strobing light adorning the name board of the coffee shop kept going on and off behind him.

He patted his jeans to feel the nine-millimetre pistol tucked securely in its place. Locked. Loaded. Ready to use. The pistol was going to play the main role today in executing the penalty the duo had long deserved. Lima was now waiting for 30 minutes past the appointed time but he made it a point that he made no calls to either of them on that day. The police, during the investigations, would pay extra attention to the calls on the day of the murder. He waited patiently. A white Ford entered the area and screeched to a halt next to the coffee shop. Lima took a deep breath and recounted the line of plan in his mind he had made sitting up on the bed the other night. Pargai and Amit walked up to him and after perfunctory greetings Lima subtly asked whether they were carrying their weapons with them. Pargai nodded.

"Things can go wrong in a gun deal," Lima said.

When asked by Lima the reason for getting late, Pargai excused himself by saying that they had been to a birthday of their friend's son.

"It's alright," Lima said. "So did you have to tell them where you were going to get out?" "No bhai. I gave them some other excuse."

Lima smiled and said, "About your weapons, have they been serviced recently?"

Lima elabourated that it was important that they had serviced the pistols to make sure they were in good condition. Pargai saw sense in what Lima was saying. He ordered Amit to take their pistols for servicing to the nearby centre and be back soon.

"That won't be necessary, Raju bhai," Lima said. "Let me check if the guns are in good shape."

Pargai didn't hesitate to hand over their weapons to Lima

Lucky along with Narendra Modi in 2010, when he was on election campaign in West Bengal.

When Lucky was inspecting weapons in Nagaland while in service.

Lucky inside the bulletproof vehicle of the Indian Army in the North-east.

Lucky receiving acknowledgment in 2018 for his intel by a colonel.

While Lucky was undergoing training in Israel in 2004.

In 2012, when Lucky was lodged in Dehradun Jail and was caught using a phone.

During an operation in Congo.

When Lucky was deployed as the security officer in Gujarat Chief Minister Narendra Modi's house in 2011.

राजू के खिलाफ दर्ज हैं नौ मामले

हल्द्वानी। राजू परगाई के खिलाफ हल्द्वानी कोतवाली में 2004 से 2010 नवंबर तक हत्या, रंगदारी, धमकाने और जानलेवा हमला करने समेत नौ मुकदमे दर्ज हैं। जबकि अमित आर्या के खिलाफ कोतवाली में हत्या का एक ही मामला दर्ज है।

कोतवाली के क्राइम रिकार्ड के अनुसार 2004 में नैनीताल रोड निवासी दयाल मेहर ने कोतवाली में नवाबी रोड की कलावती कालोनी निवासी राजू परगाई और सुरभि कालोनी निवासी राजू पुसन के खिलाफ 323, 504, 506 और 385 आईपीसी की धारा में मुकदमा दर्ज कराया था। 27 जुलाई 2007 में लालपुर नायक निवासी अमर पाल ने कोतवाली में राजू परगाई समेत अन्य के खिलाफ 323, 504, 506 के तहत अभियोग पंजीकृत कराया था। इसी माह की 30 तारीख को आदर्श कालोनी निवासी कैलाश चंद्र ने नवाबी रोड की कलावती कालोनी निवासी राजू परगाई समेत तीन अन्य के खिलाफ जानलेवा हमला करने समेत कई धाराओं में मामला दर्ज कराया था। 15 नवंबर 2010 में हल्दूचौड़ के ग्राम देवरामपुर निवासी महेश सुनारी ने रंजिशन भाई योगेश सुनारी की हत्या करने के आरोप में राजू परगाई, नई बस्ती राजेंद्र नगर निवासी अमित आर्या और तिकोनिया क्षेत्र निवासी डब्बू नेगी के खिलाफ 302 में मामला दर्ज कराया था। राजू पर गुंडा एक्ट और गैंगस्टर के साथ तीन और मामलों में कार्रवाई की गई। राजू अपने दोस्त अमित आर्या के साथ सोमवार की शाम करीब सात बजे पत्नी मधु से दिल्ली जाने की बात कहकर गया था। उसके बाद राजू कार से अमित के साथ मोहल्ले में अपने एक दोस्त की बच्ची के नामकरण में शामिल होने गया। मगर फोन पर फोन आने से राजू वहां दस मिनट ही रुका और फिर अमित के साथ चला गया।

दु:खद — अपनी दो पत्नियों के साथ राजू (फाइल फोटो)। इंसेट में माता-पिता और राजू की मौत की खबर सुनने के बाद बिलखती पत्नियों को समझाते लोग।

योगेश हत्याकांड में बरी हो चुके थे दोनों

हल्द्वानी। योगेश हत्याकांड में जिला कोर्ट ने तीन मई 2011 को राजू परगाई, अमित और डब्बू को साक्ष्यों के अभाव में दोषमुक्त कर दिया। इसके अलावा राजू सीजेएम कोर्ट से 25 अप्रैल को रंगदारी और धमकाने के एक अन्य मामले में बरी हो गया। पुलिस के अनुसार हल्दूचौड़ के देवरामपुर निवासी योगेश सुनौरी की 15 नवंबर 2010 को करीब साढ़े ग्यारह बजे नैनीताल मार्ग पर जल संस्थान के सामने टेंपो में गोली मारकर हत्या कर दी गई थी। योगेश की हत्या के आरोप में उसके भाई महेश ने पनियाली निवासी राजू परगाई, नई बस्ती राजेंद्र नगर निवासी अमित आर्या और तिकोनिया क्षेत्र निवासी डब्बू नेगी के खिलाफ 302 में मामला दर्ज कराया था। पुलिस ने राजू को गिरफ्तार कर हत्याकांड का खुलासा किया था। जबकि अमित और डब्बू को काजपुर बस स्टैंड से गिरफ्तार किया था। दोनों सीजेएम कोर्ट में सरेंडर करने की फिराक में थे। पुलिस ने कुछ माह बाद हत्याकांड से जुड़े तमाम दस्तावेज एकत्र कर जिला कोर्ट में चार्जशीट दाखिल की थी।

दो पत्नियां हैं

हल्द्वानी। राजू परगाई ने तीन साल पहले पनियाली में प्लाट लेकर मकान बनवाया था। उसके पिता लक्ष्मण छोटे बेटे रतन सिंह और जीवन सिंह के साथ नवाबी रोड स्थित कलावती कालोनी में रहते हैं। राजू यहां मकान में दो पत्नियां मधु और भावना के साथ रहता था। राजू के तीन बच्चे हैं। इनमें सबसे बड़ा आठ वर्षीय अभिषेक है। छह वर्षीय पुत्री कुमकुम और उससे छोटा डेढ़ वर्षीय पुत्र करन है।

Clipping in a local newspaper after the death of Raju Pargai, which says that Pargai had nine cases against him.

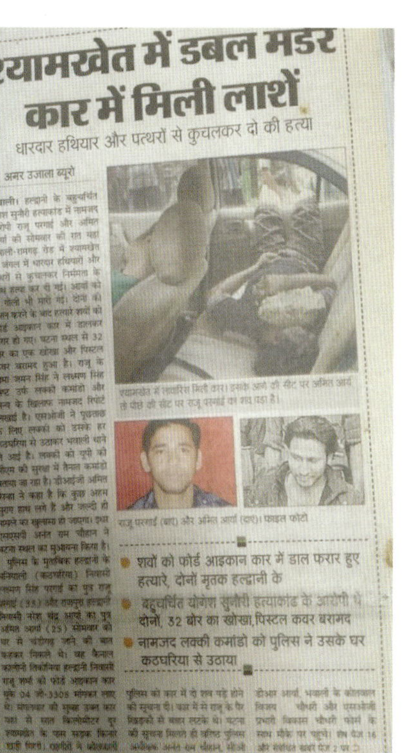

श्यामखेत में डबल मर्डर कार में मिली लाशें

धारदार हथियार और पत्थरों से कुचलकर दो की हत्या

अमर उजाला ब्यूरो

राजू परगाई (बाएं) और अमित आर्य (दाएं)। फाइल फोटो

- शवों को फोर्ड आइकान कार में डाल फरार हुए हत्यारे, दोनों मृतक हल्द्वानी के
- बहुचर्चित योगेश सुनौरी हत्याकांड के आरोपी थे दोनों, 32 बोर का खोखा, पिस्टल कवर बरामद
- नामजद लक्की कमांडो को पुलिस ने उसके घर कठघरिया से उठाया

Reportage on the double murder case of Pargai and Amit Arya.

हत्याकांड में ढेरों सवाल

श्यामखेत दो

बेहोश

जवाब चाहिए

- कमांडो क्यों करेगा अपने दोस्त की हत्या
- कार के भीतर झोंके फायर के निशां कहां
- फोर्ड कारों के अलावा दो कारें कहां गईं
- कार के अंदर कैसे राजू को कुचला

अमर उजाला ब्यूरो

A local newspaper reporting about loopholes in the murder case of Pargai.

बदला लेने को तो नहीं हुई हत्याएं!

तीसरे शख्स और लाल कार की खोज

बारबार राजू को कौन कर रहा था फोन, कॉल डिटेल से चलेगा पता

सुनौरी का अजीज दोस्त है कमांडो

साहूकार भी था

नौ बजे के बाद का ठेका राजू उठाता था

दबंगों की पंचायत

Headline in a local paper after the death of Pargai, saying the post-mortem report to be re-examined.

पोस्टमार्टम रिपोर्ट का

रि-एक्सामिन होगा

नैनीताल। एसएसपी अनंत राम चौहान ने बताया कि पोस्टमार्टम रिपोर्ट में चिकित्सकों के पैनल ने एंटी मार्टम इंजरी, शॉक तथा ब्रेन हैमरेज को मौत का कारण बताया है। वारदात स्थल पर कमांडो ने अपनी पिस्टल से गोली भी चलाई। गोली किसको लगी? इसकी जानकारी उसे नहीं है। हालांकि, पोस्टमार्टम रिपोर्ट में राजू को गोली लगने की ठीक तरह से पुष्टि नहीं हुई है। घटनास्थल से 32 बोर की पिस्टल का खोखा बरामद और पिस्टल का कवर मिला था। कमांडो के पास पिस्टल का लाइसेंस है। पीएम रिपोर्ट को री-एक्सामिन के लिए चिकित्सकों के पास भेजा जा रहा है।

Headline in local paper reads, “Police trying to find the car and third co-accused in Pargai case”.

Earlier picture of Virender Chauhan and Jitendra Kumar, when they were together in SOG.

Virender Chauhan and Jitendra Kumar, who used to work with Haldwani Special Operations Group, and were instrumental in the arrest of Lucky Bisht.

Hirdesh Kumar and his cousin, both co-accused in the case along with Lucky, outside Hirdesh's residence. Hirdesh's mother is a councillor.

Dr Sharan Dayal, Head of Forensics for Uttarakhand. He conducted forensics of the car and the bodies of Pargai and Amit Arya.

T.D. Joshi, erstwhile jailor of Haldwani Jail,
when Lucky was behind bars.

Haldwani Court, where Lucky's order of acquittal was announced.

(Above): Kotwali Haldwani (in common parlance: Haldwani Police Station). (Right): Haldwani Jail, where Lucky was lodged.

Kotwali Kathgodam. Lucky's investigation took place at this police station and an unrelenting Lucky was coerced to confess here.

(Right and Below): Nainital Jail, where Lucky was lodged.

Kotwali Bhawali, under whose jurisdiction the crime happened.

Murder spot.

Prashant Rekharia, Lucky's cellmate in various jails.

as he had witnessed the extraordinary skills Lima possessed in handling firearms at their first meeting. Pargai asked Arya to quickly grab enough packets of gutkha from the nearby paan shop to keep them satiated during the entirety of their journey. Amit hobbled to the paan shop. Lima was delighted that Pargai had done half the job and provided him the window of opportunity he was looking for by sending Amit away. Lima only wanted a few minutes with the gun alone so that he could render them useless.

"Raju bhai, we are going to strike gold soon in the form of three AK-47 rifles at a very cheap price," Lima said. "It calls for a celebration."

"What do you want? Chicken? Kebab?" Pargai asked. He touched his forefinger to his nostril. "Or something else?"

"An ice cream for now will be fine," Lima said.

There was an ice cream parlour on the opposite side of the road. Pargai ambled over to the other side to get the ice cream.

Lima had gotten rid of the duo so that he could turn their pistols into pieces of scrap by putting his incredible skills to use. In a repeat of his magnificent performance from earlier, Lima began disassembling both the pistols in a couple of seconds. He had only a few minutes before either of them would return. He undid the safety lock, displaced the piston extension and took out the firing pin and repeated the procedure with the other gun. The removal of the firing pin from both pistols meant that the weapon was now as good as a piece of stone.

At that moment, Arya returned to the car and peeped through the window. The pistols lay in Lima's hands as neatly assembled as before. Pargai returned soon after and Lima gave back their pistols to them. Pargai extended the ice cream he had bought towards Lima.

"And where's my ice cream, Raju bhai?" Arya said in a child-like voice.

Pargai and Lima looked at each other and broke into a resounding laughter. Lima turned Pargai's ice cream borne hand in Amit's direction.

"Here," Lima said. "Take mine."

Perhaps, Agent Lima wanted to fulfill a dying person's last wish. A strawberry cone was an insignificant sacrifice for the greater "purpose". All three took their seats in the car. Pargai turned on the ignition and stepped on the accelerator. A grin appeared on Lima's face as he began leading the duo to their final destination.

twenty-one

Solitary Confinement

April 2012

During his solitary confinement, Lucky was fuming desperately to square up with the jailer. He could not get over the humiliation of being put into *tanhai* as they called it in the jail. No meaningful contact with other people was wreaking havoc with his mind. He wanted nothing more than to land a punch on the jailer's face. And he started planning for the same.

A constable came to deliver lunch to him. Lucky casually asked the constable if he would pass a message to Waseem Kalia on Lucky's behalf.

"What message?" the constable asked.

"Ask Waseem to call me."

The constable was aghast. Though Lucky had played a bluff on him, the constable had fallen for it hook, line and sinker. Lucky even stuffed a five hundred rupees note in his pocket as a reward to keep his mouth zipped to make his act seem believable. The trick worked and the constable went out truly believing that Lucky had carried a phone on his person into the jail and then into solitary confinement. The constable went straight to the jailer and apprised him of Lucky's message for Waseem. The jailer decided to visit Lucky's cell and search him for the alleged cellphone on his person with no clue that he was playing right into Lucky's hands.

Prior to the jailer's arrival in solitary, Lucky was already kicking the walls and gnashing his teeth due to Ashmita's unreciprocated affection. He was pacing up and down, imagining the scene in his mind when he would break the jailer's jaw. Finally, the jailer arrived in the solitary confinement area along with an entourage of five to six policemen. Lucky could hear the sounds of the boots of the cops.

The jailer pushed the iron gate open and stepped inside. He was accompanied by a couple of policemen. The rest of them stood close to the gate outside the cell.

The jailer came close. Lucky shaped his knuckles into a fist. As soon as the target was in his range, Lucky threw a powerful punch on the jailer's face which lifted him off the ground for a second or two and flung him backwards. He landed with a thud with his limbs spread out. Lucky charged at him when the four policemen standing outside jumped inside and constrained him to the spot. The other couple of policemen helped the bleeding jailer to his feet and carried him away, each one supporting him from one side.

The news of the incident spread like wildfire. When the inmates of the jail went to court for their hearing, they would meet fellow criminals who were lodged in different jails and tell them that Lucky had broken the jailer's nose with one punch. Thus, the incident became known across the jails of Uttarakhand.

The jailer was shattered. He felt humiliated and chose not to attend the jail for the next couple of days to recover from the injury on his face. Lucky's anger had subsided by then. He realized his mistake as a matter of course and was filled with remorse.

Three days after the incident, the police constables, led by their superiors, were canvassing the entire jail, one cell at a time. They intended to sanitize the entire jail, every nook and corner of it. They took particular interest in the cell opposite Lucky's in the solitary confinement. Lucky had already got wind of the situation that apparently caused the great commotion. One of the most wanted criminals of the country, Prakash Pandey, was going to be transferred from Tihar Jail and lodged in this jail.

At eleven in the next morning, Lucky saw a number of policemen, led by the senior inspector, streaming into the corridor leading to his cell and forming two separate lines. He also saw a warden scampering between them and hauling a bag. He was followed by a handcuffed individual. The handcuffed individual's gait was as steady and solemn as the flanking policemen filed inside the solitary confinement area. The handcuffed man was none other than underworld don Prakash Pandey.

A man who had been featuring in the most wanted list of the nation for a while had finally been nabbed in Vietnam where he was living with the false identity of Vijay Sharma, a 40-year-old labourer. He had 34 cases against him at the time, 13 of which came under Mumbai jurisdiction and the rest under Uttarakhand's. From extortion to abduction to the murder of an ACP, he had multifarious crimes on his sheet.

Prakash Pandey aka Bunty Pandey was a resident of Nainital who had quickly climbed up the ladder of the mafia. He had been involved in a fake currency racket and was allegedly working for Chhota Shakeel and Dawood Ibrahim. He was also allegedly involved in the murder of encounter specialist ACP Rajbir Singh of Delhi Police.

ACP Rajbir Singh had more than 50 encounters to his credit and was instrumental in probing the terror attack on Red Fort in 2000 and the attack on the Indian Parliament in 2001. He was killed at the office of property dealer Vijay Bharadwaj who was known to him. The two had a dispute of about 50 lakh rupees. On 24th March 2008, Bharadwaj had called Rajbir to his office. The two had a round of drinks. But as tempers flared over the monetary dispute, Bharadwaj shot Rajbir twice and killed him on the spot. It is alleged that Prakash Pandey's men were present in Bharadwaj's office when Rajbir was murdered.

Pandey was average in height and had grown a paunch. He turned to look towards Lucky as he was led to the opposite cell. He appeared like a perfectly normal citizen whose face did not provide any inkling about the many grave crimes he was responsible for. He kept throwing occasional glances at Lucky who was getting uncomfortable in the heat of solitary confinement. Finally, he said: "Only a big tree can offer you the shade you need."

It wasn't difficult at all for Lucky to catch Pandey's hint. He wanted Lucky to assist him in widening his network in Uttarakhand. In return, he would help Lucky in his release from the prison by virtue of the immense power and influence he enjoyed in the underworld. Lucky told him he would think about it.

The conversation, which was so earnestly sought by Pandey, kept going for at least thirty minutes. Though Lucky only asked the reason for his transfer from Tihar Jail, Pandey jumped to the occasion and spoke vivaciously about Dawood and Chhota Shakeel. After the split between Dawood and Chhota Rajan, Pandey chose to side with Rajan and was said to have planned an attack on Chhota Shakeel in 2001. Pandey was also madly in love with a girl who now refused to even let her name be taken in the same breath as his.

Lucky got up from the far end of his cell, came near the gate, sat down and spoke through the bars of the gate. "A woman is also the cause of my present misery, Pandey bhai."

A brief moment of awkward silence descended upon the two inmates of solitary confinement. Both of them were lost in the thoughts of the women they loved. Just then a constable stepped into the space between the two cells and announced that Lucky had a visitor waiting for him in the mulaqaat room.

"Who is it?" Lucky asked the constable.

"I don't know. Appears to be some kind of a sportsperson," he said.

Lucky got up instantly and dusted his pants, visibly eager to meet the person. The constable unlocked his cell allowing him to step out. And without saying one more word he scurried towards the mulaqaat room. He was sure someone from the Agency was here to meet him.

twenty-two

Surprise Visitor(s)

Lucky could not believe his ears. Bad news in the mulaqaat room had been delivered to him by a young man, roughly of his age. Lucky had already verified the Agency's passcode with the man verbally and found it to be legit. The man had not said a single word for the next couple of minutes. The news he was sent to deliver was bearing down heavily upon him.

Lucky was unsettled by the ominous silence and prepared himself to get hit by worse. The man had finally opened his mouth to ask Lucky about his well-being in the jail and whether he was in need of some legal assistance. Pursing his lips with sarcasm, Lucky said that he was doing great.

"Just get me out of here," Lucky said. "Please."

The man cast his eyes down and finally delivered the bad news. "The government has decided to reduce your salary while you are out of commission."

"By how much?"

"You'll be paid only the basic component starting this month."

Lucky widened his eyes and shrugged as he made some mental calculations. "Why don't you tell our honorable *sarkar* to shove those basic 11 thousand rupees a month into their ass?"

Lucky's stentorian voice was echoing throughout the vacant room. The man felt embarrassed and pleaded with Lucky to calm down. Lucky explained that he did not need the Agency's sympathies. He needed his salary so that he could pay the lawyer who was charging him 23 thousand rupees for each hearing in the court.

"I am only a messenger," the man said.

Lucky realized that the man was right and was as ill-positioned to be able to alter the current situation as himself. He offered Lucky the carry bag he had brought from the Agency which contained fruits and some packets of biscuits. Lucky refused.

"Take it back and return it to them," he snapped. "Save them a few pennies."

The man trudged towards the exit when Lucky called after him and asked if he would do him a favour. Having deflated Lucky's morale with the bad news, the man was more than receptive to the idea and agreed to the favour. Lucky gave him Ashmita's contact number.

"Call this girl. Tell her that the media reports against me are false," Lucky said. "Convince her to meet me once."

The man promised to do his best. He got back to his cell with a feeling of growing contempt for the Agency's incompetence in bringing about his release from the jail. The hope he attached with the Agency was diminishing at a staggering rate.

Later in the evening, Lucky was asked to report to the jailer's office. It was the jailer's first day on duty since he had taken *that* punch on the face. Lucky was certain that it was the jailer's turn to have a go at him. He braced himself to get bound and thrashed by the constables as soon as he entered the jailer's office, until the jailer was well pleased.

On the contrary, the jailer politely asked him to take a seat, assumed a fatherly air and admonished him to maintain a distance from the hardened criminals he was sharing the prison with. He told Lucky that he belonged to a respectable family in the society and that he should be wary of joining their ranks coming under the influence of their inflammatory speeches against the authority.

"Besides, you should be the last person to go against the government," the jailer said as he concluded his counsel. "You are one of *us*. Aren't you?"

Lucky nodded. He apologized by saying that he was dealing with personal issues at the time and that the violence was the result of misdirected rage. The jailer accepted the apology. Just as Lucky reached the door, he heard some parting words of wisdom from the jailer.

"The world of crime is a bottomless pit," the jailer said. "There's no getting out once you are in too deep."

Lucky stood there for a second or two, gave a courteous nod and left. The jailer was covertly advising Lucky to not pay much heed to Pandey's offers and save himself from going down the hideous path of organized crime. Lucky understood the parable well.

Meanwhile, outside the jail, Lucky's friends and those who had as little as met him once in their lifetime were having a field day. They were extorting huge sums from big businessmen and builders and had fixed a lion's share in the gambling circuits that were popping up everywhere in the city at an incredible rate. The smear campaign run by the media channels was used as a leverage to drive fear into the businessmen and gambling houses who would turn in the money complacently as soon as *Commander bhai*'s name was mentioned. Lucky did not pay much attention to it when he got to know of it from one of the inmates on his way back to his cell after the unpleasant meeting with the Agency man.

Next morning at breakfast, a prisoner sent by Waseem came hurtling into the confinement area and called for Lucky.

"What is it?" Lucky asked.

"Good news," the prisoner said.

Lucky felt a slight twist in his stomach. It had been a while since he had heard good news.

"Commander bhai," the boy said, "one of the co-accused in Raju Pargai's case was granted bail yesterday."

"Who is this lucky bastard?" Lucky asked eagerly.

"Prakash Bora."

Lucky was relieved to know that one of the co-accused in the case had received bail. It strengthened his chances of obtaining one should he apply for it. Prakash Bora got the bail within forty-two days and it made Lucky hopeful that he too wouldn't remain inside for more than two months. He made a mental note to discuss the matter with his lawyer.

Later at night, Lucky's mind was preoccupied with Ashmita's thoughts. The rudeness with which she had spurned his requests to speak with him still pricked his heart (and his ego). He badly sought one chance to explain himself and clarify matters. The avalanche of thoughts kept him up all night. He struck a conversation with Prakash Pandey in a bid to pass the night. Surprisingly the conversation went on till morning wherein Lucky elicited all that he could from the notorious don about Dawood, his probable whereabouts, and the identity of his active shooters.

The next morning brought another round of good news when a constable arrived and told Lucky that a girl was waiting to meet him. Butterflies fluttered in Lucky's stomach. His face lit up as he pulled out a five hundred rupee note for the constable. The cop hopped forward and snatched the note. Lucky sent the constable away with a message for the jailer that he would need at least an hour with the particular visitor who'd come to meet him. He wore his best clothes and matched it up with a shimmering pair of Puma shoes.

Lucky felt so light on his way to the meeting room that he felt he was floating instead of walking. A constable standing as the keeper of the mulaqaat room greeted him and asked for baksheesh. Lucky smiled back gleefully and told him that he would give it on his way back to the cell. The constable nodded and stood there with earnest anticipation.

Ashmita was wearing a pair of blue jeans and a pink-coloured tee shirt. Lucky's heart thumped with excitement as soon as his eyes fell on her. The same hurricane of emotions he felt when he saw her for the first time filled up inside him. Watching her standing in front of him acted like a therapy that made him momentarily forget the ordeal he had been through since the past few months. There was so much to say; so much to talk. An hour won't be enough, he thought.

"Listen," Ashmita said. "My dad works for an insurance company. He is held in high esteem in the society." She paused. "My mother is the principal of a primary school."

Lucky did not know how to react, though he knew the direction in which she was trying to steer the conversation.

Ashmita broke into a nervous blabbering. "My p-p-parents—will never agree to our relationship. We have no future. Forget all about me. Forget that I ever existed."

Then she spun and rushed out of the room. Lucky's heart shattered into a thousand pieces as she disappeared into the corridor leading to the jail's exit. Lucky also made his way out of the mulaqaat room. The constable was still waiting for his baksheesh and grinned in anticipation.

"Don't even fucking think about it," Lucky said without even looking at him. Then he stomped his way back to his cell and began thinking of ways in which he could douse the fire of frustration which was burning inside the chambers of his heart.

twenty-three

Another Transfer

"The one who stands with you in your darkest hour has passed the test of loyalty," Prakash Pandey said.

He was sitting opposite Lucky in the space between the two cells of solitary confinement. Two cups of tea and a plate containing half-finished snacks lay spread out between them. Pandey was amongst the most privileged prisoners in the jail. He was now distributing these pearls of wisdom which he had gained over the years in the arena of crime.

"Unfortunately, you are at the rock bottom of your life," Pandey said as he saw that his words were making an impression on Lucky. "Good news is, there is only one way you can go from your lowest point; upwards."

The passionate counseling by Pandey since the last thirty minutes or so had proven effective in restraining Lucky from going berserk once again on account of Ashmita's refusal to maintain any contact with him. However, the shrewd and cunning criminal that he was, Pandey had ulterior motives. The content of his counsel was filled with connotations inviting Lucky to join forces. Lucky carefully tiptoed over such verbal landmines and tried to heal his wounds.

Lucky had nothing to lose. The Agency's reluctance to bring about his release coupled with the government's decision to cut down his salary to basic and Ashmita's refusal had shredded his morale to bits. But after Pandey's titillating speech, Lucky made a firm resolve to leave no stone unturned in fulfilling the goal of clearing his name in all charges and gaining financial and muscle power as well.

He sent word to his friends that they should come and meet him in jail. They were there the next day. After warning them that they shouldn't use his name to perpetuate prostitution and drug peddling, he told them that they were free to use his name to cobble gains from the gambling businesses and his "share" should reach him regularly. He'd figured that he must have access to large sums of money now that he had decided to go forward on his own.

The next move was turning the tables on Pandey. As Pandey ardently desired that Lucky came into his fold and seemed ready to bend backwards towards that end, Lucky decided to feign interest in the offer. By doing so, he gained Pandey's confidence and was able to extract everything he could about the workings of the underworld and the jail system. He planned to use this knowledge for his own benefit. He would also pander to Pandey's nature of self-amazement to elicit inner secrets related to the underworld.

Meetings between the two became frequent. For the next few days, the jail was abuzz with the news of the bonding of the solitary inmates becoming stronger by the day. One would only eat in the company of the other. The meetings in the periphery of the two cells would sometimes exceed an hour consisting of occasional bursts of cheerful laughter bustling through the vicinity. The constables passing through the area would smirk and behold the sight with a faint disdain.

Lucky wrung out of Pandey all he could during the meetings and became sufficiently informed to prevent any missteps in the process of dealing with the system in attaining his release. His portion of the share in gambling businesses reached him from time to time, a single sum of which would exceed one lakh rupees.

The authorities, however, disapproved of the union. A top personnel of the Agency coming together with one of the most wanted criminals under a common cause was the kind of event that would give endless nightmares to law enforcement agencies. Besides, Lucky was freely distributing the money amongst the impoverished inmates and the resulting affinity was an added threat for the authorities. They thought it fit to stub the fledgling flame before it developed into a raging fire.

The first action taken towards such an end came in the form of Pandey's transfer back to Tihar Jail. However, this did not affect Lucky much as he only cherished the bond he had formed with Waseem, Javed and Vimal. Pandey was just another acquaintance Lucky had made for the benefit of gaining crucial information.

Lucky had his next hearing in the court a few days after Pandey's transfer. He visited the court handcuffed with the usual posse of policemen. It was just another day at the court, marking the attendance, filling up some forms and receiving the date of the next hearing. However, he also learnt that one more co-accused, Montu Arya, had also been granted bail. The news had raised his hopes high, and he thought that the day wasn't far when he would also be let out on bail as soon as the chargesheet against him was filed in the court.

He returned to the jail with a jovial heart only to be hit by the news that an order to transfer him to Almora Jail had been issued. The van which would transport him to the new jail was waiting outside. The transfer seemed to be ordered on a whim and came across just as resentful. He sighed. Once again, he had to part with the people he had come to enjoy the company of.

Handcuffed and escorted by several policemen, he was led into the van waiting outside. Built by the British during the era of colonization when they had Jawaharlal Nehru as one of the many political prisoners, Almora Jail is situated in the Ranikhet district. The journey to it went through several steep and narrow highways delineated with colossal mountains. Already transferred a couple of times within a short span, Lucky wondered how many more surprises were left for him in store.

The jailer at Almora Jail, Aryan Saxena, seemed to have not taken a shower for eons. Saxena welcomed him to the jail. He led him to his barrack and asked him to appear for a procedural medical checkup once he had put away his belongings.

Returning to the barrack after the medical checkup, Lucky saw that he was sharing the barrack with eight to nine other inmates. Unlike the previous jails where he was paired with big time criminals, his new cell mates were charged with petty crimes. A man in his early twenties was charged in a dowry case while a middle-aged man was said to be a habitual robber. The rest of the jail was occupied by inmates charged with crimes along the same lines, something he would learn by the passing of each day in the jail.

Later in the day, Lucky expressed his desire to meet the jailer. Lucky had figured out by the appearance of the jailer that he wasn't making enough money to spend sufficiently on his own well-being. Lucky contrived to take advantage of the fact. He met the jailer at his office and as the small talk occasioned by the first meeting neared its end, Lucky thrust 10 thousand rupees in his hand. The jailer's eyes widened with surprise and he swiftly transferred the money from his hand into his pocket. His face glowed with pleasure.

"Commando bhai, if you need anything, just inform me, anything!" he said.

"I need a cricket kit," Lucky said. "Running around will keep me fit."

He whipped out an additional three thousand and stuffed it inside the jailer's shirt pocket. The jailer gave a servile smile and shoved the money deeper into the pocket.

"Yes, Commando bhai," the jailer said. "Hit as many fours and sixes as you want. But please don't break anyone's head with the bat."

Lucky nodded and came back to his barrack. A short while later a constable came to the barrack and informed Lucky that the jailer had called him to his office. Reaching the office, Lucky saw the jailer sitting behind his table with a number of tiffin boxes of different shapes and sizes strewn all over it. The food in the tiffin boxes was a range of homemade dishes which filled the air with its irresistible aroma.

"Please come," the jailer said, "my wife had coincidentally decided to prepare all this today and I thought of sharing this delectable cuisine with you."

Lucky smiled and thought that the money he had just presented the jailer was quick in showing its magical effects. He peered at the table and saw that the items in the tiffin boxes ranged from vegetarian to non-vegetarian. Even dessert was included. He gorged on the food to the jailer's surprise, who kept clutching at his pockets to feel the pleasure arising from the money it contained.

Lucky stayed there after the meal to chat with the jailer for a while before it was time to call it a night.

He came to the barrack, lay in a corner and thought of a way to avail a cellphone in this jail. He concluded his day at the new jail with a settled heart and a satiated tummy. He had already been transferred a couple of times to different jails. Each time, he had to play new tricks to find his feet in a new environment. Ironically, Lucky was the prisoner whom no jail wanted to keep behind its bars.

twenty-four

Jungle Survival

January 2005, Training Camp, Israel

Standing on an elevated position, Lucky and D'Hencho were scrutinizing the military topographic map spread out before them. The terrain offered them a vantage point which would help them chart their way out of the jungle so that they could finish the jungle survival drill within the stipulated time.

"We go two degrees north. We reach the water," Lucky suggested in broken English to his buddy D'Hencho.

"Yes, we try," said D'Hencho.

Lucky attempted to squeeze out the last few drops of water from the only bottle he had carried along with a few other supplies. The drill stretched over two days and a night where a commando and his buddy had to find their way out of the jungle from the spot where the military chopper had dropped them. They were fast running out of supplies which would eventually force them to use survival skills they had learnt in the camp. Other supplies included small amounts of dry ration, a tarpaulin, a pocketknife and a firearm.

They climbed down the steep treacherous terrain by holding hands so that in case one of them slipped or stumbled the other could prevent his plunging all the way down by quickly pulling him back by his hand. The rays of the setting sun were largely hindered by the dense canopies of the overwhelming trees. Overarching mountains that lined the forest accentuated the darkness. Lucky knew that a night in the jungle brings along a distinct set of dangers. The setting of the sun also meant being deprived of the crude method of charting the way ahead to which he was taking recourse up until now by studying the direction of the sun and the bending of the trees in relation to it. He felt a dire need for a source of light which would enable them to progress further in the direction of their desired spot as well as keep all possible nocturnal threats at bay.

Lucky scoured the ground beneath their feet and picked up a dry bark lying in the midst of a sea of leaves, broken twigs and branches. D'Hencho understood that Lucky wanted to light a fire by employing the friction method. He would use this fire to create a flame torch. D'Hencho hastened and sculpted a spindle out of the small wood lying nearby with his pocketknife. Lucky cut the bark with precision and built a long shaft to grit the spindle against.

Lucky snipped a V-shaped notch on the shaft and slit the adjacent part to form an oblong slot to drive the produced ember down which could then be transferred to the tinder that D'Hencho was piling up next to the arrangement. Lucky placed the spindle on the notch and started rolling it vigorously while moving his hands up and down its length. The exercise, trivial on the face of it, demanded a lot of exertion.

Lucky endeavored with the spindle for a while before a tiny speck of ember popped out of the surface of the shaft which was immediately collected and transferred to the tinder by D'Hencho. He blew onto it relentlessly before the tinder caught fire and they gained access to the proverbial light at the end of the tunnel. D'Hencho held the fire torch and led the way whilst Lucky followed holding the chart in his hand. He put the skill he had learnt in the training of finding the directions with the help of the positioning of the moon and the stars to its utmost use.

They finally reached a river stream and replenished their water bottles, freshened up and decided to spend the night after finding a safe space a few yards away from the stream. D'Hencho stood under a huge oak tree and pointed to the ground and decided to set camp. They spread the tarpaulin on the ground and dug a mini trench around it from all sides.

D'Hencho jumped into the trench and they both peed into the trench, each covering one half of it, and after finishing they moved out. The trench and the urine were a part of the safety measures against the wild animals and venomous reptiles. The trench would discourage a ferocious animal from coming anywhere close to them and the rancid smell emanating from the urine would put the venomous reptiles off. It was an animalistic way of marking "their" territory which was pretty effective in the current environment.

Dawn came as eagerly as the night had fallen. The forest came alive once again with the cooing of the birds. Vivacious sunlight illuminated the entire expanse. Lucky took out the last remaining stock of dry ration from his backpack and scarfed it. Then he unfurled the map, studied it carefully and after finalizing their next line of route, the pair set off for their final day of the drill.

Reading a military map is an esoteric exercise of sorts. Only those who are well versed with the skill can comprehend the puzzling lines and graphs on the parchment. Lucky and D'Hencho were among the handfuls whose expertise prevented them from deviating from the appropriate course of route.

The sun had risen fully now. Flora grew thinner. With every step, they inched closer to the end of the jungle. Lucky was wiping the sweat from his forehead when he saw a mass of clustered leaves ahead of them rustling while a hissing sound emerged as it moved. It was a cobra. Lucky and D'Hencho exchanged excited glances. Their lunch had arrived!

Lucky followed the rustling mass of leaves and found a medium sized cobra rearing its head up facing the opposite side. He walked nimbly, half crouched and hands spread in an attempt to catch hold of the serpent by its hood. Lucky was successful in clinching it correctly.

After slashing the reptile's neck, the rest of the procedure in making it edible was a piece of cake, thanks to Zora Singh's impeccable teaching methods. Lucky even remembered Zora Singh's adage that the commando who can eat a snake will never die hungry.

Now it was D'Hencho's turn to read the map and show the direction while Lucky led the way for whatever was left of their journey in reaching the camp. They managed to find their way out of the jungle and into the camp without facing many complications and were the first to finish the drill with nearly half a day to spare. The pair who stood second in the drill reached the camp a whole three hours after them.

Lucky, as he had done in his second attempt of the sprint drill, outclassed his peers by an incredible margin and was successful in regaining Zora Singha's respect and admiration which he once feared he was on the verge of losing. This drill had prepared Lucky to survive in the harshest of conditions and find his way out of impossible situations. He was now confident of using these skills in the real world.

twenty-five

I Am Lucky Commando

June 2012

Jeetu Arya, who worked with the Special Operations Group of Uttarakhand Police, visited Lucky in Almora Jail accompanied by Virender Chauhan. Since they both were friends with Lucky, they were sent by the authorities to elicit anything untoward which he might have been up to in this time. Jeetu had brought plenty of fruits along with him. The jailer also accompanied him to the cell. A lengthy conversation did not yield any reason to suspect Lucky. On the way out, Jeetu told Lucky that he could convey a message to him through any of the constables in case he needed anything. The jailer walked up to a constable named Vikas who was struggling to stand still.

"You are adamant at ruining your father's legacy," the jailer said. "Your drinking habits will land you out of your sarkari job."

Vikas, whose father had also been a constable, had given in to the temptation of uninhibited drinking. He had inherited this job after his father's death. His salary could only afford country liquor but that never stopped him from seeking ways to buy bottle after bottle of desi tharra.

Lucky spotted an opening and decided to make use of it. He took advantage of Vikas' weakness for liquor and drew him closer by keeping him furnished with enough money to buy imported alcohol. In return, Vikas was tasked with passing on any information that could prove useful for Lucky. Once, during his return to the cell after the evening stroll, Lucky met Vikas and slipped a bundle of cash into his pocket. The amount summed up to five thousand rupees.

Lucky drew him near. "I need a cell phone to be sneaked into my cell," he whispered.

The constable looked around, made an attempt to pull himself out of insobriety and gave a stealthy nod. The five thousand rupees was just Vikas' fee for the job. Lucky told him that his men would pay for the cellphone separately. Lucky was sure that Vikas would have done the job at a much lower price but he wanted to keep the man happy.

Vikas was truly elated with the arrangement and he came back to Lucky's cell the following night with the device. He told Lucky that he bought the sim card registered in his name as nobody was ready to help him with their id.

"Commando bhai," he said, "talk as much as you want, my only request is please do not issue threats from this sim card. I am holding this job only as a favour coming out of my father's demise."

Lucky kept the phone concealed behind a brick of a wall which he had managed to dislodge from its place in a feat of marvelous craftsmanship. The brick came off easily when removing the cellphone and went back just as easily, taking the cellphone inside along with it. Nobody could spot the irregularity in the wall once the brick was put back in its place. He used the cellphone to establish contact with his friends outside and inform them of some ingenious methods by which they could get his "money" to reach him.

Lucky also wasn't able to get Ashmita out of his mind. The same perennial delusion of "getting one last chance to explain himself" afflicted him like most men who had faced rejection from the love of their lives. He would pull out the phone each night while being fully determined to give her the dreaded 3:00 am call.

He would dial, listen to the ring as he would wait for her to pick up the call and hang up as soon as she said "hello". This went on for some nights. Ashmita's bitter remark of the two having no future had become imprinted on his mind indelibly. The sentence would play in his mind word by word as soon as he would hear her voice saying *hello* which would force him to cut the call, fearing receiving even more scathing words from her this time. He grabbed the phone on one of these nights, went through the process and once again hung up as soon as she picked up. He was about to put the phone away as usual when he received a call back from her.

He hastened to receive the call. A fretful voice spoke from the other end. "Some local goons are harassing my friend Megha," Ashmita said, "please do something to stop them."

Without bothering to listen any further, he cut the call. He paced up and down the cell to calm down his nerves. His phone rang again with her number flashing across the screen.

What has she taken me for? A hoodlum? A fucking gangster? Meanwhile the phone kept buzzing. *And why should I help her friend if she had been acting so rude all along?* The ringing died down. But a few moments later, as the emotional upheaval was starting to subside, he called her back.

"Why can't your friend just change her number by simply buying a new sim card?"

Ashmita explained that her friend, Megha, had tried but that did not stop those miscreants from getting her new number every time and continuing to keep on harassing her.

Lucky asked her for the boy's number which she dictated to him rather quickly. Lucky hung up the call and dialed the given number immediately. The call was answered after a couple of rings by a young boy.

"Oye bhenchod," Lucky said. "Why have you been calling a girl named Megha?"

"Who are you?" the boy said and mocked Lucky. "Her brother?"

"I am Lucky Commando," said Lucky. "You better stop calling her or I'll break your knee-caps."

The media had already created a "bhai" type image for Lucky. For the entire state, Lucky was an organized gangster. Lucky knew that all of Uttarakhand was well-versed with his (perceived) terror. He felt that the boy would cower in fear on hearing his name. But the boy, who seemed to be drinking with his friends at a bar, turned to his friends and insulted Lucky in a way he had never imagined.

"Hey, listen to this chutiya. He is claiming to be Lucky Commando." A chorus of loud laughter sounded out before the boy spoke to Lucky again. "If you call me again, I will kick your scrawny ass."

The line was dead from the other end before Lucky could get a chance to establish his identity. He was taken by absolute surprise. He pinched himself to make sure that he wasn't dreaming. That he had been humiliated and abused in an unprecedented manner was something which had never happened before. He called on the number again with the intention of talking some sense into the boy by making him understand that he was indeed speaking with *Commander bhai*.

"Oh hello?!" the boy said in the same caustic tone. "Don't try to impersonate a badass and think you can scare us."

"Listen carefully. I am Lucky Commando. And I am calling straight from the jail."

"If you are Lucky Commando, then I am James Bond."

The boy snickered. Roaring laughter was heard in unison from the background yet again. Lucky held the phone for the next two seconds wearing an expression of utter bewilderment. He was melting in embarrassment.

The next day, Megha called Lucky from Ashmita's number. She requested Lucky to stop threatening the boy as his calls had irked him even more. Now he was calling her relentlessly from different numbers and heaping even worse abuses upon her. Lucky was infuriated. It had come down to saving his face in front of Ashmita more than helping her friend out of the sticky situation. In a fit of anger, he called the boy again and asked him for his current location.

"Trikonia Chauraha," the boy said with an air of impudence.

"Just wait there for fifteen minutes," Lucky said. "I'll show you who I really am."

"Pfft," the boy said.

Lucky called his men and instructed them to reach Trikonia Chauraha. He ordered them to give this rascal the beating of a lifetime. His men promised Lucky that they will teach him a lesson he will never forget. Getting into a Scorpio car, they sped towards the location. But when they reached, the boy was nowhere to be found. They called Lucky to apprise him of the situation. Lucky immediately called the boy again.

"You dumbfuck," the boy said. "Should I wait for your men all day?"

"Where are you now?"

"Near the Sutta Bar Cafe. Come here with your men and I'll beat all of you black and blue."

On Lucky's instructions, his men got back into their car and rushed to the spot to find that the boy had vanished once again. Lucky understood that his rival was merely playing with him. He was the kind of dog who could only bark but not bite. He called the boy again and hurled the choicest of abuses. The boy made a joke out of Lucky again and told him that he was now sitting in the Anu Badshah's Stone Crusher cafe.

"If you are man enough," the boy said, "come here in the next 10 minutes."

Lucky then called his men, gave them the cafe's name and told them to get the number of the cafe's resident manager. He spoke with the manager who informed him that it had only been a short while before he had opened the cafe for the evening and that he was still waiting for the first customer to walk in.

In the midst of all the drama, Megha kept calling Lucky, requesting him to stop calling the boy. Lucky thought it was better to put a stop to all the fuss. The bloody boy was just not ready to take Lucky seriously and that was irritating him more than anything else. Lucky called his men and told them to end the pursuit.

He was nonetheless piqued at the fact that he wasn't able to fulfill the only request that Ashmita had asked of him. Swallowing his pride, he called the boy and said that he was sorry. He did this to ensure that the boy did not try to take revenge on Megha for the calls.

"I am Megha's classmate in reality," he said. "Pardon me for impersonating Lucky Commando."

"That's more like it," the boy said. "It's good you apologized. Otherwise I would have castrated you!"

Lucky hung up and stowed the phone back into its hiding place. The predicament however did not end there. The boy gave Lucky's number to all his friends and asked them to harass him. Lucky too kept getting calls from different numbers in which he was endlessly abused. Things came to a point where Lucky stopped answering phone calls from unknown numbers.

Fifteen days passed. In a twist of fate, Lucky received a text on his phone from the boy's number. *Lucky bhai, we are sorry. Please forgive us. Please. Please!!*

Lucky called the boy immediately. "What happened now? Why are you apologizing?"

"One of my friends visited the IG's Office yesterday," the boy said in a trembling voice. "He sneaked a peek into a file and saw your photo and phone number listed on the top."

The police department, sooner or later, would be tipped about the inmates who possessed phones inside the jail. They would seize these phones from the inmates whom they reckoned as inconsequential. But they would let the inmates from whom they wanted to extract some crucial information to keep using the phone so that they could snoop and gain the information they were after. Lucky realized that the tables had turned.

"You asshole," Lucky roared. "Now I will parade you naked throughout the entire town and you can bring your father along for company."

The boy begged him for forgiveness and to forget everything that had happened between them.

"Not so easily," Lucky said. "Go to Megha's house and beg for forgiveness at her feet."

"Sure, commando bhai," the boy said.

"My men will be there at your place if I don't get a call from Megha within an hour. I can get your address from the IG's office."

Half an hour later, Lucky got a call from Ashmita who thanked him immensely before passing on the phone to her friend Megha who also did the same. The boy had literally put his nose on her sandal and sought her mercy. Lucky's heightened nerves came to rest after a long period of time. He spoke to Ashmita for a while and then hung up the call feeling elated. Finally, he had made his way back into Ashmita's good books.

twenty-six

Political Winds

Lucky had an unusual visitor in the jail. His growing prominence in Uttarakhand drew the attention of a local politician, Sukesh Tiwari. He was a local politician from a national party who was famous for becoming a Block Development Council (BDC) member at the young age of 15 and who now had the aspirations of becoming a CM. He had come so far to meet Lucky in the jail. The duo was seated in the mulaqaat room. Tiwari was speaking under his breath as he offered Lucky a hefty sum of money. Lucky was well aware of the reason behind the politician's generosity. The money was the price for permission to use Lucky's name to garner a higher number of votes in the future elections. Lucky politely refused.

"Consider me as your brother, Lucky," Tiwari said. "Don't worry about returning it."

Lucky, to speak the truth, was finding it difficult to refuse the huge sum. But he would never want to see his name being used to propagate a system, or a party for that matter, which dupes people by giving them false hopes and promises but ends up stripping them of even basic honour and dignity. After much insistence on Tiwari's part, Lucky finally agreed to take the 50 thousand on the condition that it should be considered as a debt and not as a price paid to enable Tiwari to use his reputation for gaining votes. Lucky took the money.

"Of course, of course." Tiwari grinning. "Return it as per your convenience."

Straightening the white kurta he was wearing, Tiwari acted as if he was clearing his throat. Then, casting a furtive glance around, he left whilst being flanked by a couple of bodyguards. Being a politician, he treated the promise made to Lucky in the jail in exactly the manner his profession demanded. No sooner had he stepped out of the jail, he directed his men to spread the word that Lucky Bisht aka Lucky Commando was now endorsing his party and had asked his followers to support his party.

Few days later, Lucky saw the same kind of cacophony building up in the jail which was similar to what he had witnessed on the day that preceded Prakash Pandey's arrival in the previous jail. But this time, the jail was waiting to welcome a different candidate who was perhaps, equally, if not more dangerous than Pandey.

Dr Rajendra Kumar, a 28-year-old MBBS-turned-criminal was set to be lodged in their jail the next day. He was charged in an unprecedented murder of four policemen. Lucky was keen to find out how the jail would treat its newest guest.

A couple of days passed after Dr Rajendra's admission into the jail. Lucky hadn't had the chance to meet him as he was lodged in a different barrack. He was completely oblivious to the fact that Dr Rajendra was seeking to make contact with him desperately.

Rajendra was successful at last when he was returning from a routine medical checkup. He made mention, assuming an air of pretentious casualness, to the escorting constable of the amount of money he was ready to part with to gain an audience with Lucky even if only for a few minutes. The quoted figure effected a change of heart in the constable and he took him straight to Lucky's cell.

Dr Rajendra was a handsome man in his late twenties. Fair skinned and bespectacled, he had a disarming look on his face that would make it impossible for its beholder to believe he was capable of executing a gruesome feat like murder. The incident involving the policemen had occurred on the day when Dr Rajendra was being taken to a hearing in the court in Ranikhet district. He was charged with multiple offenses, the prominent among them being theft and murder, in states such as UP, MP and Delhi at the time.

At the time, he was charged with some offenses and was lodged in the Almora Jail. The van in which he was being transported was escorted by four policemen. They had reached halfway when he complained of the handcuffs being too tight. The policemen scoffed at him, an argument ensued and it quickly devolved into the trading of insults and abuses. He was filled with vengeful rage.

A short while later, he asked the policemen to lend him a mobile phone as he wanted to arrange for someone to bring him an application to the court which he wished to submit that day. Not finding any reason to be suspicious, one of the policemen handed him the phone. He informed the caller of his location on his way to the Ranikhet Court.

"Do bring the application with you," he said. "My release depends on it."

With a wide grin, he gave back the phone to the policeman, who took it haughtily not knowing that the *application* stood for the guns and the man he was talking to was one of his lackeys who was already on his way to gun them all down.

A Tata Sumo car came hurtling in front of the van when they were not far away from the court, forcing the van to screech to a straggling halt. Four men, armed with pistols, got down and opened fire at the affrighted policemen. They were caught off guard. All the four policemen were dead in a matter of a few seconds. Dr Rajendra got into the Sumo quickly and fled before he was eventually arrested again.

Lucky was well informed on the man's history to know that Dr Rajendra was granted safe haven by two prominent politicians. The first was Mohammad Shahabuddin, a member of Parliament from Bihar who was convicted for the murder of a communist activist and accused of killing 15 others. And the second was Mukhtar Ansari, a gangster-turned-politician who along with being an MLA held his criminalistic sway over major districts in UP which included Ghazipur, Varanasi, Jaunpur and his own, Mau. The liaison proved catalytic in Dr Rajendra holding law in little regard and ultimately evolving into a cold-blooded murderer. Lucky tread with caution.

"Commando bhai, I am Doctor Rajendra," he said to Lucky through the bars. "The two of us will make very good friends."

This was all that he could manage to speak given the constraints of the time and place. As the days progressed, Rajendra figured out ways to run into Lucky and speak to him elabourately on the subject of huge rewards that the underworld bestowed upon a person who joined the right organizations. He was trying to talk Lucky into pledging allegiance to the mafia so that he could exploit the influence Lucky now possessed over the state.

"I am scheduled to be taken to MP court for the hearing this time," he told Lucky during one of his run-ins. "Get your men to lay siege to the train and make way for my escape."

Lucky was amazed. "While you are being escorted by 12 policemen?".

"Gun them all down!"

Lucky was astonished at his propensity to kill people without any sign of remorse. He realized then that he was dealing with a maniac. Sticking to the complexity of the exercise as an excuse, he refused to be complicit in his bloody plan for escape. Despite the hatred he had developed with law in general and police force in particular, Lucky fulfilled the vow he took at the time of becoming a commando, that he will protect his country and his fellow security personnel from all departments at the cost of his life. He intimated the Agency of Rajendra's plan of fleeing to Bangladesh and cautioned them to never transport the man via train. He advised them to ride him in a police van which must always be accompanied by a pilot car.

On the next hearing to the court, Lucky's mother came along with his father to the court. Lucky wasn't quite happy with his father's decision to bring his mother besides appointing a new lawyer who charged 25 thousand rupees per hearing. Getting out of the court after fulfilling the formalities, Lucky witnessed a scene that rendered his heart asunder.

His mother stood, joining her hands in front of the assembled media, which would swarm the premises on each occasion of Lucky's hearing, and implored them to stop showing her son in bad light.

"My son is innocent," she spoke in the flurry of mics stretched in front of her face.

He shuddered to see the crumpled figure of his mother standing before the media with her shoulders slumped and her hands joined in earnest prayer. He walked up to her, took hold of her with his handcuffed hands and withdrew her from the spot. The media personnel followed and the wild army of excited journalists trickled down slowly to the place where Lucky was heading towards the van with his hands around his mother's shoulder.

A volley of questions as well as mics came his way. He kept moving while swatting the oncoming attack of mics with his bounded hands as best as he could to protect his mother. Just then one of the journalists asked, "Lucky, when do you think that you will get a bail now that one more accused, Virender Bohra, has been granted it while one other, Sanjay Arya, will probably get it in a week?"

Though the news wasn't a revelation, as his lawyer had already informed him about it at the time of getting out of the court, the question still went piercing through his heart like an arrow. His only comfort was holding his mother in his arms. He bid goodbye to her, not knowing when he would see her again.

He got into the van. The door was shut and the van started off. He saw his parents from the meshed windows. He could not take his eyes away from them and the expressions of despair and dejection that loomed on their faces. A thought, transitory yet powerful, crossed his mind. *Dr Rajendra, who holds the law in as little regard as the law holds us, isn't wrong after all.*

The van exited the court premises and took a turn. His parents were no longer in sight. But he was determined to not see his parents in such a condition again. Lucky was now going to try everything in his power to get an acquittal as soon as possible.

twenty-seven

The Last Ride

September 5th, 2011

Meanwhile, Lima continued leading Pargai and Arya to the valley of no return. Few miles down, the road was about to connect them to the highway. Agent Lima asked Pargai to let him drive on the pretext that he had never driven a Ford before. With slight hesitation, Pargai conceded to the request and pulled the car to a corner. They exchanged seats.

Lima started the car and resumed the journey. The move by Lima was a measure taken to ensure the security of his life against any probable harm coming from any one of the two. Lima wasn't ruling out the possibility that Pargai could have second guessed him regarding the whole affair. They were highly unpredictable even if it seemed like they had walked into his trap. Even though he had disarmed their weapons by removing the firing pin of their guns, the duo had the advantage of numbers. There was a possibility that Pargai could try to strangle him from the backseat.

So Lima had decided to stay in control of the car until the "time" was ripe. The path through which he had planned to take them featured mountainous roads with a deep gorge running along one of its sides. A careless turn here or a needless swerve there would either result in a terrible collision or the vehicle losing control and falling headlong into the gorge, either of which would lead to certain deaths of all the occupants of the car. Pargai wouldn't attempt to kill the person driving the vehicle in such a situation which would leave the car to fend for itself through the treacherous plain. Although Lima wouldn't hesitate, if it was the only way, to toss the car two hundred feet down the gorge in case the situation turned dire. The two had become like an incurable disease for the nation and Lima was determined to eliminate them at any cost.

Agent Lima's amazing ability to foresee the future and plan accordingly did not end there. He had spent the previous day planting alibis to cover his backside if he eventually got charged with the assassination of his fellow travellers. The Agency had established contact with some of the local persons around the place Pargai and Amit lived and paid them handsomely to be of assistance to Lima in his covert mission. Lima met them one by one, all three of them, and asked each one of them to call him at a particular time tonight and hang up after some time. He put his cellphone on auto answer and left it on the table before coming to the appointed place near the coffee shop.

The route from Nainital to Chandigarh was a regular highway bustling with vehicles. The roads were lit up by bright lights of streetlamps that lined across both sides. Lima was constantly on the lookout for a spot to carry out the "deed", but the conditions were most unsuitable to carry out an assassination. He had to take the car down an obscure path which would be poorly lit and less frequented by vehicles or people so that his final act invited as little attention as possible. He adjusted the back view mirror just enough to monitor Raju's movements. His eyes were fixed on the windscreen and upon Pargai in the mirror while his left hand rested near his waist over the cocked pistol. He was constantly in a "shoot to kill" mode, all ready to blow the men's head off if he found anything even slightly suspicious.

"Raju bhai, I'll take a small diversion," Lucky said looking into the rearview mirror. "I need to receive a payment of three lakh rupees from one of my previous deals from a client."

"Sure," Pargai said. "The cash may come handy in the AK-47 deal also."

Pargai's greed got the better of him. He thought that the extra cash may help him in getting more AK-47s if the dealer had them on offer. Lima briefly stopped at the crossroad. One route led to Nainital via Chandigarh and the other went to Bhimtal, a long stretch carved out of mountains which was bereft of streetlamps and vehicular traffic. Lima steered the vehicle towards Bhimtal.

With each stride, the car climbed the steeper. Darkness grew denser while the gorge that ran across the side appeared deeper. Once reaching a considerable height, the only lights that offered them some visibility were the headlights of their car and that of the other vehicles which passed them on rare occasions. The path ahead for the criminal duo started to turn bleak in more ways than one. A song began playing on the radio and Lima sang along as the car cruised through the valley. *Kare chaand taaron ko, mashhoor itna kyun, kambakht inse bhi khoobsurat hai tu ...*

Arya tuned in to complete the lines from the newest Salman Khan movie—*Bodyguard*—which had released only a few weeks ago. "I love you-u-u-u."

The three men laughed together. But Lima hadn't let his guard down. Whenever he noticed a vehicle appear in the rearview mirror, he would slow down the car and let the approaching vehicle overtake him before driving back to normal speed. He did so in order to make sure that Pargai's men were not tailing their car.

Around 12:30 am, the date had already changed to 6th September 2011. The journey was turning out to be quite uneventful with little change in the terrain. Visibility grew fainter by the minute. Pargai asked Lima to stop the car at a *safe* spot so that he could pull out some bottles which were stocked in the back of the car. Lima kept driving for a while until he came across a police station which was a shanty and snuggled up in a corner with a tube light hung over its entrance. He steered the car a few paces ahead of the station to the corner.

"Get those bottles," Lima told Pargai.

Pargai got down. He smirked when his eyes fell upon the tube light which was illuminating the board of the police station. "You had to stop here of all places!"

Lima smiled casually. "You asked for a *safe* spot."

The two men burst out in belligerent laughter. Pargai went around the car and grabbed the liquor bottles lying in the car's trunk. Lima noticed a couple of policemen on their bike near the police station who were apparently on patrol. *How come they hadn't crossed the patrolling cops all this time?*

He warned Pargai to not get overly drunk as he wanted to hand over the steering to him.

Pargai and Arya were seasoned drinkers. A few pints weren't going to dull their senses to the point of incapacity. The journey resumed once again with Pargai in the driver's seat. A slight drizzle began.

On the pretext of taking a leak, Lima asked Pargai to stop in the car near Shyamkhet. When he returned, he tapped on the window which was rolled down by Amit Arya. And the rest, as they say, is history. *Agent Lima successfully eliminated two of the most dangerous criminals in the country with a single bullet.*

twenty-eight

The Trial Begins

November 2013

The news of the rejection of his bail had left Lucky fuming. He simply couldn't wrap his head around the enormity the court had committed by rejecting his bail even after the filing of the chargesheet which contained glaring lapses and an absolute dearth of evidence. He decided to call the Agency and take them to task for their impotency in influencing the case. Lucky pressed the phone to his ear and his expression was a mix of gloomy and wrathful. The ring continued for a while before the call was answered.

"For how long is the Agency going to sit on its ass and do nothing?" Lucky said. "Why the fuck am I still rotting in jail?"

"Calm down Lucky," the Agency's representative said. "We are more worried than you about your bail."

The Agency man revealed that the current government was expected to lose power in the upcoming general elections in 2014 which would improve his chances of being cleared in the case. Lucky was aghast. "Don't expect me to sit behind bars until then," he said. "Need I remind you that you are speaking with the person who's managed to give a slip to even the stringent Bangladesh Rifles custody and run scot-free? I will break out, one way or another!"

Lucky grunted and hung up abruptly. He was sick of being given the same false promises over and over again. He was well aware that the court had rejected his bail under political duress. His men had informed him that Neeraj Joshi, one of the high-ranking politicians from the ruling party, was seen around the court a few hours before the court declared its decision of rejecting his bail plea. He called Neeraj Joshi and inquired about the reason for his visit to the court.

"Legal work," Neeraj answered.

"You went in an Alto," Lucky said. "What made you travel in a low-end Alto car when you own a fleet of high end expensive cars? You think you can fool me by hiding in a common car?"

Neeraj Joshi seemed to be at a loss for a response and there was complete silence.

"Start praying Joshi ji that I never find out that the decision of the court was influenced by you," Lucky said. "Because if that turns out to be true, I will not hesitate gunning you down in the middle of the street. And I won't give a damn that you are always accompanied by a dozen of your men."

And he hung up the call. Lucky was feeling cornered, beaten up and knocked down. His faith in the Agency was shaken to the core. Feelings of self-doubt and helplessness kicked in. His resolve to fight it out till the end started to wane.

He wished to talk to Ashmita to assuage the feelings of despair and gloom invading his being. He texted her, asking if he could call her. No reply. He put the phone away. When he checked the phone later, the screen displayed several missed calls from her number. He called her immediately. But pinning his hopes to Ashmita to pull him out of his miseries turned out to be, as usual, a terrible mistake. He had learnt, in the course of his conversation with her, that she was seeing a boy who held a B. Tech degree and was on the path to a successful and bright future. He congratulated her and drove the conversation to a premature end.

It took him some days to recover from the shock. But with renewed vigour, he began preparing to appear in court for the first day of his trial. He phoned the owner of the Levi's store, who had his shop near the jail, and ordered him to send five pairs of jeans and matching shirts.

"It is the first day of my trial," he said, "Media will be present in full force. Your younger brother should look like a hero, right?"

"But I don't have a younger brother," the shopkeeper said.

"You do," Lucky said. "I am as good as your younger brother, ain't I?"

The shopkeeper understood that Lucky was issuing a veiled threat to him. He tried to wriggle his way out of the situation.

"But my shop is closed on the day of your trial, Lucky bhai," the store owner said.

"Your shop will get closed forever if I don't get my clothes," Lucky said.

The shopkeeper understood and turned up with bags of jeans and shirts a day before the hearing. The next day, Lucky got down from the van in his Levi's ensemble amidst the incessant clicks and flashes of the cameras totted by the media personnel. He was handcuffed and escorted by a band of policemen who exerted great force to contain the unruly crowd. One media person managed to slip in and pose the question, "Laxman Bisht, why do you think the government is refusing to grant you bail?"

"Good question," Lucky said, smiling. "But you need to ask that to the government."

The policemen hustled Lucky into the court's foyer with swift strides which compelled the media persons to abandon the pursuit and turn their attention instead to the remaining accused: Sanjay Arya, Montu Arya, Virender Bora and Prakash Bora. The four were being led to the court by a small group of policemen and attracted less public attention.

Once ushered into the courtroom, they were made to stand together in one box while Lucky stood in another box. Alone. Two policemen stood guard at each of the two witness boxes.

The courtroom was teeming with people from the last row to the first where Lucky's parents, together with his two younger sisters, sat with their eyes fixed intently upon him. Lucky gave them a passing smile, attempting to convey that he was in a superb state of mind and he was going to pull it off without much difficulty.

The courtroom was buzzing with the murmurs of attendants and all the hustle that went into the preparation of the commencement of the trial. A number of curious lawyers were also seen standing wherever they could find a space across the courtroom to witness the proceedings of perhaps the biggest and most sensational murder case of the town. The lady judge ordered for the first witness of the prosecution to be presented in the court.

Raju Pargai's uncle, Jaman Singh, was ushered into the courtroom and in the witness box. An autorickshaw driver by profession, Singh was Pargai's maternal uncle and the first person to register an FIR against Lucky. He was perhaps the greatest benefactor of his nephew's death. Pargai did not get along well with his brothers which is why he had bequeathed all his wealth to his uncle, Jaman Singh.

Singh was rather quick in taking possession of everything that belonged to Pargai, including his two wives, with whom he was currently living. The judge directed the court to start with proceedings and at once a pin-drop silence was observed in the court.

The prosecution was represented by one of the top criminal lawyers in the state. He rose from his place carrying a few pages from the FIR in his hands. He came near Lucky and the other accused and began reading. The papers stated that Jaman Singh had seen his nephew, Pargai, and Amit Arya in a car with Lucky and other co-accused on the night of the murder. It asserted that Jaman Singh was informed of the murder at around 8 am in the morning and he went to the local police station to file an FIR against Lucky and the other four accused (mentioned as unidentified men) at 9 am.

The public prosecutor turned his attention towards the lady judge and stated Jaman Singh's testimony was clearly naming Lucky and the other co-accused who were accompanying Pargai and Amit in their excursion to the place where their dead bodies were found. "Lucky and his friends are the perpetrators of this brutal double murder," he said.

At the judge's request, Lucky's lawyer began the cross-examination by walking up to Jaman Singh.

"Mr Singh," he said dulcetly, "how did you learn that your nephew was murdered?"

"The police informed me in the morning."

"At 8 am, yes? Then what stopped you from filing an FIR right away? Why did you wait a full hour before filing an FIR against my client and the other accused when you had seen them together the previous night?"

"I was in total shock," Jaman Singh said after a moment's hesitation. "I took some time to gather myself before visiting the police station."

"Very well. But why does your initial statement to the police not make any mention of Lucky Bisht's name. Why?"

Jaman Singh looked flustered. After swallowing what seemed like a lump in his throat, he answered that Pargai had only mentioned going to Chandigarh with Lucky. Lucky realized that the cops had done a very shoddy job in weaving the case together which was intended to frame him. Indeed, Jaman Singh had not named Lucky in his first statement and had been tutored by the cops to take Lucky's name in his subsequent statement.

"Please explain Mr Singh," the defense lawyer said, "what makes you sure about my client's role in the case? You didn't even know him."

"He is friends with Sanjay Arya who was loyal to Yogesh Sunehri, who was allegedly murdered by my nephew. That is enough motivation for him to kill my nephew."

"Your logic should make Sanjay the prime accused, not my client. And when did you learn that my client was friends with Sanjay Arya?"

"Some fifteen days before the murder."

"And yet there's no mention of my client in your initial complaint?"

Jaman was cornered, a perfect moment to land a knockout.

The lawyer's voice echoed through the courtroom. "Who informed you Mr Jaman that my client was friends with Sanjay? And please don't lie."

"Police." Jaman cried

"How very strange!" the lawyer announced. "It looks like our witness is reading from a script he received from the police."

The witness was knocked out alright. Lucky's lawyer did not stop there. He decided to grill the knocked-out uncle of Pargai some more.

"Yogesh Sunehri has a younger brother with a criminal past," the lawyer said. "He is more than fit to avenge his brother's murder. Pray tell Mr Singh, why would my client dabble in such a case which had nothing to do with him?"

After dismantling all of Jaman's illogical reasoning in accusing Lucky, the lawyer asked Jaman if he had anything to say about the reason behind his accusations against Lucky. Jaman made a last attempt to get back into the fray by saying that he identified the pistol cover recovered from the crime scene which he knew belonged to Lucky.

At this point, Lucky called his lawyer near him and whispered something in his ear. The spectators as well as the judge watched him in amazement. The lawyer walked back and stood in his place and told the judge that the pistol cover that Jaman was talking about was nothing but an inner holster which always remains concealed behind the person's pants.

"Our witness is only putting himself in a more awkward situation," the lawyer said, addressing the judge. "He claims to have seen the inner holster on Lucky several times when such a holster is always concealed inside the clothes."

Jaman Singh was flustered. Lucky's lawyer said, addressing the judge further, that the witness had been led by the cops in falsely implicating his client in a case that reeks of a high-profile political conspiracy. He added that Pargai and Amit were renowned gangsters who had earned many rivals during the course of their mafia career which eventually became the reason for their deaths. "They were probably killed by their enemies, but not by my client," the lawyer asserted and took his seat.

Lucky smiled. The lawyer had done a good job. The court was adjourned and the judge announced the date of the next hearing. Out of the court, Lucky met his family, sought blessings from his parents and exhorted his younger sisters to take care of them and not let the troubles he was going through affect their studies adversely. Lucky then asked the policemen to excuse him for a moment to speak with his lawyer in private. He discussed with his lawyer the action plan to be adopted in the future proceedings and asked for a copy of the chargesheet before he headed back to the jail.

Reaching the jail, he scrutinized the chargesheet and quickly got in action to call his lawyer. He asked his lawyer to delay the testifying of the next witness, who was an important piece in the case, until he had figured out certain details about her which could bear heavily upon the statement she had made in the FIR. His lawyer made the necessary arrangements. The next hearing was postponed as one of the co-accused, Montu Arya, reported high fever and was unable to turn up in the court.

Lucky's lawyer gleaned all the information requested by Lucky until the next day of hearing had arrived. This witness, a crucial one, was none other than Raju Pargai's first wife.

twenty-nine

Mrs Pargai's Blunders

Pargai's first wife looked like a reticent figure. She stepped into the witness box and stood with her gaze fixed on the floor. The prosecution lawyer strolled up to the witness box and began to read out the statement of the witness. It said that she had identified Lucky Bisht as the accused who had visited their house with Pargai about a month before the murder. It further said that she had heard Lucky mentioning about their trip to Chandigarh to which Pargai gave a nod, telling the accused about the successful arrangement of five lakh eight thousand rupees required to close the deal.

The prosecutor claimed that the testimony of Pargai's wife clearly proved that Lucky had planned a trip to Chandigarh with Pargai. And the money found in the car was arranged and carried by Pargai only at the behest of the accused. Reiterating to the court that Lucky was the author and chief perpetrator of the dual murder case, he walked back and took his seat.

Lucky's lawyer rose from his place for the cross examination. He shot his questions exactly in the manner Lucky had asked him to after perusing the chargesheet.

"How long were you married to Raju Pargai?"

"Seven years," she said.

"What did your husband do for a living?"

"He was in real estate and would deal in properties."

The lawyer asked about the location of the office from where he worked. She told him that Pargai had no office and operated from home. The lawyer retorted by saying that the entire town knows very well that her husband was a big-time gangster and that she was spinning lies in order to implicate his client falsely.

She jerked her head back. "My husband was a property dealer. That is all I know."

The lawyer scrambled to his desk, pulled out a few sheaths of paper that were stapled together and passed it to the judge. While the judge went through the documents, the lawyer explained that the documents contained the records of witness' visits to the jail where her husband was imprisoned during the period in which he was charged with Yogesh Sunehri's murder.

"Thirteen times, your honor!" he said. "Thirteen times she visited Raju Pargai in jail. The documents in your hand are ample evidence of her lies. Yet she says that she had no clue about her husband's shenanigans."

He drew the court's attention to the incredulity of an event wherein a wife remains totally unaware of her husband's real occupation while her husband has been charged with eighteen criminal cases, all of them being offenses of the highest order.

"When did my client come to your house?" he asked her. "Remind me, please."

"Around a month before the incident," she repeated.

"That's another lie Mrs Pargai. My client was not even present in Uttarakhand a month before the incident. His service record can show that."

He then asked her whether her husband possessed the license

for the pistol that he openly carried around while wandering on the streets of Nainital. She replied in the negative. The lawyer used it as a proof of Pargai's blatant disregard for the law which was a further indication to the fact that he wouldn't hold back from meddling into affairs which could potentially cost him his life. All this while, Pargai's wife stood with her gaze fixed down on the floor and made no attempt to look Lucky or his lawyer in the eyes.

The lawyer concluded his cross examination by declaring that the discrepancies in the statements of the witness were far too conspicuous as to be overlooked. She was just trying to toe the line by fabricating stories so as to give strength to the false charges pressed against his client.

The court was adjourned and the lawyer met Lucky outside and informed him that he was going to apply for bail in the High Court now that the first two cross examinations had clearly gone in their favour. Lucky had immense confidence that the court would have no reason to turn down his bail plea this time.

While exiting the court Lucky noticed a man who wasn't taking his eyes off him. He then noticed a Honda City car following the van which took him to the court. He understood it was the same man in the car who he realized was none other than an Agency personnel. The Honda car stopped right where Lucky's van took a halt near a hotel to eat and freshen up. Two men came out of the car and, walking up to the group of policemen, they inquired about the jail the policemen belonged to. Lucky was attentive.

"Why do you ask?" One of the policemen asked them.

"Our bhai, D.P. Yadav, is going to be lodged in Dehradun Jail soon," they said.

Lucky understood he was up for another transfer and this time it would be Dehradun jail where he was required by the Agency to get close to D.P. Yadav.

After returning to the jail, a transfer order was passed, proving

Lucky's assumption to be right. He was transferred to Dehradun Jail. He was first taken to Haldwani Jail where he was to spend a day before they would transport him to Dehradun. The Haldwani jailer frowned at the news of Lucky spending a day in his jail. But owing to the unavailability of the escorting policemen, Lucky's stay extended to 11 days.

Dehradun Jail was considered as an aberration as far as the administration of the jails across the state was concerned. The superintendent, Mahinder Singh Gwal, was a person known for not letting even the slightest of excesses committed by the inmates go without a severe punishment. He believed in putting the offender through mental torment rather than just beating them up.

As usual, Lucky gelled with the inmates in his cell and he initiated the practice of playing Ludo inside the cell. Once, Lucky was walking to his cell. But he flinched when he saw that one of the inmates was being bathed in jaggery water and left to dry outside under the scorching sun. Such were the kind of punishments which Gwal would put offenders in his jail through.

Gwal however was a superintendent which freed him from the necessity of attending the jail every day. He would pay regular visits and leave the responsibility of jail administration in the hands of an equally strict and cunning officer, Verma.

Verma was a man of colourful personality. He would too, like Gwal, not let any nuisance committed by the inmates go unrequited. But at the same time he would not hesitate to go an extra mile in helping the prisoners who he knew were put into the jail wrongfully.

Verma was a well-read and a resourceful man. Not only would he keep himself fully informed on the cases and the charges each criminal was put in jail on account of, he also commanded a big network of informers and news bearers which enabled him to remain one step ahead in his game.

The news of Lucky violating the rules and playing Ludo inside the cell did not go down well with him. He summoned Lucky while he was playing football in the jail premises and advised him against playing games of dice.

"I feel bored," Lucky said with no signs of inhibitions. "How am I supposed to pass my time in the cell?"

Verma caught the ball that came racing towards him and glanced at Lucky with an expression of surprise. Lucky stood unmoved. Verma then went on to enlist the ranks and positions Lucky had held during his period as a trainee and then as a certified commando. Lucky was amazed at the jailer's intellectual prowess and impeccable knowledge. But he remained tight-lipped, neither confirming nor denying the jailer's claims. Lucky had also learned to stay in touch with Verma's moves. He was well aware that Verma was an informant to the STF and therefore it was in his best interests to remain silent.

"What do you like other than Ludo?" Verma asked Lucky.

"Cricket," Lucky said.

"Okay. There's no need to play Ludo from now on."

Verma had a cricket kit arranged the very next day. For the first time in the history of Dehradun Jail, the inmates were seen playing cricket. Lucky was just happy that he would get some physical activity in the form of a sport.

Meanwhile, Amar Mani Tripathi, the accused in the Madhumita Shukla murder case, was lodged in the Gorakhpur Jail along with his wife. The four-time MLA from Uttar Pradesh was now being transferred to Dehradun Jail for his role in the crime.

On 9th May 2003, Madhumita Shukla, a 24-year-old budding poet, had a couple of visitors in her two-room apartment in Paper Mill Colony. The visitors gunned her down from close range and escaped from the site. The postmortem report revealed that Madhumita was seven months pregnant with Amar Mani Tripathi's child.

After investigation, in September 2003, Amar Mani Tripathi was arrested on the charge of the girl's murder with whom he was found to have had an extramarital affair. Calls leading to the murder were traced down to his wife's number. Tripathi's wife was also arrested a few days later for complicity in the crime.

Dehradun Jail was teeming with a number of wanted gangsters and criminals. The offenses for which they were put inside varied from murder to extortion to gross embezzlement. The most serious case was that of two IAS officers whom Lucky had met inside.

The duo, who were now in their eighties, had embezzled 500 crores in a scam some 30 years ago. When Lucky asked how they managed to evade conviction for 30 years, they answered that they simply challenged the conviction and raised it to the High Court. The High Court had convicted them this time. But they were confident of being granted bail in 12 days. They further told Lucky that they would pull some strings, pass a portion of the pilfered money high up the order and voila—they'd be out.

When Lucky inquired about them on the tenth day of their claim, all their prophecies had turned out to be true. They walked out. Just like that.

A few days later, a suspended police inspector visited Lucky in the jail and told him that D.P. Yadav, one of the local politicians, was soon going to be lodged in Dehradun Jail. The officer advised Lucky to look after the minister well who could in turn help him get out of the jail.

Yadav was a four-time MLA and held the office of an MP in the Rajya Sabha and Lok Sabha. His criminal aspirations, unsurprisingly, preceded his political aspirations and he allegedly stepped into the world of crime by bootlegging in collusion with Mahendra Singh Bhati, a three-time MLA from Dadri constituency in Uttar Pradesh.

By the time Yadav had reached his forties, he had not only held several offices but also had a number of criminal cases filed against him that ranged from illegal liquor trade (which had resulted in 350 deaths at one instance) to dacoity, kidnapping and murdering his erstwhile mentor, Mahendra Singh Bhati.

Yadav and his men arrived in the jail a couple of days later and Lucky managed to establish contact with him. Yadav offered to get Lucky released on the condition that, once out, he would look after his illegal liquor trade business. Lucky discussed the offer with the Agency, which advised him to steer clear of such unlawful deals and put his faith in the rule of law to secure a release. Lucky heeded the advice.

He remained close to him as was asked by the Agency. He was able to win the politician's trust and extracted out of the man all he could about his illegal ventures. The most insidious was Yadav's partnership in a betting racket that spanned from India to Pakistan to Dubai. The racket was weakening the country's economy by allowing the cash to flow in other countries via the route of the expansive betting rackets. Lucky passed the awful information to the Agency quickly which resulted in a series of crackdown in the year of 2016 where the police busted the high scale betting racket. The seizure also made its way into the major news editorials and it took the entire political system of the country by storm.

The day of the third hearing in the trial, where Pargai's second wife was going to appear as the next witness, had arrived. The hearing did not continue for long as she was, for obvious reasons, unable to legally establish her status as Pargai's second wife. The judge dismissed the hearing on the grounds that the prosecution had attempted to deceive the court by producing a false witness. Another day had gone wrong for the prosecution.

All this raised Lucky's hope of getting the bail this time for sure. He went about carrying an air of joy and cheer that came as a result of the anticipation of certain bail. But one day, he picked up the daily newspaper and was shocked as soon as his eyes fell upon the headline of the news that was printed on the first page—"High Court turns down Laxman Bisht's bail plea once again" read the headline.

The court had repeated its act of turning a blind eye to the facts and proofs presented before it in the three hearings that took place. Lucky was sure that the politicians who were close to Pargai did not want him to be set free.

thirty

Exercise Breakdown

January 2005

Exercise Breakdown, a drill which was true to its name had just ended. Lucky's team had emerged first in this drill and won plaudits from Zora Singh. But Lucky's ears almost began to bleed when another team of commandos received a verbal lashing from Zora Singh. The trainer hurled scathing reproaches and scornful remarks at them with abandon even as the veins stood out on his neck. The other team of commandos hung their heads in shame. Lucky could barely contain his laughter as he was, in great measure, responsible for the misery being heaped upon his fellow trainees.

Zora Singh was making the other team repeat phrases that would prick their soul. At his command, the boys were shouting "we are the traitors of our nation". There could not exist a greater insult or humiliation for a soldier.

But Lucky seemed to be enjoying the whole ruckus. The rest of *his* team, though standing in a somewhat slumped posture, had great pride written all over their faces which resulted from defeating their opponent batch and coming on top in the drill.

Exercise Breakdown was aimed at training the commandos to work as a team with the goal of sneaking into the enemy's territory with arms and ammunition, setting up an explosive and retreating in due time. Therefore, the key pieces of this drill were the explosives and the commando who would carry it.

As the drill was just a reenactment of the actual scenario, the commandos were made to carry wooden logs as sniper rifles and rocket launchers. Couple of jute bags, each containing 20 kgs of gravel, were deemed to be the explosives. The bags were sealed with the training centre's stamp, which would mean that no commando would dare to open it and lessen the weight along the way to their target point. A commando whose bag was found short even by a kg from the original amount during the surprise inspection would have to do a 16-kilometre run at night after the rest of the commandos have gone to sleep as a punishment; for seven days consecutively. Each prop weighed the equivalent of the arm or ammunition it represented.

Zora Singh laid out a map and briefed the participating teams about the territory in which the drill was to be conducted. He marked the spot where the enemy's base was supposed to be located. The explosives were to be planted at this spot.

Each batch was divided into two groups. One group was assigned to be the snipers while another was assigned to carry the rocket launchers. One commando from each batch was going to be the main man who would carry the explosives. He would see to it that no team member was left behind. If a commando got sick, hurt or wounded such that he seemed not in a position to carry on, then it was the main man's responsibility to direct the team members to bring him along by carrying him on their shoulders. Zora Singh glared at Lucky, announced his name and brought forward the two bags filled with gravel, the centrepiece of the drill—the explosives.

Zora Singh pointed at the jute bags. "Commando," he said. "Pick up the explosives."

Lucky's heart flew with joy. He was reveling in the responsibility which Zora Singh had bestowed upon him. But when the weights were strapped to his shoulders, Lucky realized what he had signed up for. He felt as if he was carrying the weight of the world on his shoulders. Zora Singh had already flung one of the two bags on his shoulder and was ordering him to carry the other. Lucky was awakened to the fact that the drill was going to be especially challenging for him given the kind of job he was tasked with. Another commando from the opposing team was assigned to carry the explosives for his unit.

Deep into the drill, Lucky was scouring the ground under his feet intensely for spending the night. Darkness of the night brought along the gloominess of a humiliating defeat in sight as the navigator of Lucky's batch had been performing poorly. They had digressed from the original course a couple of times now. The commandos were deprived of light as well as food and were too worn out to successfully heave the load up to the finishing point. Lucky was suffering the worst due to the huge amount of weight he was laden with.

Halfway into the drill, when the relentless pattering of the rain turned the treading ground all wet and slushy, Lucky's buddy—D'Henco—came to his rescue. He took one of his bags and heaved it for a good five kilometres in addition to the load he had carried.

The path to the point they had reached now was filled with numerous risks and challenges. Lucky's body was covered with welts and bruises received as the team cut their path across the large swathes of jungle landscape that abounded with prickly wildflowers and thorny bushes. While they were ankle deep into the water crossing one of the brooks, Lucky decided to ditch his bags of explosives. He just could not carry it anymore.

His chance came when they stopped at a place for spending the night. The commandos weren't permitted to fire a torch or get access to light by any other means as it potentially reveals the commandos' location to the enemy in a real scenario. They were supposed to do the operations at night by treating the darkness as the best cover against the enemy. The sheer darkness of the night would provide him enough cover. The despair caused by the awareness of their trailing far behind their opponents had brought their morale down. So, Lucky emptied the gravel and started the morning burden free!

Finally, the group managed to reach near the finishing point from where they would be lifted back to the camp by a helicopter. Lucky saw their opponent team was passing time by lounging or loitering around and had not planted their explosives yet. They were acting like the rabbit who decided to rest before the finish line, thinking that the tortoise was far behind.

Lucky, with help from D'Hencho, had refilled his bag with the sand he had gathered before reaching the finishing spot. None among the opponent team could spot the anomaly. Soon Lucky's eyes fell on the main man of the opposing team who was lying under a tree, catching a nap. The jute bags containing explosives, with the seal intact, lay near him unattended.

Lucky walked in a leisurely manner towards the man while D'Hencho sat next to the bag feinting to wipe clean his launcher. Lucky squatted and lugged the sealed bags carefully towards him. Once sufficiently within his reach, he lifted the bags and walked back heaving them as coolly as he had walked to them. The duo then emptied the bags they had brought with them quickly and threw them away so that it didn't lead anyone to their trickery.

It wasn't long before the air above them was blaring with the sound of a helicopter. The chopper descended on the spot. Zora Singh descended from the helicopter and asked which team had reached first. The opposing team eagerly claimed their spot to the first place. But when Zora Singh asked them to show their explosives, they were at a loss!

Lucky stepped forward and showed *his* bag of explosives which was intact. Zora Singh awarded the first place to Lucky's team. But Zora Singh was furious with the other team.

"Repeat after me," Zora Singh bellowed, "*We are the traitors of our nation because we lost our explosives.*"

The opposing team had no option but to comply. They had reached the finishing spot first but the loss of the centrepiece meant that the team in question hadn't even performed the drill to begin with. No one among the losing batch could report the robbery of their explosive bags since being responsible for one's own arms and ammunition were one of the main values the drill was supposed to instill into a commando.

Lucky couldn't hold it anymore. A muffled laughter escaped his mouth. The commandos standing close to him cast a confused glance at him. D'Hencho took notice. His eyes bulging out, he threw an incisive glance at him, gesturing to him to get a grip on himself. It was the day when Lucky had proved that he was the kind of commando who was ready to resort to whatever it took to gain victory over his adversary, be it honest work or timely wit. All was fair in love and war. And this was war.

thirty-one

The Commando Returns

Lucky stood at the edge of one of the four diving boards over the swimming pool with his hands and legs bound firmly with a thick rope. The same was true for the three batchmates who were standing on the edge of their boards. The pool was nine feet and 10 inches deep (three metres). Lucky took a deep breath, held it there and jumped into the air with his arms tied behind him. He pierced through the wheezing wind in the direction of the pool at an incredible pace. Splash. He went piercing through the mass of water and found himself submerged in the pool in no time.

As the training neared its completion, the trainees were now spending more time learning the psychological skills which were deemed as essential for the success of an operation as being skilled with the weapons. Drills requiring physical exertion became less frequent and drills demanding performance under pressure became the flavour of the season. One such drill was the Advanced Swimming Drill. It was designed to test a cadet's ability to remain calm and composed in a situation that could potentially lead to death.

Lucky allowed a couple of seconds to regain the senses

befuddled due to the immersion. Then with a smooth movement he flipped himself over, face up and twisting into a ball-like shape he reached his mouth to the rope tied to his hands.

The drill was about releasing oneself from the clasps by the prompt application of appropriate wit and judgment demanded by the situation, emerging out of the bottom onto the surface and swimming out of the pool.

It was an unyielding knot. It demanded extreme physical exertion which made the shortness of breath even more which also led to persistent blackouts before Lucky's eyes. Struggling with the knot started to feel like fighting death itself. Finally, deciding to keep his eyes closed, he went for the knot with full vigour and this time managed to prise it open. He immediately began tugging on the rest of the coil which made his head throw back with each pull. Soon, his hands were released from the bond.

In between, Lucky took short, insufficient breaths underwater. Bubbles of air came out of his mouth. Instead of reaching directly for the legs, he waddled with his now freed hands once or twice so as to curb the fear and panic arising as a result of the shortness of breath. Having achieved such a state of mind, he pulled on the knot binding his legs at once with utmost dexterity.

The knot gave way quickly. Flinging it aside, he swam towards the surface. Not once did he care to look around and check the status of his opponents as he dashed forthright in the direction of the side of the corner marked for him to exit the pool. Though deprived of air for a relatively long time, he only breathed in accordance with the discipline the art of swimming demands.

Zora Singh stood at the finishing spot with his arms folded over his chest. Slamming his fists against the edge of the pool, Lucky pushed himself out of the pool swiftly to finish the drill.

Standing on the ground, he finally had time to look around and check on the position of his three opponents. One of them had just emerged out of the water, closely following him and another was swimming his way to his finishing mark.

But the next moment, Zora Singh dived into the pool and disappeared under the water. He emerged a few moments later, heaving the third cadet along who had fallen unconscious while the rope tied around his legs was still intact. The team of on-site medicos rushed to the spot once he was placed down on the ground by Zora Singh in order to tend to him and administer the treatment required for the resuscitation. Lucky heaved a sigh of relief that he had topped the drill.

A few days later, Lucky was sitting in the classroom along with his batchmates. Zora Singh was lecturing them on the equal importance of mastering psyops while being a warrior skilled in the use of weapons. It was the last lecture of the official tenure of their training period.

"A commando needs to be extremely cautious at all times when executing a covert operation," Zora Singh said. "There is no room for oversight. None."

The slightest mistake on the ground could lead to the failure of the entire operation and could even result in a number of deaths.

"You must have listened to the operating principle of a *single bullet per enemy,*" Zora Singh proclaimed. "But I am telling you—a single bullet per leader. You get rid of the leader, you get rid of his entire herd."

D'Hencho and Lucky paid undivided attention to Zora Singh's words. They were quite intrigued by the rich content of the instructions.

"Listen to what your adversary's eyes say," said Zora Singh. "The rest of the body may lie, but eyes, they never lie."

Zora Singh added that obsession with three of the most enchanting desires in the world can invariably compromise a mission. These three desires were the need for money, drugs and sex. He counseled that a true commando should prioritize his country above everything and not give in to such vices. He also imparted a secret that a commando should make the darkness his intimate friend.

"Never let your guard down." Zora Singh was now trudging around in the class carrying his swagger stick in his hands. "Blend with your environment."

An undercover commando should always wear common clothes, sport a common hairstyle and follow an ordinary routine; being careful to not deviate from it even in the least. Vice versa, they should always be on alert to spot even the slightest of signs that appear out of the ordinary.

"Let not the enemy predict your next move," Zora Singh added, "the greatest weapon of a commando is *surprise*."

Lucky was getting obsessed with the subject as Zora Singh went on from touching on one aspect of psychology to another. As a result, Lucky ended up passing the written examination conducted on the subject with flying colours.

On the last day of training on the ground, Lucky picked up a fistful of mud and packed it in a small pouch of cloth. He intended to keep this mud as a souvenir and a reminder of his times in Israel. In Indian tradition, the land or stage where one performs is held in high esteem. Though Lucky was emotionally attached to the land of Israel now, he finally decided against taking the mud of the land back home. His rationale was that, at the end of the day, there was just one country that had his undying loyalty. That country was India; and only India.

The Agency threw a farewell party on the evening of the last official day of the training. An array of dishes featuring different cuisines was served for dinner. The music also played its part to relax the commandos after a grind that seemed like it would never end. Trainees across batches and nationalities mingled with each other as well as with their superiors.

Zora Singh seemed like a different man that day. He was completely relaxed and not uptight at all. Lucky, D'Hencho and a few other distinguished trainees from the batch huddled around Zora Singh. He was sitting near the counter and sipping on his whiskey. He had abandoned the severity of a trainer today and had been entertaining the flock of trainees with his quips and jokes.

"Sir," Lucky said. "Should we shout so that your wife knows you'll be home in a few minutes?"

"No," Zora Singh said. "That won't be needed."

"Why sir?"

"Because I am not married." Zora Singh winked. "Never was."

Saying this, Zora Singh gulped down his glass and laughed like a child who'd been tickled furiously. Lucky and D'Hencho looked at each other. The next moment, the entire group of commandos burst into unanimous laughter which drowned the sound of slow music.

Next morning, the Tel Aviv Airport was bustling with overjoyed trainees waiting to return to their homeland after two-and-a-half years. Lucky and D'Hencho stood at the spot from where they had to part ways, probably for the rest of their lives.

Lucky and D'Hencho bumped fists and exchanged last words in their characteristic broken English to demonstrate the care and concern which had been fostered by their camaraderie. But D'Hencho had something on his mind with which he sought to measure the degree to which their friendship had grown.

He placed his hand on Lucky's shoulder. "In future, if our countries fight, will you fire a bullet at me?"

Lucky thought about it for a moment. "Yes," he said with finality. "I will do anything for my country."

The excitement from D'Hencho's face vanished almost

immediately. Lucky felt his stomach twitch. His companion wasn't expecting the answer which he had just given. To defuse the situation, Lucky asked the same question to D'Hencho, hoping that he would make the same choice and then realize that there was no other answer to such a question.

But D'Hencho gave no answer to Lucky's question. He merely stepped forward and hugged Lucky. Then he turned around and headed in the direction of his flight. That moment was very painful for Lucky. His pain eased only when he landed at Delhi International Airport a few hours later. Finally, he was home. But soon, he was going to be deployed to foreign lands.

thirty-two

Will Lucky Bisht Remain Behind Bars?

December 2013

Relentless slandering by the media had taken an ugly turn. News channels were constantly spawning outrageous theories which ranged from depicting Lucky as a mafia mastermind and connecting him to the top criminals in the state. The authorities, out of their depths as usual, resorted to the only measure they knew best and decided to transfer Lucky to Tehri Jail. The idea was to cut him off his home ground and sever all the routes through which he could be in touch with his men and local people by sending him 300 kms away.

It took them 12 hours to reach the jail which was situated in Garhwal. He hid large amounts of cash in the soles of his shoes before getting out of Almora Jail. He had no idea what the new jail and jailer was going to be like and he did not want to take chances. Moreover, so many transfers within such a short span meant that the authorities were watching him closely and the new jailer wouldn't allow him to carry so much money inside the jail.

Frequent transfers and awful long journeys in the dysfunctional vans were getting on Lucky's nerves. He had even quipped about the ordeal to one of the elderly policemen accompanying him in the journey to the jail.

"*Chacha,*" he said in a caustic tone, "how do you make a criminal confess?"

"Our *danda* makes them talk," the elderly constable said.

"A trip in these scrappy vans can make an elephant confess that he is a rabbit," Lucky said.

Even the cops burst out laughing. When they reached Tehri Jail, the jailer who was nicknamed "Tempo" by the inmates, walked Lucky to his cell. He was infamous for taking every penny from the pockets of prisoners. On his way to the cell, he caught hold of one of the prisoners, frisked him and took the five rupees coin lying in his pocket.

"You might use it as a weapon," he said to the prisoner with glee.

Lucky heaved a sigh of relief that he had hid the money well under his shoes while it was also no less good news that the new jailer was bribe-able.

There he met two of the most dreaded criminals in the state, Jittin Rawat and Sachin Khokar. Khokar was Sunil Rathi's brother whose unusually daring feat of murdering another prisoner, Munna Bajrangi, inside the jail had become a household tale.

Munna Bajrangi, charged with various crimes such as murder and extortion was shifted to Baghpat Jail on July 8th, 2018. At the same time, Sunil Rathi was serving his term on charges that ranged from extortion, murder and other high-profile offenses. Bajrangi was scheduled to be taken to the court the next day for a hearing in one of the extortion cases he was charged with. But a ringing sound of a pistol was heard from the jail.

Authorities rushed to the spot and found Munna Bajrangi lying on the floor in a pool of blood while Sunil Rathi stood over him wielding a pistol, the wisps of smoke still trailing from the barrel of the weapon. When asked about the reason for killing Bajrangi, Sunil Rathi said that he had insulted him by calling him "chubby". This was not the first and certainly not the last internecine incident in the prison.

Lucky's knack to bond with the inmates was on display once again as he was quick to develop an affiliation with the two gangsters. Jitti Rawat had his influence in the city of Dehradun while Sachin Khokar's dominance was widespread in western UP. However, the jailer, Tempo, would get nervous on the slightest of developments. Growing affinity between Lucky and the two gangsters had him in a state of paranoia much sooner than any of the jailers that Lucky had before in the previous jails. But, like every mortal, Lucky too had his fair share of days when he would feel extremely sad and sorrowful. And it was on such days that the short heights of the walls of the mountain top jail would become tempting.

"In fact, one of the jailers had filed a plea before the court requesting that Lucky should be moved out of his jail," said Balvinder Singh. "The jailer was worried that Lucky would climb these walls and run away from the jail as he was a trained commando."

Activating his network from the jail, Lucky nominated one of the college students as an independent candidate to contest in the upcoming college elections. He had instructed his men to take care of the boy and provide him with the necessary support. The move by Lucky to step into the political world through a proxy was seen as a threat by one of the top ministers of the ruling party. Soon, Lucky started getting messages from an intermediary who warned that a local don named Manish would break the legs of the candidate if he didn't opt out of the elections.

Lucky felt a dire need for a cellphone as he knew that one call would put an end to Manish's mischief. "Lucky had once taken a jailer to task. He was adamant that he should be provided with a mobile phone inside the jail, otherwise he will climb the walls of the jail and escape," said Bhupinder Rawat, a journalist who had covered the case widely.

Lucky came up with yet another ingenious plan to smuggle the phone inside.

A few days later, one of his friends came with an earthen pot for a visit. The guard at the gate checked the pot. It appeared like just another earthen pot which was perfectly empty from inside. So, the guard allowed the pot to be taken inside.

The friend gave the pot to Lucky. On the same evening, Lucky dropped the pot accidentally while trying to shift it from one place to another. A cell phone emerged from the broken pieces. Lucky had instructed his men to hide the cellphone in the pot by engraving it inside at the time of molding the pot. Once the phone was in his possession, he did not lose another second before making the call that would send tremors across the ruling establishment.

"Manish," Lucky said, "this is Lucky Commando calling."

There was a pin drop silence for a moment before he received a response.

"Yes, what is it?" Manish said.

"The next time you send your men to threaten my boy, I will shoot your head off."

The call made its way to the headlines of the major newspapers the next day. The ruling party was flustered. The concerned minister came out on the streets and called for legal action to be taken against Lucky. Questions were raised about the integrity of the jail security department. In response, Uttarakhand STF conducted a raid and canvassed the entire jail and its premises but did not get anything. Lucky hid the mobile phone in a flowerpot by shoving it well down into the pot deep inside the mud. He also sprinkled some water on the top to avoid suspicion. He watched with bated breath till the end of the raid, as surfacing of the phone in the raid would result in the wholesale suspension of the entire police department of the jail.

But cries for a full investigation of the matter did not stop and it was SP Sadanand Date who eventually took charge of this case. But he was himself a victim of the minister's unbridled meddling in the affairs of law and order. Date gave a clean chit to Lucky. His investigation report said that there was no mobile phone found in Lucky's possession and therefore the call was nothing more than a fantasy that the media so readily loves to indulge in.

Tempo, the jailer, however, was losing his grip. He was contemplating transferring Lucky from his jail before something horrendous took place. Lucky had sent a word to him advising him to drop the idea of one more transfer as no jail would be ready to admit him anymore. Tempo paid no heed to that advice.

The day of the next hearing had come which meant an arduous journey of 350 kms had to be suffered in the same miserable van. Lucky was visibly frustrated by the frequent transfers and the grueling long journeys to and from the court. To top it all, Tempo was successful in getting a transfer order from the magistrate and Lucky was set to be transferred once again back to Haldwani Jail.

Reaching Haldwani Jail turned Lucky's trepidation of no jail admitting him to be true. He was kept waiting in the jailer's office for hours on end. The company of policemen who escorted him to Haldwani Jail from Tehri Jail also had to stay back with him until he could be duly admitted into the cell. He couldn't take it any longer and asked one of the policemen to call Tempo.

After reminding Tempo of his advice against the transfer, Lucky said, "I have been waiting outside all day. If I do not find myself lodged inside a cell in Haldwani in the next 10 minutes, I will reveal all details of your *rishwat-khori* in Tehri Jail to the SP."

Tempo was drowning in sweat. He called each person he knew who could help him get Lucky lodged inside the jail. He was successful at last to convince the Haldwani jailer to admit him for a night into his jail. SP Sadanand Date was kept up all night owing to the endless calls he got from Tempo who begged him profusely to make sure that Lucky wasn't sent back to his jail. The SP had to give in to his insufferable entreaties.

Next morning, a van, which was bound for Pauri Jail, was idling outside the Haldwani Jail. A handcuffed Lucky and a usual posse of policemen were sitting inside apparently waiting for someone before they commenced their journey. SP Sadanand Date strode towards the van in his gym outfit. He looked at Lucky ruefully for a second or two.

"I was kept up all night because of you," he said. "The jailer kept calling me the entire night, pleading to not send you back to his jail."

Lucky tried to suppress a giggle.

"Your days in jail are numbered Lucky," Date said. "Why don't you chill and spend them without getting yourself into trouble?"

Date had done him an immense favour by granting him a clean chit in a case which would otherwise have put him into a lot of trouble. He nodded courteously and the SP gave a strident call to the driver to get going. The van started and Lucky was on his way to yet another jail.

Once done with the formalities, he was lodged in the barrack where he met the infamous Maoist leader, Prashant Rahi, once again. He tried to brainwash Lucky into joining him in his cause. He would constantly try to bring his attention to the fact that the country and the government hadn't been as faithful to Lucky as he had been in serving them, otherwise he should have been out of jail by now.

"Tell me one thing Commando bhai," he would say, "does this country belong to only a privileged few? What about the countless poor workers who can't earn their daily bread?"

Lucky noted the truth in the people's opinion about the Maoist leader. Of course, he had the gift of bringing the entire system down to its knees without picking up a single weapon, namely the gift of oration and eloquence. Since Lucky was furious with the system and government, he feared that Rahi's tantalizing speech would creep its way into his heart and he would end up rebelling against his own country. He thought it fit to maintain a distance from him.

Through newspapers, Lucky consumed the daily news, kept himself informed and looked forward to the bail which would allow him to put the gained knowledge into action more effectively in getting an acquittal from the court. However, the headline in one morning's newspaper forced him to rethink his strategy: *Kya salakhon ke peeche hi rahega Lucky Bisht?*

And this headline was followed by an article which said that Lucky's plea for bail had been rejected by the court.

thirty-three

The Accursed Gold

Tempo, the jailer, took early leave from his workplace that day and headed straight for the jewelry shop. He was vigilant throughout the journey, trying earnestly to latch on to the gold which was hidden under his shirt. He planned on selling this gold to the jeweler and making a quick buck out of it. It was an unusual sight that a man who would try his best to evade buying the ticket while traveling in the bus was seen taking a cab to the jewelry store.

The jeweler scanned the gold very carefully before asking Tempo to wait for a moment as he vanished inside the workshop. He returned with a pleasant smile and asked Tempo to wait for some time as the party interested in the piece of gold was arriving shortly. Hardly 10 minutes had passed when a group of policemen entered the jewelry shop and marched towards Tempo. He shifted uneasily from his place.

"Here Inspector sahab," the shopkeeper said and pointed in Tempo's direction. "This thief was trying to sell me this fake piece of gold!"

The inspector grabbed the gold and looked at Tempo menacingly. Tempo glanced at the slab of gold with disbelief. He swallowed, rose from his place clumsily and identified himself as the jailer of Tehri Jail to the party of police who had surrounded him.

"Doesn't matter," the Inspector said. "The case falls under the jurisdiction of the local police station. Come with us."

Tempo was about to drown in his sweat. He knew that it wouldn't take much time for the incident to become a scandal which would certainly cost him his job. He requested the inspector to have a word with him in private for a moment. The inspector, on cue, nodded in agreement.

"I am sorry that you had to come all the way up here by leaving the comfort of your police station," Tempo said. He dug into his pocket and a couple of seconds later pulled out a bundle of notes to offer it to the inspector. "Please accept five thousand rupees as a token of my apology."

"I wasn't the only one who had to leave the comfort of the police station," the inspector said and looked over his shoulder at the group of police constables standing near the counter. "Not a single paisa less than 10 thousand will do."

Tempo grimaced. He slipped his hand inside his pocket ruefully and handed the inspector what he had asked for. Then Tempo returned to the jail with a sullen face. Who would have believed that the man known for filching even five rupees from the inmates would be made to cough up 10 thousand rupees at one go? But Lucky had a knack in pulling off the impossible. He controlled his laughter hard as Temp narrated the incident to him.

"You fucked me today Lucky," Tempo said to Lucky.

"I am sorry Sharma ji," Lucky said. "How would I know the veracity of that gold if its duplicity escaped your shrewd eyes?"

The flattery worked. A smug expression washed over Tempo's face before he turned around and strutted off without speaking any further. Lucky burst out laughing as soon as the jailer was gone. The memory of the day when the fake piece of gold had come to his possession returned to his mind.

Around August 2011, a man named Nabbu Kura was digging up the ground around his house at night. He was deeply immersed in digging, working the shovel on the ground labouriously when suddenly he struck gold, or so he felt.

Nabbu Kura was one of Lucky's close friends. He had tasted very little of the real and savage world. When Lucky was in the town on his brief vacation, Nabbu showed him the gold and asked him to sell it. Nabbu was thinking he'd make a couple of lakhs on it. Lucky asked one of his men to take the gold to the jewelry shop and find out its value. Much to Nabbu's disbelief, the piece of gold turned out to be fake.

Nabbu was devastated. He handed the gold to Lucky as he couldn't bear the piece of sham. "Get rid of it!" he told Lucky.

Kishan Kaliya lived in the neighbourhood and knew Lucky casually. Kishan came to know that Lucky had come in contact with a portion of gold. He called Lucky and invited him to his place for dinner. Lucky was surprised at the invitation and said that he would try to visit him and hung up the phone with no intention of obliging.

But Kishan's obsession with the *gold* made him call Lucky relentlessly till Lucky ran out of excuses and had to accept the invitation. After drinks and dinner, Kishan Kaliya broke the suspense and requested Lucky to give him a chain made out of the gold he had with him. Lucky was, fortunately, sober enough to stop himself from bursting out laughing. Lucky merely said he would give it a thought and forgot about it after the night passed.

However, Kishan Kaliya soon found himself behind bars. After the police had picked up Lucky in the murder case, they discovered that his phone record was filled with Kishan Kaliya's calls around the time the murder took place.

The cops picked up Kishan. He was beaten ruthlessly by the policemen who were trying to implicate him in the crime. They began asking for names of his accomplices. Shocked by the beatings, Kishan blurted out the first name that came to his mind: Deepak Patni, his best friend.

A couple of hours later, Deepak Patni was behind bars too. The cops began beating both of them together. Patni was just as clueless about the crime he was mercilessly being beaten to confess about. Hours later, the cops took a break to get their breath back before another round could begin.

"Why did you give my name to the cops?" Patni asked Kishan. "What have I got to do with this case?!"

"You are my best friend," Kishan said. "I couldn't think of any other name."

"Best friend?" Squealed Patni. "You are not a friend but a stupid ass."

Patni threw a punch across Kishan's face which broke his nose. The accursed gold had brought misfortune upon so many men before Lucky came up with the idea of handing it over to Tempo as a bribe. He was sure Tempo's greed would turn him blind and land him in trouble, and so it did.

The next day, Lucky was waiting in his cell for the policemen to arrive and take him to the court for his next hearing. The team arrived. The escort group consisted of usual members except a young policeman who seemed to be a new recruit. He stepped into the jail to frisk Lucky before leading him to the van. The guy sounded oblivious to the identity of the man he was dealing with. He spoke to Lucky in the tone characteristic of a snobbish policeman dealing with a small-time hoodlum.

"Take off your shoes," he ordered Lucky, who was surprised at the man's impertinence.

He looked at the congregation of 12 to 15 policemen standing outside the cell and smirking.

"Remove your socks," the young policeman continued while maintaining the harsh tone. Lucky had begun to lose his temper. He looked at the elderly policeman who was standing close to the bars. The policeman scrunched his face at Lucky, gesturing to him to control himself. Lucky was handcuffed only in one hand while the other cuff hung loose from the other wrist.

"Be quick," the young cop said to Lucky.

"Listen you motherfucker," Lucky roared. "One smack on your head from this loose handcuff will crack your skull open."

Lucky decided to provoke the young chap further so that he did something untowardly and ended up inside the jail with him. The elderly policeman hopped inside. Tugging at the young man's arm, he dragged him outside the cell quickly.

"*Array chutiya,*" Lucky called from behind the bars. "Have you ever fired that pistol? Or is it just hooked to your ass as a showpiece?"

The young policeman struggled to meet Lucky's eyes. Once inside, Lucky thought, it wouldn't take much effort to shut the man's disgusting mouth forever and pass it off as one more mysterious death inside the jail. Lucky was totally ready to go for it when the elderly policeman entered the cell, reached out to him and tried to calm him down. He pleaded with Lucky on the young man's behalf and requested him to forgive the young policeman and bury the hatchet. Lucky listened to the old man's pleadings out of respect and walked out of the cell coolly and made his way to the van. Lucky never saw the young policeman after that day as he was transferred to a different jail with immediate effect. Many police personnel became reluctant to accompany him to the court from that day. They feared losing their job, if not their lives. Such tales of Lucky's terror amongst the policemen proved successful in garnering him even more respect from the inmates.

thirty-four

Pandey's Plan

Lucky watched Prakash Pandey with amusement as he issued dire warnings on the phone. Pandey was speaking with the parents of a young doctor who was lodged recently in the Dehradun Jail. The parents of the prisoner were also doctors. The young medico was arrested in the case filed by a woman, one of his patients, alleging inappropriate advances.

"Storing so much cash in the house must be quite a burden, Doctor Saheb," Pandey said. "Allow me to relieve you of this burden."

Pandey, who was transferred to Dehradun Jail along with another big-time gangster Amit urf Bhura, had made an entry to the jail with a purpose this time. He wanted to expand his criminal network further in the state of Uttarakhand. To this end, he had resorted to various methods with which he would harass rich prisoners and fleece money from their families. The parents of the doctor caved into Pandey's demands.

"Please. I beg you," the father said to Pandey, "25 lakhs is too much. How about 20?"

"How about me showering behind your son in the jail? And

imagine what can happen if he accidentally drops the soap, huh?"

The father gasped.

"Alright...alright. Take all my money," the doctor pleaded. "But please don't harm my son."

The money reached Pandey via the network of a handful of policemen complicit in the act. Each policeman would keep his share and pass it down the line until it reached Pandey.

Pandey would make use of his dominance and influence to intervene and stop any mistreatment done with other criminals who were of use to him. The move would prove effective in impressing a godfather kind of image on the minds of these young men who would eventually end up getting recruited as members of his mafia gang. To convince Lucky to help him in building his network in the regions where Lucky now held sway was also central to Pandey's plan.

Lucky, on the other hand, was miffed by one more bail rejection by none other than the High Court. He was drowning in the sea of continuous disappointment and was ready to clutch at any straw to save himself from completely drowning. Pandey sensed this and invited him over to his cell for tea.

Pandey put forth an offer asking Lucky to help him establish a network in Dehradun and its outskirts. In exchange, Lucky could claim a portion of the money Pandey would extort from the wealthy inmates. The deal was done and Lucky put in a request asking for a transfer to Pandey's and Bhura's cell. The request was granted and the young doctor became the first victim of Pandey's extortion plans.

Lucky instructed one of his men to mark himself as Pandey's visitor in the register when they were next going to pay him a visit in the jail. They did as asked and Pandey set the first step towards establishing his presence in Dehradun and its surrounding region by using Lucky's contacts.

Mahinder Singh Gwal came to the jail for a routine inspection. After having a word with Amarnani Tripathi, he summoned Lucky. Rather short in height and possessing features characteristic of the people of Nepal, Gwal was a well-spoken and genial man. He advised Lucky to keep himself away from Pandey and his ilk. He also assured him that he wouldn't remain in jail for long as the case against him did not hold much water.

Pandey's adventures of looting the wealthy inmates had reached Amarmani Tripathi as well as Sunil Rathi who was transferred to Dehradun jail at the same time Pandey was transferred. His growing influence and hype among the fellow inmates were envied by the two gangs and they too started to indulge in shenanigans similar to Pandey's. A fierce battle between the three gangs in the quest to gain an upper hand ensued.

Rampant extortion in the jail continued until Verma got the information from one of his informers in the jail. He took action by calling for the transfer of several prisoners who had played the part of being foot soldiers for the heads of their respective gangs.

With almost all the inmates leaving the cell, Lucky, Pandey and Amit Bhura spent more time together which eventually set them on the path to become an inseparable trio in the coming days. Amit even managed to sneak a cellphone inside by hiding it in a bag of fruits and vegetables. The cell phone was shared by the three of them where one would stand guard if another was speaking on it. Amit was seen making incessant calls sometimes with Lucky standing close by to provide him cover. The reason for his frantic calls was soon going to prove a nightmare for the authorities.

Forty-five days had elapsed since the last hearing. Now, Pargai's younger brother—Brijesh—was to appear as the next witness to testify against Lucky.

A young boy in his mid-twenties, Brijesh looked nothing like his eldest brother. His criminal record was as unblemished as the colour of his skin He was ushered into the witness box by a posse of policemen while Lucky stood unfazed in his new Levi's outfit. The judge called for the hearing to begin and the prosecution lawyer read the statement of the witness aloud.

On the night of the murder, the witness claimed to have seen his brother with the accused in a car near Chaupala Chauraha while he was on his way back from his shop. He saw Lucky in the driving seat of the Ford car with Amit sitting next to him. Raju Pargai, claimed Brijesh, was sprawled in the backseat.

After reading out minor details related to the time and place of the sighting, the prosecution lawyer made his point that the accused was indeed with the victims on the night of the murder. He took his seat. Soon after, Lucky's lawyer came up to Brijesh and began cross-questioning.

"Mister Brijesh, when do you usually close your shop?" asked the lawyer.

"9 pm," he said.

"What time did you close your shop *that* day?"

"7 pm."

"May I know why?"

"Raju bhai had asked me to visit him at his house."

"For what business?"

"I don't know. And now I will never know."

The lawyer asked him why he took a longer route through the Chaupala Chauraha while the bridge that goes through Kusum Kheda was the obvious route one should take to reach Pargai's house from the location of Brijesh's shop as it would save the traveller nearly half an hour. Brijesh stood stunned and wasn't able to respond.

"What was the time when you saw the car?" Lucky's lawyer asked.

"Seven, I guess."

"Someone's life is at stake, Mr Brijesh," the lawyer said. "Guesses won't make the cut. I need to know the exact time. *Please.*"

"Ten minutes past seven."

The lawyer then observed that during that season and hour, dusk usually falls early and renders visibility to a minimum. He added that there were reports where people could not distinguish one person from another due to the pervasive darkness at such times.

"So Mr Brijesh," the lawyer said, "Please shed more light on your impossible feat of identifying my client, your brother and Amit Arya in such circumstances! Didn't the car's flashing headlights block your vision?!"

Weird silence followed. The witness was seen casting frenzied glances all around, even looking at the prosecution lawyer, for a cue, who quickly turned his gaze away. Lucky's lawyer appealed to the judge that the witness was concocting lies with the aim of misleading the court.

"After reaching your brother's home, Mr Brijesh," the lawyer said, "did you inform your brother's wife that your brother was travelling in a car with Amit and my client?"

"N-n-no."

"Strange. You went to your brother's house on his request. Yet you did not find it important to mention to his wife what could allegedly explain his absence."

The lawyer concluded his cross-examination by asserting that the witness' clear failure to provide convincing answers was fraught with deliberate lies. The judge announced the adjournment of the court on the above note.

Seeing that one more cross-examination had gone in his favour, Lucky decided to put in a plea for bail in the High Court once again. This time, he hired a criminal lawyer who practiced in the Supreme Court of India and charged 1.5 lakhs per hearing. Lucky was now staking his freedom on one more deposition swinging in his favour.

thirty-five

Perils of Protecting

In the jungles of Congo, in Central Africa, Lucky was standing with his right foot planted firmly on the rebel's right hand as he lay sprawled on the open field. The year was 2007 and Lucky was into the early stages of his career as a professional commando. This mission was part of the operations conducted by the United Nations aimed at putting an end to the growing dominance of the rebel outfits in Congo. Lucky was among the few chosen commandos that constituted the fighter team in the troop. He carried a special forces cover ID.

Scorching rays of the sun fell on the rebel's face. The wincing outlaw tried to yank his bullet ridden hand out from underneath Lucky's foot. Lucky and his team of 45 men from various nationalities, clad in battle gear, had encircled the man with their guns pointed at the man who was on the verge of death. He was left behind by the group of rebels the night before after the coalition troops had zeroed upon them.

The coalition forces had been informed of the location of the rebel group hideout by the intelligence earlier in the day. The spot was situated in the heart of a sprawling forest. The team had to make their way to the location by wriggling, crawling and sometimes squirming through the narrow pathways surrounded by tall grass on all sides. Dusk had started to settle in and navigation was getting tougher by each passing hour.

Oral communication between the troops was forbidden. They were supposed to communicate by tapping on the shoulder of the personnel moving ahead. Each instruction was represented by a specific number of taps. So, if a personnel sensed some kind of danger in their path and therefore wanted the troop to stop in its tracks, he had to tap two times on the shoulder of the personnel moving ahead of him, who in turn would tap the same number of times on the shoulder of the personnel before him and so forth. The domino effect would eventually bring the entire troop to a halt. A gap of at least three metres was to be maintained between every two commandos in a team. This ensured the impossibility of the entire team coming into the enemy's firing range all at once. Moreover, the commando at the end of the team would walk backwards so as to offer protection from any threats approaching from behind. This commando would exchange position with the penultimate commando in the line after every two minutes.

The rebels somehow got tipped about the incoming coalition forces and immediately began planning for an ambush. Being locals, they knew the place like the back of their hands and laid siege to the exact lane through which the troop would pass to reach the place. They took position, set up their MMG guns and waited for the coalition forces to arrive.

As soon as Lucky's team reached the spot, one of the rebels opened fire. The bullet however got stuck in the chamber and the MMG failed to fire. The resonating sound of the trigger renting the air, however, alerted Lucky to the position of the rebels.

The next moment, a barrage of bullets came showering towards the rebels. A fierce gunfight followed. Soon, the rebels began abandoning their position. All of them fled except one. This rebel was unable to move due to bullets piercing his right shoulder and left leg. But he kept firing bursts at regular intervals so that the troops wouldn't get near him. One of the bullets even whizzed past Lucky's ear.

The team decided to wait till dawn and move at first light. But the morning began on a bad note when Lucky saw that the head of the friendly personnel right behind him had been blown off by a hail of bullets which the lone rebel had kept firing through the night. The coalition forces moved in to neutralize him.

After the man was incapacitated, Lucky brought his rifle forward and aimed it at the rebel to take the final shot. The rebel had resigned to his impending fate. Lucky saw the outlaw's quivering lips. He was trying to say something. Lucky waited until the rebel spoke after gathering the last vestiges of strength in his body and spirit. "Your God was by your side today," he said. "Mine wasn't."

Lucky couldn't agree more but chose to remain silent. A single shot of MMG fires 246 rounds, enough to blot out Lucky and his whole team of unsuspecting eleven fighter commandos.

The rebel seemed at peace after making this statement and closed his eyes. Lucky took a moment to gather himself. Lucky's gun and his bullet were his god at this time. He pulled the trigger with a cold stare. That was all. Lucky's achievements in the years after his return from Israel had gone a long way in commissioning him to be a part of many such operations launched by the United Nations.

After returning to India, Lucky was allowed to remain in his hometown for a few days before he was summoned to resume further training which would take him to different parts of the country. The next module was conducted at the Infantry School in Belgaum. The 39-day training was followed by a month of vacation.

Next, Lucky was sent to the Infantry School at Mhow. This training was especially designed to improve a commando's sniping skills besides enlightening him on the tactics needed to identify and drive the commander of the opponent army to the desired spot before putting a bullet through him.

He was also made a part of several counter insurgency operations during this period which had tired him to no end. He requested for a break on the grounds that he had been through relentless training and operations for seven years since he started his training in 2003 and he badly needed a cool off period. His request was granted and he was given National Security Guard's (NSG) cover ID in March 2010.

Thereupon he underwent training with the NSG to gain the skills required to become a Personal Security Officer (PSO) who can provide personal security to the VIPs and VVIPs of the country. The training spanned 45 days after which he was posted as the PSO to the then CM of Punjab, Prakash Singh Badal.

During this period, Lucky learnt the perils of being a protector. One day he was sitting in the CM's bulletproof Pajero Car which was to depart towards Panchkula where the CM regularly paid religious visits. The standard operating procedure (SOP) in such situations mandated that no one except the PSO could accompany the CM in the car.

The car was to be followed by a procession of other vehicles which were occupied by the CM's family and other high-ranking officers and ministers. The convoy was about to depart when a high-profile officer, clad in civil clothes, came up to the CM's vehicle. He had the DIG and SSP in his company.

"The CM's son will also travel in the CM's car," he said to Lucky rather tersely.

"Sorry sir," Lucky said. "That is not allowed."

The officer repeated the request and Lucky also repeated the same response. *Not allowed*. The officer felt offended. The DIG shuffled in front and spoke with Lucky. But Lucky didn't budge. He merely repeated, "Not allowed, sir."

The DIG kept insisting despite Lucky's reluctance. In the midst of the back and forth, Lucky pulled out the declaration form from the dashboard of the car and passed it to the DIG.

"Kindly submit your order in writing," Lucky said. "Only then I can comply."

The DIG's gaze swept from the form to Lucky in absolute amazement. He also invoked the CM's son's position, which was Deputy CM, to get Lucky to acquiesce, but to no avail. His face was suffused with palpable anger. But Lucky was merely doing his duty. As per protocol, even the CM's wife or son were not to be allowed in the car with the CM. Written records were supposed to be maintained of any digression from this rule.

Sensing that a written note would go against his case, the DIG finally gave orders that the CM's son would follow in another vehicle, right behind the CM's vehicle. He was rankled nonetheless at the notion that a PSO had shown the audacity to not submit to his bidding.

By the time the visit came to an end and the convoy returned to Parkash Singh's place, it was communicated to Lucky that he had been transferred to Assam where he would be posted as PSO of the youngest person to become a CM, Prafulla Kumar Mahanta. Lucky was well aware of the reason behind his transfer. He had ruffled high ranking feathers. Nevertheless, he flew to Assam at 7 pm on the same evening.

A few days passed since he was assigned as the PSO of Assam's then CM Prafulla Kumar Mahanta. Lucky was enjoying his stay in Assam. CM Prafulla Kumar had been involved with the All Assam Students Union (AASU) which had spearheaded the "Assam Movement" between 1979 and 1985. The movement was known for its aggressive stance in detection and deportation of migrants.

Once, when Prafulla Kumar was out on one of his campaigns, he was surrounded by swarms of people who came to greet him. Lucky was finding it extremely difficult to keep the excited crowds of admirers at a safe distance in his bid to protect the CM. He was particularly vexed by a woman who was constantly trying to slip her way into the inner circle of the security perimeter.

While he managed to contain the unruly crowd by flailing his hands about him, he kept nudging the woman with his elbow which threw her off every time she came anywhere close to the CM.

The woman, however, seemed to be quite adamant in her desire to get close to the CM. Lucky sensed danger and decided to act without making the situation volatile. When the woman came close next time, he stepped onto her sandal from behind and as she tried to yank it off in her attempt to take the next step, the sandal snapped and broke down. She was left far behind the procession as she struggled to walk in a broken sandal.

Returning to his office after the campaign, Praffula Kumar summoned Lucky to his chamber. Lucky thought that the CM would have noticed his efforts and would probably praise him for his quick thinking. But Lucky was in for a surprise. The CM smiled and first told Lucky that he did a good job. Then he said, "My wife, however, is not a threat to me."

Lucky stood there puzzled. His mind flashed back to the woman who was trying to get close to the CM. He realized that he had broken the sandal of none other than the CM's wife! Lucky looked at the floor in embarrassment. He thought he would be transferred once again.

But the CM guffawed. "Relax," he said. "It's alright."

Lucky also heaved a sigh of relief and quickly stepped out of the CM's room.

thirty-six

Disillusionment

August 2011

Lucky's face appeared pale. He had returned to his quarters only a minute ago. His current assignment was to protect "Papa Seven Two" which was the codename for a prominent politician of the opposition party of the day.

Past midnight, Lucky hadn't even got a chance to change from his PSO uniform. His morale had reached an all-time low. After ruminating on his next step of actions, Lucky made a rather tough and unpleasant choice. He reached for the landline kept on the table beside his bed and dialed the number of one of his friends, Naveen Kura, in the Agency.

"Do me a favour," Lucky told his friend. "I need an emergency leave. Dial the Agency and tell them that my mother has taken ill."

"Why?" the friend asked. "Is everything okay?"

The question pierced through Lucky's heart like an arrow. He stumbled in his attempt to give a simple answer to an apparently simple question. His lips trembled, cheeks flushed red and he had almost decided to vent it all out when suddenly his commando instinct took over and he ended up hiding his emotions. His mother, by the grace of God, was fit and fine. Yet Lucky was forced to a point where he had decided to cover the truth with the veil of a lie.

"I'll explain everything later," he told his friend. "For now, just do as I say."

Lucky then got out of his bed and poured himself a glass of water. He took small sips and tried to swallow the rage running fiercely in his veins. Each sip was followed by a long pause during which his eyes were stuck on the telephone in anticipation of a call from the Agency directing him to leave for his home to attend to his supposedly ailing mother. He was in need of the break, especially after what had transpired that day while performing his duty.

Following his stint as PSO of Assam CM, Prafful Kunar Mahanta, Lucky was appointed as the PSO for the politician who was codenamed "Papa Seven Two" by the security agencies. Being a prominent leader of the opposition, the politician was based in Delhi. Though Lucky had always wished to spend some time in Delhi which would allow him to visit some of the famous historical sites, the job of providing security to Papa Seven Two was not a simplc task by any means.

A list of checks and scans had to be carried out before the elderly politician could even step out of his house and get into his car. Starting with donning a 15 kg fighter vest, the next step was to inspect each of the leader's cars, ensuring none of them were riddled with any kind of security threats.

A few times during this period, he began feeling that the top class training he went through was being wasted in performing such duties.

Lucky was given a room in the minister's house for his stay. He was given a logbook in which he was to note down the schedule for the whole week. He would check it once every night before going to sleep so that he could make security arrangements as per the schedule fixed for that day. He had the habit of rising early in the morning to stretch and do some exercise before eating his breakfast. The politician normally wouldn't set out before nine in the morning.

On that night, one of the leader's personal assistants (PA) happened to pass by his room. Lucky had kept his door open and was sitting topless. The blister rashes that he had acquired during a recent training period had caused him great irritation which had compelled him to sleep without a shirt for some comfort.

The PA cast a disapproving glance at him as she crossed the door. Lucky realized that the PA had perhaps taken offense and seen his action of not wearing a shirt while keeping the door open as impertinent. He did not give it much thought once the PA left. Little did he know that the PA would return, pretending to walk by, to check if Lucky was repentant for his "supposed impropriety". But Lucky was engrossed in checking his diary and still hadn't put on a shirt.

Ten hundred hours. Lucky made a note that the politician was going to get out of his home at 10 am. He shut the diary and prepared to go to sleep. No more than five minutes had passed and his landline buzzed with a ring. The PA had called to inform that the politician's schedule for the morning had been revised. Instead of 10 am, Papa Seven Two would be starting at six in the morning. Lucky was surprised. The politician had never before started so early in the day. He said okay and hung up.

He had to miss his breakfast in the morning in order to make everything ready before the minister arrived for his day's trips. In an extraordinary display of expedience, he led the entire operation of checks and scans and brought it to completion 10 minutes earlier than the normal time. Then, carrying the 15 kg weight on his person, which included a couple of heavy weight guns, he stood near the leader's Ambassador car in an attentive position.

Ten minutes turned to 30 minutes which in turn became an hour but there was no sign of the leader. Lucky was hungry and miffed. He thought of slipping into the room for a cup of tea during the long wait. But SOP demanded that the PSO would have to go through the entire procedure of checks and scan all over again in case he stepped away from the vehicles—even for a moment. Lucky dropped the idea. A cup of tea was not worth an hour of additional work.

Three hours later, Papa Seven Two emerged from his house accompanied by his daughter. They went to a cinema hall hosting the premiere of a movie based. The politician's daughter had produced the picture. Several high-ranking officers were also attending the show.

The entire function finished at two in the afternoon after which they headed for the leader's home. Before entering the house, the PA asked Lucky to wait for a few minutes after which they had to visit one of his party colleagues who was admitted to a hospital. Lucky forced a smile on his face. His tummy lurched on account of extreme hunger and five minutes was not sufficient time to get to his room, eat something, get back and get done with all the procedural security checks. He stood next to the car laden with the intolerable weight of his security gear whilst trying hard to suppress the pangs of hunger.

It turned out that the PA had misinformed him once again, as he got out of his house after another three hours, i.e., at five in the evening. Lucky, by this time, had lost his bearings and was feeling like smashing and crushing anything and everything that lay in his way. Nevertheless, he went on with the diplomatic air of calm and civility which he had learnt to muster in such situations. They stayed back at the hospital till 11 in the night. He reached his room at 11:30 after he had dropped the minister at his home—safely.

Lucky unloaded the 15 kg weight by doffing the security gear. Not bothering to change the uniform, he went straight out and sat in his car, seething. The DIG of the police happened to pass by the area and found Lucky sitting in his car with the uniform still on. The DIG engaged in some conversation during which Lucky narrated to him the ordeal which he believed he was deliberately made to go through throughout the day.

As he spoke, Lucky realized that he no longer wanted to work for the government. The kind of experience he had while serving as a PSO to some prominent personalities of the country had made him disillusioned with the system of the country and its polity. His unwavering determination of putting the country and its caretakers before one's life was at the precipice of a total collapse. Lucky grimaced. *I was trained to be a soldier. This was not what I signed up for.*

He decided that he needed to take a break from the PSO duties, go back home and try to drive things in a different direction. He hatched a plan and strode back to his room. Throwing himself on the bed, he picked up the receiver of his landline and dialed his friend in the Agency and provided his mother's fake illness as an excuse for his emergency leave.

Finally, his wait was over. He got a call from the NSG informing him that a reliever will be arriving soon at Papa Seven Two's house and that Lucky should start packing for his trip to his home to attend to his sick mother. The reliever was there within 45 minutes and handing over the charge of duty to him, Lucky bade farewell to Papa Two one's house at 3 am the same night.

And on 25th of August 2011, Lucky boarded the flight from Delhi airport to Uttarakhand, not knowing that his fate was going to change forever in the next few weeks. Soon after he reached home, Agent Lima had taken down Pargai and Amit Arya. And Lucky was arrested as the prime suspect in the case.

thirty-seven

Old Habits Die Hard

December 2014

In the mulaqaat room, Lucky was sitting next to Amit Bhura. The inmates would sit in a line on a long bench made of concrete before they were allowed to go meet the visitors who had come to see them. A few metres away, a man, probably in his late 30s sporting Ray-Ban goggles and dressed up primly was speaking with Mahendra Singh Gwal.

Once the conversation with Gwal was done, the man approached the sitting area and asked Prakash Pandey to make some space so that he could sit. Pandey did not like the tone of his voice. He pointed to the chairs that were lying vacant further ahead and told the man to go and sit there. The man was equally pissed to be told off. He kept insisting that Pandey should move. Lucky hadn't said a word up to this point as he was busy resenting the pompousness in the man's demeanour.

But Amit Bhura could not hold back and intervened at this point. "Start walking off before I break your legs," he said.

"Mannerless bastards," the man scoffed and began moving ahead.

Lucky asked the man to stop. Walking up to him, he took the man's glasses off gingerly and placed it in his pocket. Then he folded his fists and landed a powerful punch on the man's jaw. The man's face swung violently to his right, and a spittle of blood emitted from his mouth. He fell down on the floor.

Mahendra Singh Gwal turned around to see what the commotion was all about. The man was stretched out on the floor. A furious Pandey had mounted on top of him and began throwing punches on the man's face with incredible rapidity. Gwal realized that the same man he had been chatting with a few moments ago was being pummeled. Lucky and Amit Bhura had also joined the party and began punching and kicking the man.

The jail alarm went off. A group of constables rushed to the scene and dived into the fray to tear the inmates away from the man. Lucky, Pandey and Bhura were the last ones to come off the man whose white shirt, soaked in his blood, had turned red. As he was being hauled by the constables, with much difficulty, he turned his head around and yelled that he would take the matter to the highest institutions of law.

"Sure. My next hearing is in 12 days in Nainital court," Lucky scoffed, "let's see what you are capable of."

Then addressing the policemen taking him away, Lucky said, "Better get him out of my sight soon if you don't want to face a Section 303 offense committed in your jail."

Half an hour after the incident, Lucky, Pandey and Amit Bhura were standing in Mahendra Singh Gwal's office. The officer was infuriated by the hooliganism. He cast a fierce glance at Lucky, who was standing with a stooped posture while his two brawl buddies stood as if nothing had ever happened.

"Do you have any idea who that man was?" Gwal roared.

"He's a construction tycoon and an important person in politics."

The revelation did not affect any change in either of the three. Pulling a file out from the pile lying on his desk, Gwal pushed it to the side of the table.

"He's filed an FIR against all three of you," Gwal said. "But he's still willing to accept an apology. The apology will include an undertaking that none of you will put a finger on that person again."

A quick discussion between the three prisoners followed and they agreed to go with the apology. Gwal revealed that the man was a decent civilian who had never allowed himself to participate in such riotous activities.

"Sir, I am sure he hasn't," Lucky said, "but being a decent man he ought to know that the prisoners are a spoiled lot and he shouldn't rub them the wrong way."

"So you consider yourself to be one of them, Laxman, a gangster?" Gwal asked.

"I have been declared as one in the media."

Gwal didn't know what to say. He looked exasperated and sat with his face buried in his hands. He dismissed them by telling them that the apology papers will be sent to their cell which they should send back with their signatures on it. Nothing of this sort had ever happened in his jail in his nine years as the superintendent. But Lucky had taken on an outsider for the sake of the inmates and gained more respect from all prisoners. The bond between Bhura, Pandey and Lucky also grew stronger as the days passed.

One day, Prakash Pandey was taken to the Gujarat court as he had a case against him where he was charged with the murders of a couple of rich diamond traders in Gujarat. He was going to be absent from jail for two days. The same day Amit Bhura was taken to the UP court for his hearing.

Meanwhile, Lucky was on his way to Nainital Court for the trial. When the van was about 80 kms from reaching the Nainital Court, the policemen escorting Lucky started receiving multiple calls from the headquarters which made them visibly flustered. Lucky figured from their horrified faces that something of a very extraordinary proportion had taken place. The van made a U-turn and headed back for the jail. In the night, Lucky saw the entire police department gripped in a kind of cacophony that lent the jail a very baleful appearance.

"Commando bhai," one of the inmates said, "Amit Bhura escaped from police custody! He also snatched three AK-47 rifles from the policemen in the van."

Lucky was astonished. The news spread like wildfire even in the neighbouring states of Haryana, Punjab and Rajasthan. It shook the entire political and judicial system of Uttar Pradesh. Amit Bhura was a dangerous man without a weapon. But with three AK-47s in his possession, which actually belonged to Dehradun Police, he was absolutely lethal.

Amit urf Bhura ("bhura" indicated to his light skin colour) started his criminal career at the age of 16 with a robbery. The nature of robberies grew with his age. In 2002, he was accused of murdering a diamond trader from Gujarat after coming in contact with two gangster brothers, Neetu Kail and Bittu Kail of Muzaffarnagar. Later, the mafia led by Suni Rathi recruited the young man into its fold. He committed at least four more murders in the course of a war that had broken out with one of the rival gangs. He was caught by Delhi Police on February 2nd, 2010, when he was on his way to rob a toll booth. Charged with several cases of murder and robbery, he was thrown inside the jail.

His daring escape made the headlines in all major newspapers. Articles reporting the incident minced no words in slamming the police department for its laxity. Serious questions were raised regarding the security of the state and the nation as the three lethal rifles now lay at the mercy of a hardcore criminal.

The police department of the entire state was in a state of chaos. They had to recover the three AK-47s at any cost; to nab Amit Bhura nudged to second priority on their list. Frantic search operations were carried out throughout the jail. Pandey, as was the same with Lucky, had to lose his expensive (25 thousand rupees) pair of shoes as they were ripped apart during the search operations. A day later, the SP of Haridwar came to visit Lucky in Dehradun Jail. They met in Verma's office.

"I need some answers," the SP said in a crass tone.

Lucky took immediate offense. "Do you have the court's permission, huh?"

Verma stared in horror. He told Lucky to show the man some respect as he was the SP of Haridwar.

"Tell the *respected* SP of Haridwar to seek the permission of the court before asking me any questions," Lucky said and stalked out of Verma's office.

Next day, an order was passed for transferring Prakash Pandey to Haridwar Jail. Sadanand Date, the SP who had done Lucky a favour by giving him a clean chit in an earlier incident, intervened and requested Lucky to help the cops. He extolled Lucky to help the law as he had sworn to do after completing his training. Lucky thought over it and agreed to help. This time the SP of Dehradun came to see Lucky on Date's recommendation.

Lucky was able to tell that the visiting SP was trying to get him emotional by reminding him of his grandfather's martyrdom and his father's selfless service for the nation to elicit a confession. He, nonetheless, assisted him in recovering the weapons keeping in mind the threat the misplaced weapons posed to the security of the nation but chose to remain silent regarding Bhura's whereabouts in honor of the many meals they had had together.

"Conduct a search operation in Santosh Singh's house. You may find what you are looking for," Lucky told the SP.

"He is a powerful politician," the SP said. "No one's going to sign such orders."

"Then search the house of Rombit Shaukeen, the cousin of politician Neeraj Bawana. The rifles will be in your possession within three days."

Lucky rose and started walking out of the office. Suddenly, he turned around and looked at the SP. He wanted a message delivered to Sadanand Date. "Tell Date sir that I've returned his favour. We're square now."

The SP did as told by Lucky and they were able to recover the rifles from Rombit Shaukeen's house. The police department heaved a sigh of relief and regained some of their lost pride.

But how had Lucky come to know of Bhura's plans or the locations where he was planning to hide the weapons? The answer was hidden in the days before Bhura's escape when Bhura and Lucky were jailed in isolation along with Prakash Pandey. Each of them were using Pandey's phone to speak with their friends and acquaintances.

Back then, Lucky had overheard Amit Bhura planning his eventual escape. He had also caught the names of Rombit Shaukeen during one of Amit's conversations on the phone. As soon as he heard the news of Amit's escape, he joined the dots easily and figured out the most likely places where the guns could be found.

Lucky, by choosing to divulge the whereabouts of the weapons and violating the strong bond he shared with the fugitive criminal, had chosen to side with the law this time.

thirty-eight

The "Not So" Ok Hotel Story

On a crucial day of the trial, Devendra, elder brother of Raju Pargai, was going to testify before the court. Lucky walked into the court flanked by a couple of policemen and stepped into the witness box. A sacred scripture was brought before him. Placing his hands upon the scripture, Devendra took an oath that he would speak nothing but the truth before the court.

The prosecution lawyer began the proceedings. He asked Pargai's brother to identify himself to the judge, which Devendra quickly did. Then the lawyer peered into the documents he was carrying in his hands. And then for some reason, instead of reading out of it as usual, he decided to lay out its contents before the court in the form of an interrogation. He walked back to his desk, opened the file lying on top and stuffed the documents inside it. He got back to the witness box. Lucky watched anxiously.

"Mister Devendra," the lawyer said. "Please tell the court what you saw on the night of the murder."

Devendra was a man of average built and unremarkable personality. He possessed features that bore only a faint resemblance to his brother, Raju Pargai. He clearly did not possess the gall required to hold oneself together in such trying situations. His eyes weren't settling at one place, his hands were fidgeting and beads of sweat had already started to appear on his forehead.

"As soon as I stepped near the hotel," he said, "my eyes fell upon a Ford car sprinting across on the highway."

"What was the name of the hotel?"

"OK Hotel."

The lawyer interjected. "And who was sitting in the car?"

"I saw this man," he said, pointing at Lucky. "He was driving the car. Amit Arya was sitting next to him and my brother, Raju, was in the backseat. A Chevrolet car immediately followed the Ford. Four men were seated inside it."

He gave the number of the two cars which he claimed to have noted down from their registration plates. The prosecution lawyer motioned towards the other witness box in which Sanjay and the other three accused stood.

"These are those four occupants of that Chevrolet car?"

The witness nodded and agreed.

"That's all your honour," the lawyer said addressing the judge. "The witness saw the main accused in that same Ford car with the victims in which they were found dead. The other four accused were also seen following the Ford car in their Chevrolet."

He said that the witness' account clearly proves that the main accused, Laxman Bisht aka Lucky, was the last person to be seen with the victims before they were murdered. "He was driving them to their death," the lawyer said. He further claimed that the other four accused had tailed them in their Chevrolet car to finish the job once he had shot them. Hence the bodies of the victims were found in such a horrifyingly mutilated condition.

"Your honour," he said raising his voice, "the accused, Laxman Bisht, is not only a murderer but also a ruthless and apathetic social being. I plead to the court to punish the accused in a manner befitting the monstrosity with which he has murdered Raju Pargai and Amit Arya."

The prosecution lawyer lumbered to his desk and took his seat. Lucky's lawyer had already stood up to proceed with the cross examination. Devendra pulled out a handkerchief from his pocket and wiped his forehead. Lucky's lawyer waved the copy of the FIR he had in his hand.

"Mr Devendra, can you please remind the court of the name of the hotel you had sighted the car around?" Lucky's lawyer asked.

"OK Hotel," Devendra said.

"What were you doing around this OK Hotel?"

Devendra cleared a lump in his throat. "I'd gone there to buy … vegetables."

"There are at least 15 vegetable vendors who stop their carts near your house daily. What made you travel all the way to the OK hotel which is one-and-a-half kilometres from your place?"

Devendra stood as if he had seen a ghost. He gawked at the lawyer for a second or two before answering that Amit Arya's brother had asked to meet him at the hotel. After confirming that the route on which Devendra saw the cars was a National Highway, Lucky's lawyer asked him to recount the entire incident once again. Devendra recited the entire account exactly as he had done during the prosecution. The lawyer inquired if the Ford car belonged to his brother. The witness replied in the negative.

"Can you tell the court the number of the car which must have passed before or after the two cars you noticed?" the lawyer asked.

"I can't," Devendra blurted.

Observing the fact that the site of the alleged sighting was a National Highway, where cars pass at great speed, Lucky's lawyer expressed his astonishment that the witness's eyes fell upon exactly the same car which his client was supposedly occupying alongside Pargai and Arya.

"Pray Mr Devendra," he raised his voice high enough so that the already affrighted Devendra would cower and speak the truth. "What was so special about this car which caught your attention?"

The witness seemed to be at a loss for a response. He took out the handkerchief once again from his pocket and swept it all over his face. Murmurs were heard from the direction where the spectators sat. The judge ordered complete silence and the murmurs died down. Then the judge asked the lawyer to continue.

"What was the time when you saw the car?" the lawyer asked.

"Thirty past seven," said Devendra.

"And when did you file the case?"

"Around seven, the next morning."

"It took you almost *12 hours* to realize that your brother could be in danger as he was seen in the company of my client?"

"I hadn't had any clue at that time."

"I am sure you must have gotten the clue in the 12 hours that passed." He paused. "Did you mention my client's name to the police in the statement which you recorded the next morning?"

"No."

"How curious, your honour!" the lawyer said, raising his voice once again, "this man bore no suspicion towards my client in his statement to the police. And yet, for some strange reason, he is confident now that my client murdered his brother and his sidekick Amit."

The witness was dumbfounded just like witnesses who had preceded him. The lawyer concluded the cross examination by making the closing remarks wherein he requested the court's attention to the glaring inconsistencies in the witness' claims and his statement. He reasserted that, much like the previous witnesses, the present witness too appeared to have been roped into the sinister plan of framing his client in a case that showed clear signs of being mired in a political mess.

The lawyer took his seat. The judge scribbled in her file before putting it away and passing an order for the adjourning of the court. Lucky came back to the jail with a sense of triumph mixed with a hint of sadness. Triumph because this hearing too had been a success as far as he was concerned. Sad because of the fact that all the savings that he had kept for the marriage of his two sisters were being spent in fighting the case. Overtook by this bittersweet emotion, he pondered that although the battle was not yet finished, he could now see a ray of hope after a long spell of darkness.

thirty-nine

Timely Intervention

For the first time in his two-and-a-half years, Lucky was compelled to enter the kitchen in the jail. He stood before a pile of burning coal, took a deep breath and thrust his right hand inside. He held it there long enough to burn the tips of his fingers which would allow him to be exempted from registering for the Aadhar Card.

Aadhar Card is a unique identity proof that grants each resident of India a 12-digit identity number based on their biometric information. The Unique Identification Authority of India (UIDAI), statutory authority established by the GOI in 2009, had started collecting data of the citizens for the purpose of creating the unique Aadhaar IDs which were supposed to be used for availing benefits of government schemes. But critics and privacy watchdogs also alleged that it was a method of the state to track each individual citizen as the Aadhar would be linked to bank accounts, tax returns and even loan applications.

The jail authorities pressed the inmates to submit the information required for creating the ID to the point of compulsion. Lucky was strictly warned by the Agency to refrain from submitting the details as it could be used by the cops to track him once he was out of the jail.

Lucky asked the jail authorities to be allowed to abstain from submitting his details. The authority refused to grant his request. Personnel from UIDAI visited the jails a few times before it was the turn of the inmates from Lucky's cell to be registered. Fingerprints from each hand were necessary for the creation of the Aadhaar ID as it represented the biometric information of the applicant. Seeing no scope for talking his way out of the Aadhar registration, Lucky resorted to the extraordinary measure of rendering his fingers unfit for imprinting by burning his skin off in the pile of burning hot coal!

"What happened to your hand commando bhai?" Baba, a diehard fan of superstar Sanjay Dutt, said.

Baba was imprisoned for making country-made pistols and illegally trading them. But it was his extreme obsession with one of the leading actors of Bollywood, Sanjay Dutt, that earned him notoriety in the jail. His ability to imitate the actor was remarkable. He would walk with the same swagger, his head tilted downwards and shoulders squared. By letting the hair flow long down up to his neck, he carried himself exactly like the *Khalnayak* actor.

"Nothing," Lucky said and tried to change the topic. "When is your next hearing?"

"Tomorrow," Baba said while swaying side to side in his favourite actor's style. "But I don't have enough money to enjoy my day out."

Lucky realized that Baba had come to him in the hope of receiving some money. He took out five hundred rupees from his pocket and put it into Baba's pocket swiftly. Baba's face brightened and Lucky saw him leave in Sanjay Dutt's signature gait.

A day later, Lucky saw him back in the cell and heard that he had been convicted in the case. Lucky approached Baba with the intention of consoling him. Lucky, however, was shocked to see Baba in a curious state of self-contentment and inquired about the source of his unnatural delight despite being convicted.

"Commando bhai, I got convicted alright!" Baba said. "But at the same time, I also managed to screw the policeman who had arrested me."

"How?" Lucky said.

"The pistol they had produced before the judge as the incriminating evidence wasn't copper. So I told the judge that the cops had planted this evidence because I only make and deal in copper pistols."

Two cops were suspended due to Baba's shenanigans. Lucky was about to burst out laughing but he did not want to ruin the joy that Baba was basking in as it could help him spend some days of his term blissfully before realization dawned upon him. Lucky secretly chuckled at Baba's naivety and wondered what a funny character he was. But Baba was not alone when it came to the colourful characters Lucky shared the cell with. There was also the curious case of Ampu.

Thirty-three years of age, Ampu was arrested in the double murder case when he was only 21. He eagerly made friends with Lucky and would look forward to meeting him frequently. Being an SSC pass out at the time of being lodged inside the jail, Ampu was pursuing a graduation from the Dehradun Jail with the aim of securing a job in a factory as soon as he got out. He was expecting a release soon as his family had filed a petition to the governor of the state pleading for an early release after he would complete 14 years of incarceration. One day, he came up to Lucky beaming and happy while holding a piece of broad paper in his hand.

"Look, Commando bhai," he said, handing the paper to him. "I have passed the second year of my graduation."

Lucky took the paper and regarded it carefully. Ampu scurried out of the cell and came back a minute or two later with more marksheets and certificates from earlier years. He was showing them to Lucky with the pride of a student who had topped the class.

"What are you going to do with these certificates?" Lucky asked.

"I will take them to the interviews, get a good job and earn lawfully. I will live my life like a good citizen!"

"Good thought, Ampu," Lucky said. "But there is a slight problem in your plan."

"What problem?" Ampu scowled.

"These certificates say that you earned your degree whilst you were in Dehradun Jail. Who the fuck is going to give you a job with such a degree?!"

Ampu's face lost colour. He whipped the certificates out of Lucky' hands and glanced anxiously at the portion where this was mentioned. Indeed, such a remark was printed at the bottom of each certificate. He was visibly upset. He did not wait for long after the damning revelation as he stomped into the kitchen and flung all the certificates into the flames! Lucky laughed at first but later felt guilty that he had burst Ampu's bubble. Hope was as precious as a diamond in the jail.

That night Lucky's eyes were glazed with tears. The day in the Congo when he had to witness an innocent man being shot in their bid to nab a terrorist of Boko Haram group flashed before his eyes. They had received the information from the intelligence about a terrorist of the wretched group taking shelter in a certain place. They carried out a cordon and search operation (CASO) in the area and nabbed the guy. They put him through relentless torture in a bid to make him speak. But by the time they could learn that the information on the terrorist was flawed and the man they caught was just an ordinary citizen, they had gone too far. The torture inflicted upon the man was too great to have him released, thus allowing him to sue them in the international court. Their doom was certain. Lucky volunteered to take the fall and insisted upon releasing the man. The perplexed army chose not to listen to Lucky and they shot the man dead to dodge the grim repercussions.

He wasn't able to get the terrible scene out of his mind. Each night he would think that his present plight is the punishment of the wrong they had done to an innocent man that day which he was a part of. He closed his eyes tightly, a tear escaped from each eye and he drifted off to sleep.

The day for the next hearing in the trial had arrived. Lucky reached the court only to be informed that his case had been transferred to the Haldwani Court and there will be no hearing that day. It pissed him no end. Each 300 km-long and tiring journey to the jail used to cost him 15 thousand rupees as he had to bear the expenses for food and entertainment of the policemen escorting him so that they would not create any difficulties for him during the trip. Now that Prakash Pandey had already been transferred, Lucky was short of cash which Pandey used to bestow upon him quite generously.

There were only two reasons, he thought, that could have spurred the unceremonious transfer of his case to a different court. Both reasons were centred around the uncompromisable honesty of the lady judge, Meena Tiwary, who had presided over his case at Nainital Court. One, she might have recused herself from the case as she must have been pressured by the powers that be to turn a blind eye to the evidence and announce her verdict in the favour of the prosecution. Second, the powers that be had brought the transfer themselves as they knew that the judge, being an upright person, was bound to give the final verdict in Lucky's favour. Whatever the reason, it did not help to assuage Lucky's rage at the decision. It was only in the wise words of Zora Singh, *"The one who fights until his last breath is never a loser",* in such situations that he used to find solace.

Now that all of Pargai's relatives had testified before the court, Amit Arya's father was due to appear as a witness against the defendant. The change of location did not make any difference to the number of people assembled near the court to catch a glimpse of Lucky Commando. Huge numbers of media personnel and curious onlookers thronged the premises.

The statement of Amit's father in the FIR made a mention of the time since his son was absent from home and the time when he was informed about his son's killing the next morning. Yet he claimed to have known Lucky during his deposition before the court as he had allegedly seen him visiting Amit at their house on the night of the murder. He added that he even heard Lucky telling Amit to get ready to go to Chandigarh.

During cross examination, Lucky's lawyer asked him the reason for the omission of Lucky's mention in his FIR statement if he saw him picking up his son for the alleged trip to Chandigarh. To this he replied that he was shocked at the news of his son's death and was mentally unstable to recollect all the details at the time of filing the FIR.

"How many days were you in shock, Mr Arya?" asked Lucky's Lawyer.

"Around 10 days."

Lucky's lawyer held out his hand in which there was a piece of paper and requested Amit's father to read aloud the date mentioned at the top of the document.

"10th September," he said meekly.

The lawyer snatched the paper back from his hand and proclaimed that the piece of paper contained Arya's second statement in which he had allegedly seen Lucky visiting their house who took his son along allegedly on a trip to Chandigarh.

"Four days after the date of murder, he claims to have seen my client visiting his son. By Mr Arya's own admission, he was mentally unstable for 10 days since the day of the murder. I believe the respected judge can do the simple math and see that such a statement cannot be admissible in the court. The witness is merely parroting the police's version of the story with the intention of maligning my client. That's all, your honour."

The lawyer went back to his place. After declaring that the evidence provided by the witness cannot be deemed eligible due to above stated reasons, the judge announced the dismissal of the court and the date for the next hearing. Lucky by this time had seen and known enough to understand that applying for another bail was going to be an exercise in vain even after what had transpired that day during the hearing. He had run out of patience as well as hope. Therefore, he planned to apply for a 15-day parole.

After smuggling a phone inside the jail, he made relentless calls to his close aides and acquaintances to plan an escape to Nepal once he was let out on parole. The creation of a fake passport for the purpose of crossing the border was underway when he got the news that his application for parole had been rejected as well. He suspected that the Agency had managed to snoop on his calls through some means and thus blocked his parole and his planned escape from the country. His suspicion turned out to be true as a high ranking official from the Agency visited him the very next day.

"One wrong move Lucky," the official said at the end of his lengthy exhortation, "and you'll drown so deep that even we won't be able to pull you out."

He warned him repeatedly to refrain from doing anything

as foolish as crossing the border illegally while carrying a fake passport. Lucky realized that the Agency had stepped in in time and stopped him from ruining his case even further. He accepted the officer's advice with an open heart which also contained suggestions to spend his time in productive activities such as exercise and sports. And thus, he set out to put it into practice as soon as he saw the dawn of the new day.

forty

Bail

March 2015

Unlike the witnesses that had preceded him, those who claimed to have seen Lucky near or about their locality, the next individual to appear before the court was quite a departure from this norm. A key witness—local resident Karan Paneru claimed to have seen Lucky with the two victims on the night of the murder, 40 kms away from Haldwani. He was considered the ace card of the prosecution whom they had saved for the last, waiting to unleash him when the time was right.

Lucky's lawyer had already apprised Lucky of the seriousness of Paneru's deposition in the court. He had opined, and rightly so, that the nature of the statement which Paneru was set to make before the court could open a new doorway for the prosecution, enabling it to spawn more theories and drag the case for another year. Even Lucky wondered how Karan Paneru had got involved with the case. His testimony would hold water with the judge if he did not have any ulterior motive to frame Lucky.

To Lucky, the almost complete lack of information about the man's identity was the biggest problem. Just a random passerby, claiming to have seen him in the car with the two victims that night appeared pretty out of place. Lucky wasn't buying that crap and he rang his friends in the Agency and outside. He asked them to dig out every detail about Karan Paneru and get back to him. ASAP.

They got back with the information four days before the hearing. Paneru turned out to be a friend of Pargai's uncle Jaman who was the first witness to testify against Lucky in the court. The revelation of the man's link to one of Pargai's relatives revealed the motive behind the testimony he was willing to give against Lucky.

Lucky, by this time, had Karan's phone number as well as the phone number of his entire family. He called Karan's brother-in-law, Yogesh. An auto driver by profession, Yogesh was shocked that he had received a call from "Lucky Commando" straight from Dehradun Jail. After invoking the fellowship that he and the other accused shared with him as innocent human beings, he assured him that he hadn't called to threaten him.

"I am not asking you to have Karan speak in my favour in the court," Lucky said. "But he must speak the truth. Understand?"

"Yes, Commando Bhai," Yogesh croaked.

"The moment he starts concocting stories at somebody's behest, I swear I will take out every single one of you," Lucky said. "Not even the *kutta* of your house shall live to tell the tale."

Lucky hung up. The call made the desired impact. Yogesh did not waste a single second before rushing to his wife (Karan's sister) and berating her on her brother's foolhardiness. He told her to ask her brother to take back the statement or be ready to leave the house for the sake of his and his children's safety.

Karan's sister informed Karan about Lucky's call and pleaded with him to not make the mistake of giving false testimony in the court. She made further entreaties by telling him to consider the threat that all of them, including her little children, would come under if he decided to go ahead with the deposition.

Karan contacted Lucky and confessed that he had not seen Lucky with Pargai and Amit that day and that he was going to give false testimony in the court only on the request of his friend Jaman. After having apologized, Karan asked Lucky to help him out of the ugly situation as the prosecution party was equally capable of harming him in case he chose not to appear for the deposition. Lucky called up some contacts outside the town, a few among many he had helped to set up their businesses and told them to make arrangements for Karan's lodging and boarding on his behalf till the time he called them again.

Karan's no-show at court created quite a scandal. His absence baffled the prosecution. After asking the court to delay the hearing a couple of times, the prosecution lawyer finally requested the judge to postpone the date of the hearing. He told the judge that he needed some more time as he hadn't come fully prepared. After bashing the lawyer for wasting the court's time, the judge announced the next day as the date for the next hearing and dismissed the court.

Meanwhile Lucky was finished with all the arrangements needed to escort Karan safely to the court for the hearing the next day. Karan got down from the car disguised as a police constable. Flanked by a couple of Lucky's men, he walked past the prosecution party who stood gaping at him in surprise. In the court he confessed that the statement filed under his name in the FIR is false.

"Why did you give the false statement?" the judge asked.

"There was no statement when I signed the paper presented to me," Karan said. "Inspector Daanu just said that I ought to sign the blank papers to help the police nab the murderer who could become a security threat for the country."

The prosecution lawyer lashed out at the witness and kept on yelling that the witness was lying and turning hostile. The judge directed the lawyer to maintain decorum. The court was adjourned till the date the next witness, Amit's brother, was to appear to testify before the court.

Back in Dehradun Jail, Lucky also came in contact with two of the most notorious gangsters of the state, Shekhar Upreti and Yogesh Rautela. Charged with offenses such as dacoity and murder, the couple had spent almost a decade in the jail now and built a strong network of supporters within the inmates of the jail. They knew that Lucky worked for the Agency and thus looked at him as a proxy for the Agency.

The duo harboured deep hatred for the Agency as they had been supposedly duped by them. The Agency had used them to conduct some of its dirty business and then disposed of them like a use and throw razor. Their involvement in washing the Agency's dirty linen became the reason for their landing up in the jail. Word started doing rounds that the duo was planning an assault on Lucky to extract their revenge from the Agency as Lucky was deemed to be an Agency man.

Lucky made the first move as he got on talking terms with them over the cricket matches they used to play every day. During the course of these conversations, he got first-hand experience of the duo gangsters' extreme hatred for the Agency.

"The Agency is *tezaab*," Upreti said. "Pure acid. They burn anyone they touch."

Lucky thought there was some truth in that. The duo was mad at the Agency for supposedly contracting them secretly to eliminate Dawood Ibrahim in the 2000s but bailing out at the last moment and leaving them in the lurch. Lucky, in order to win them over to his side, chimed that he too had been the victim of the Agency's cunning and was left to fend for himself once put inside the jail.

"So who was the target assigned to you by the Agency?" Rautela asked.

"A certain man in Nepal," Lucky replied, putting up an aggrieved pretense. "But they dumped me nonetheless."

The tactic worked and the duo accepted Lucky as one of their own. They shared plenty of stories with him about their daring adventures in the world of crime. Once getting rid of the threat that the duo had posed, Lucky turned his attention back to the hearing. The next witness in line to testify against him in the court was none other than Amit Arya's younger brother.

An 18-year-old, Amit's brother was comfortable with the world of crime only as much as a fish would be when breathing outside of water. He was never seen picking up even a verbal fight against someone, let alone guns and rifles. Lucky planned to take advantage of this fact. He deliberately asked his men to spread out the word that Lucky had been seeking information about Amit's reclusive brother as he had never seen the fellow. This got Amit's parents worried. They feared for the safety of their son's life as they were well aware that the statements given in the FIR were all untrue.

The plan worked just as Lucky wanted. Amit's brother refused to turn up in the court on the day of the hearing. He sent a message to the court that he was mentally unwell and wasn't fit to appear and testify before the court. The judge struck out his name from the list of witnesses and announced the date when the next witness, a certain Kothari, was supposed to appear before the court. Lucky had, almost single-handedly, shifted the last two hearings in his favour.

Coming back to the jail, Lucky sought to establish a contact with Kothari. Pargai had borrowed the Ford car from Kothari in which he was found dead along with Amit Arya. Lucky obtained Kothari's contact number and dialed him to understand his role in the case. After answering his query, Kothari asked Lucky to excuse him as he wasn't interested in becoming a witness and testify against him in the court. Subsequently he filed a petition in the court requesting to be excused from appearing for the deposition. The court rejected his plea and sent him summons to appear for the hearing on the due date. Kothari had to comply.

During the prosecution, he told the judge that he wasn't related in any way with the case except that Pargai had visited him along with Amit Arya on the evening of the murder to borrow the car on hire from him along with a sum of money.

"How much money?" the prosecution lawyer asked.

"Five lakh eighty thousand, sir," Kothari said.

"What did you lend him so much money for? Pargai must have mentioned something."

"None of my business, sir," Kothari said firmly, "I am a professional lender. I even have the legal receipt of the transaction."

"Are you sure, Mr Kothari? Didn't he mention anything about a trip to Chandigarh with someone?"

"Objection your honour," Lucky's lawyer shot up from his seat. "The prosecution is trying to lead the witness."

"Objection sustained," the judge said.

"Didn't you see this man with Pargai?" the prosecution lawyer asked, pointing to Lucky.

"No sir," said Kothari. "I'm seeing him for the first time."

As the witness had said nothing worthy of cross-questioning, the court was dismissed. And as Kothari was the last witness in the case, the judge also announced the conclusion of the legal proceedings of the case.

"Cases were registered against other accused for threatening witnesses in this case to not give statements," said Balvinder Singh. "But there was no case against Lucky. However, even in the threat case, all the accused were acquitted."

Lucky's lawyer filed a petition for bail. He reasoned that since the trial had come to an end, there was no more possibility of his client harming the witnesses and as such there was no ground to keep him under restraint anymore. The court granted the plea to Laxman Bisht aka Lucky Commando. For the first time since his arrest, Lucky was escorted by policemen out of the jail with no handcuffs on his wrists.

forty-one

Sister's Wedding

As soon as Lucky stepped out on bail, he saw a Scorpio waiting for him outside to drive him home. His father got down from one of the cars and came forward to receive him. Lucky hastened towards his father and bowed at his feet. His father lifted him up by grabbing his shoulders and hugged him. Lucky climbed into the car with moistened eyes. He saw new faces inside the car except for one of his friends who explained to him that the vehicles were sent by Hitender, a business tycoon in Haldwani. Lucky was overwhelmed.

A surge of inexplicable emotions and thoughts rushed through his mind as soon as he reflected upon the fact that he was going to step inside his house, free and unfettered, for the first time in three years. He was going to meet his two sisters and more importantly, his mother; the same inconsolable mother whom he had promised that he'd be back soon while he slipped his feet inside his flip flops to follow the policemen who had come to arrest him three years ago. He was feeling a little less cheerful as he had dearly wished to take gifts for each one of them at home. But he was down to only 610 rupees in his bank account.

It took seven hours to reach home. As soon as Lucky got out of the car, one of Hitender's men came up to him and offered one lakh rupees sent by Hitender. Lucky refused to take it at first. The man called Hitender asked Lucky to keep the money as he must be in need of cash. After insisting a couple of times, Hitender told Lucky to treat it as a debt and return it as and when he found it easy to do so. No man who was running as dry as only 610 rupees in his bank account could resist such an offer. Lucky took the money and thanked Hitender for the support.

Evening, 9 pm. It had only been a day since Lucky was home and he hadn't even got used to the home-cooked food again. He was suffering from bouts of indigestion. While he was sitting with his father in the room, the landline buzzed. His father waved at him to relax and got up to receive the call.

"Hello." The voice was brassy and inane. "I am calling from the Agency's office. May I speak with Mr Laxman?"

Lucky's father gestured to Lucky to take the call. "Agency," he breathed in Lucky's ear as he came and stood next to the phone. Lucky returned an annoyed look and took the receiver.

"Laxman Bisht," the caller said, "you are required to report to the Agency's office in Delhi in the next 24 hours."

"But sir, it has hardly been a day since I got back home." Tinges of frustration were evident in Lucky's voice. "Please grant me a week's time at least."

"Orders are orders, Lucky. We'll be waiting for you. Tomorrow."

The caller hung up. Lucky's frustration peaked when he placed the handset back on the receiver and asked his father to say that he's not at home if they got calls from the Agency in future. The court had apparently informed the Agency of Lucky's bail as soon as the order had been passed.

But Lucky abhorred the idea of going back to the Agency.

He was disillusioned with the system as well as the Agency, both of whom had considerably fallen short in recompensing him for what he had done for the country. The authorities had chosen to disassociate themselves from him in the last three years. All this had made him sore and bitter. Moreover, he wanted to stay back home so that he could give his undivided attention to the case till the remaining hearings were done and he could be cleared of all charges. For the time being, he decided he wasn't going to report to the Agency. That was final.

Summons from the Agency for Lucky kept pouring in the days that followed to the District Magistrate's (DM) office. The DM would pass it down to the SSP who in turn would forward it to the local kotwali. Six to seven policemen from the local police station would then visit Lucky's place for the formality of passing the summons to him and reminding him that he was supposed to comply. But Lucky played smart here as well. The cops kept returning to the police station with their pockets full of gifts which Lucky bestowed upon them. They would pass the message to the DM's office that they didn't find Lucky at home!

All of that wasn't going to distract Lucky from conducting his sister's wedding, which was round the corner those days, with much pomp and glitter.

The house was covered in layers of ornate draping that bore intricate designs which were dotted with twinkling lights. Huge processions of guests were seen filing in and out of the house in the days leading to the wedding. Elabourate feasts, pre-wedding functions and ceremonies based on traditional beliefs and practices were held. Far from laying low, Lucky fared forth in the open, sending a clear message to the Agency as well as the state government that he was going to enjoy his much deserved release on the terms he thought fit.

13th December 2015

The day of the wedding. Lucky was dressed in a glamorous kurta salwar suit and a pair of traditional mojdis. The fact that the crowd turned up for the wedding consisted of an equal number of guests as well as officials from the police and LIU (Local Intelligence Unit) did not escape his wary eyes. The wedding was also attended by prominent local politicians and businessmen. He got out of the house to join the procession which was supposed to accompany the bride to the wedding hall amidst raucous beating of drums and melodic tunes of shehnai. Small boys would light firecrackers every now and then and quickly retreat, giving a wide berth so as to watch the cracker burst just before the procession trod the path.

Just when he was about to get into the crowd and join the party, his phone began vibrating in his pocket. He stopped, fished out the phone and saw an unknown number with Nepal's country code flashing on his screen. He picked up the call. A pyrotechnic rocket shot up in the air and burst after gaining a certain elevation, filling the sky with streaks of luminous rays of light.

"Hello," Lucky said. The noise coming from the procession filled with overzealous participants and the relentless beating drums seemed to make it difficult for Lucky to listen to the voice coming from the other end. "Hello?"

"Laxman, I have called you on behalf of Nana," the caller said in a grim tone. "Join our gang. And congratulations on your sister's wedding."

Lucky was furious. The man being referred to as Nana was none other than underworld don Chhota Rajan. But the veiled threat made Lucky lose his temper. They'd mentioned his family and he wasn't going to take this even if it came from the man who gave Dawood Ibrahim a run for his money.

"Listen you shitbag," Lucky bellowed, "I'll rip your heart out and eat it raw if you dare to put a finger on my family. Now just shut your filthy mouth and get back to licking your master's feet."

Lucky ended the call and scuttled to catch up with the procession. He weaved his way into the gathering with the ease of a man who hadn't received a threatening call from one of the most dreadful dons of the country a mere couple of minutes before.

He did not talk about the phone call to anyone. But that did not keep it from making into the headlines of the next day's newspapers. Lucky got visited by a couple of police personnel who offered to provide him security against the caller if he wished. Lucky told them clearly that he didn't need protection against puny gangsters. And with that he got back to preparing for the next hearing in which the court was going to hear the forensic expert's testimony.

forty-two

Guilty Or Not Guilty?

Lucky was accompanied to the court by his father. In spite of the living hell that he was made to go through when he was first arrested, he had been successful in pulling the wool in the forensic expert's eyes on the second day of his unofficial arrest. He was going to hold back and let things unfold on their own when the expert would give his statement in the court. It had taken him a lot of cunning and fortitude to trap the forensic person and the police department in the ploy he had crafted. Today was the time to reap the fruits of that labour.

Lucky got into the witness box as usual. The courtroom was teeming with people and curious lawyers who awaited the witness' arrival with bated breath.

The forensic expert stepped into the witness box amidst the relentless murmuring and chattering of the crowd. The judge asked for complete silence while the witness took the black rimmed spectacles out of his shirt's pocket and put them on. His action reminded Lucky of the moment when Lucky had dictated the fake phone number to him. After noting it down, the forensic expert had put those specs in his pocket with the air of an extremely pleased person and walked out of that dingy torture room. At the time, he had no clue of Lucky's intentions.

Now, the expert had been called by the defense to testify. This move had flummoxed even the prosecution. Nobody, except Lucky and his lawyer knew that Lucky had already trapped the forensic expert in his trap during their earlier meeting.

Lucky's lawyer came up to the witness and asked him to identify himself. After identifying himself as Dr Dayal Sharan, the fingerprint expert in the case, the witness was asked by the lawyer to reproduce his statements to the police.

Dayal said that he was called upon by the Investigating Officer (IO) Vijay Chaudhary to the murder site on September 6th, 2011. Upon reaching the spot, he saw two badly mutilated bodies stretched out in the backseat of a Ford car. He collected the necessary evidence, oversaw its proper sealing in the plastic bags and took leave.

"The following day," Dayal said, "the IO asked me to come to the Bhowali Police Station to collect the hand and foot prints of the prime accused in the case." He paused. "I reached the police station and collected the hand and foot prints of Mr Laxman Bisht, signed the documents and left."

"That's all, your honour," Lucky's lawyer said and took his seat.

The prosecution lawyer was confused. Where was this heading? All of it was going to be unveiled soon. With clouded judgment, the prosecution lawyer said that he didn't need to cross-examine this witness. The judge asked Dr Dayal Sharan to be present on the day of the next hearing as well at the request of the defense.

The next and last and perhaps the most important hearing was that of the Investigation Officer (IO), Inspector Vijay Chaudhary. Inspector Vijay got into the witness box as did Lucky and both exchanged hostile glances. The prosecution lawyer asked Vijay

Chaudhary to narrate events that transpired on the day of the murder.

Vijay Chaudhary said that after discovering the bodies of the two gangsters, he initiated an enquiry and sent a word to his informants to apprise him with anything they knew about the murder. It wasn't long before Jaman, Pargai's Uncle, came forward to submit his statement to the police that he had seen Laxman Bisht with his nephew and Amit on the night before the murder and that he strongly believed that it was him who had killed them.

Inspector Chaudhary reached Lucky's place immediately to take him into custody. But when he didn't find him home, he got a tip-off that Lucky was at large and was planning to escape to Nepal to evade arrest. "We quickly got into action," Chaudhary said, "and were able to seize Lucky at Bhakra Nangal Forest on the 8th of September along with a shotgun and a pistol which were found on his person."

Vijay Chaudhary concluded his statement and the prosecution lawyer returned to his place. Lucky's lawyer came forward for the cross-examination. He tottered to the witness box. With a wide grin, he turned his attention from Vijay Chaudhary to Dayal, the forensic expert.

"Mr Dayal, please remind the court of the date on which you collected the fingerprints of my client while he was in the police custody."

"That was the 7th of September," Dayal said.

The lawyer turned back to the witness, the grin still spread on his face. He asked, "Mr Vijay Chaudhary, when did you arrest my client? Please repeat the date for the benefit of the court."

Chaudhary's face blanched. A faint smile appeared on Lucky's face. It was for exactly this moment that he had led the police on a false weapon trail for nearly two days after he had duped the forensic expert to sign the official papers bearing the date of 7th of September.

"8th of September," Vijay Chaudhary said in a quavering voice.

The lawyer sniggered. The spectators watched bemused at the glaring hilarity of it all and several of them were even seen tittering.

"How is it possible Mr Chaudhary?" the lawyer asked. "The forensic papers say that Dr Dayal took my client's fingerprints on the 7th while according to you he was arrested on the 8th?"

Vijay Chaudhary stood there without saying anything.

"This proves your honour," the lawyer continued, "that either Mr Chaudhary is not speaking the truth or my client was illegally detained for one full day before the police decided to initiate an official inquiry. Doesn't matter which one, but either fact is enough to put the whole investigation by the police under serious suspicion."

Indian law mandates that a person should be presented before a judicial authority within 24 hours of his arrest. The IO had not followed such procedure and resorted to fudging the records to cover his tracks. The IO had shot himself in the foot as Lucky's lawyer gestured "that's all" to the judge and waddled back to his seat.

Successful in baiting the fingerprint expert to sign the collection samples with the date of 7th September, Lucky took almost the entire police department on a wild goose chase in pursuit of weapons that didn't exist for the entirety of the following day. Thus, eluding the presentation in the court within the 24 hours of the forensic expert signing the official papers. Vijay Chaudhary was left with no choice but to present Lucky in court on the day they returned from their trip—9th September. And, in order to cover the illegal arrest, the inspector marked the date of arrest from 24 hours before the presentation, i.e., 8th of September!

A few days later, the two lawyers were supposed to deliver a final closing statement before the judge. After the prosecution lawyer had delivered his closing statement, Lucky's lawyer came out in the middle.

After repeating that the accounts given by the witnesses were all riddled with gross contradictions and clear discrepancies, the defense lawyer went on to draw the court's attention to the fact that his client could have gained nothing by getting his hands dirtied in the petty gang wars.

"My client," the lawyer said, "is a respected soldier who has many accomplishments to his record. A person of such a stature has no need to participate in a petty gang war."

The lawyer also reiterated that Lucky's acquaintance with Sanjay (the co-accused) was on account of being neighbours and he barely knew the other three. There was no sense in assuming that Lucky would go out of his way to kill the murderer of Yogesh Sunehri, Sanjay's gang leader, on Sanjay's behalf, for the sake of such an ordinary relationship.

"All the witnesses who came forward to testify against my client," the lawyer said, "were the relatives of the deceased persons who seemed to have been planted by the prosecution. Your honour, there is not a single evidence the prosecution has produced to prove unambiguously that my client is guilty of the crime."

"Objection, your honor," the prosecution lawyer rose from his place. "My dear colleague is forgetting about the holster that was recovered from the site of the crime."

"And is my dear colleague also forgetting that the holster does not bear the identity of its owner?" Lucky's lawyer said. "Two or more persons can have holsters that look alike. I am amazed that the prosecution lawyer reckons an ordinary and common holster found at the crime site as proof of something."

"Why does the defendant lawyer not say anything about the cartridge found at the site of the murder?"

"Your honour," Lucky's lawyer said, "here is the report from the prestigious Chandigarh Forensic Labouratory where the cartridge along with my client's pistol was sent for the testing." He paused. "The lab has concluded that the cartridge belonged to a different pistol from the one submitted with it."

"What about the forensic expert's report then?" the prosecution lawyer asked. "It says Mr Laxman's pistol was found to be last fired not long before the day of his arrest."

Lucky's lawyer smiled. "I have a car which I rarely take out due to increasing traffic and congested roads. It remains parked in the parking lot most of the time. So will you please help me figure out when was the last time I took my car out for a drive?"

The prosecution lawyer stared in confusion. "How can I tell that?"

"By looking at its odometer," the defendant lawyer said coyly.

"That's ridiculous!"

"Exactly." Lucky's lawyer shuffled to address the judge. "Your honour, just as one cannot tell the last time the car was driven by looking at its odometer, one cannot tell exactly when the pistol was last fired on the basis of a report that simply says it was fired *recently*. It could have been fired a day before, two days before or as far back as one week."

In retrospect, several people associated with the investigation believed that the gun handed over by Lucky to the police station was his service revolver, but the weapon used by Lucky to kill Pargai and Arya was a different weapon. Hence, they were not able to piece this together about the weapon being used by Lucky.

But at the time, the contention was met with complete silence. The opposition lawyer looked as if he was struggling to find a response and after trying in vain to come up with one, he crashed into his chair and sat there resignedly. The judge drew his file close and after a moment's scribbling, he announced the adjournment of the court and proclaimed that the judgment would be reserved until next week, i.e., 6th of March.

6th March 2018

The court was turned into a fortress and surrounded by a huge number of policemen clad in riot gear and wielding AK-47 rifles. The area abutting the court premises was cordoned off. The streets were deserted and no one was seen wandering about except the police vehicles that kept patrolling the area. The authorities feared that riots would break out in case the decision went against Lucky. The curious crowd of locals however thronged the area outside the restricted zone in thousands.

Lucky reached the court in a procession with 150 men consisting of his friends and well-wishers. Two cars drove in the front, both driven by Lucky's men from Nepal. He had come prepared to escape to Nepal in case the judge announced the verdict against him. He would rather escape, or even die in the attempt rather than go back to jail.

The procession came streaming towards the court but wasn't allowed to continue after a certain point. The policemen standing guard only let the four accused cross the demarcated point. Media personnel flocked outside the cordon.

Cops from nearby districts were called to ensure tight security outside Haldwani Court where around 1000-1500 people had already gathered from the morning. From 11:30 pm onwards, there was a curfew-like situation in the town. In fact, Pargai's family members—Jaman Singh and Ratan Singh—who had come to court, were picked up by the cops and dropped back at their residence. Cops were deployed at their residence to prevent them from moving out.

Lucky and the four accused were led by five policemen. The judge entered the courtroom, opened the file and was seen signing on some papers before raising his head and looking at Lucky and the other accused. Lucky looked back with a mingled expression of hope.

"All the five accused are acquitted," the judge said in a single breath.

Lucky heaved a huge sigh, his eyes welling with tears. He grabbed the wooden railing of the witness box and cried with joy while his nose flared with years of pent-up frustration. Lucky's lawyer also pumped his fist and gave a thumbs-up sign to Lucky. Soon the news spread and the entire city broke into celebration. Scenes of people bursting crackers, frolicking and shouting slogans were witnessed throughout the city and especially in Lucky's town.

"The order was pronounced at around 4:45 pm. But the media and supporters of Pargai and Lucky were thronging the court since morning," said Balvinder Singh, Lucky's lawyer. "There was a buzz that Lucky would be convicted. No one knew he'd got acquitted because only the lawyers and the five accused were allowed in the court. Then we came out and gave the information to the media."

Lucky was given a grand welcome when he got back home from the court. His mother stood near the doorstep. She hugged him as he got there, performed prayers and blessed him before allowing him to enter the house. On 6th March 2018, Lucky stepped into his house once again—as a free man.

The following day he was seen strolling the street across from Ashmita's house, an exercise that would become a part of his daily routine for the next couple of months. He wanted to share the joy of being given an acquittal, the joy of being cleared of all the heinous allegations that made her end the relationship with him. After trying in vain to catch a glimpse of her from across the apartment, he would make his way towards her house. But as soon as he would get near the house, his feet would freeze and he would stand, staring at the building blankly. The vicious memory of the day when she asked him to stay out of her life would attack his heart like a sharp sword and he would turn back and return to his home.

Even after Lucky was acquitted, Pargai's family maintained the animosity against him. They wanted to avenge Pargai's death. One day, after conducting a recce, they ended up at his house just as Lucky was about to step out of his house as per his regular schedule. They knocked at his door but Lucky did not entertain them. Eventually Lucky had to call cops and ensure that the mob from Pargai's gang was taken away.

"Ever since, I noticed that Lucky was skeptical of walking in smaller lanes. He would always prefer meeting someone on main roads," said Bhupinder Rawat, a journalist.

forty-three

Once a Soldier, Always a Soldier

Now that he was acquitted and cleared of all charges, Lucky's lawyer informed him that he could get his weapons, a shotgun and a pistol, released from the police. But Lucky did not seem to be in a hurry to get his weapons released. Not this soon, he thought. Similar to the news of his bail, it took no time for the news of his acquittal to reach the Agency. He kept getting summons which he kept ignoring until 16th July when one of his juniors informed him that the Agency was preparing to pick him up from his home.

The Agency had obtained the permissions from the Defence Ministry as well as the Home Ministry required to legally pick him up from his house. Lucky fled and remained absconding for two days from his home. He showed up at the Manipur camp of the Agency on the third day. The Agency got into action as soon as they came to know of Lucky's arrival in Manipur and it immediately set a "court of enquiry" against Lucky into motion.

Several charges were pressed against Lucky on account of his absence from the Agency after he got out on bail. Lucky chose to represent himself at the court of enquiry instead of using the services of a lawyer from the legal branch of the military. Lucky had come under attack of several allegations where he had to prove his innocence yet again.

The Agency officials in Manipur got a call from their counterparts in Delhi who instructed them to keep an eye on Lucky and make sure that he didn't give them a slip this time. Lucky spent his days in Manipur refusing to work and asking for an audience with the Brigadier as he intended to resign from the Agency.

Several days passed during which he wasn't granted his request of meeting the brigadier. Equally stubborn, Lucky continued to refuse to go back to work. Lucky was becoming increasingly resentful. One of these days he got rid of his shoelaces, belt and lanyard and told his senior to allow him to meet the brigadier as he wasn't carrying anything on him from which the brigadier would fear getting harmed. The senior did not respond as he knew that Lucky was seething and he was simply trying to mock the Agency and its senior members.

Meanwhile the arrangements were made and Lucky was brought to the court to face the trial. The proceedings began in the presence of several high-ranking officers including the brigadier while the colonel of Indian Army, Manoj Mishra, led the hearing. The grilling began.

"Mr Laxman Bisht," Manoj Mishra said, "What can possibly explain your absence from the Agency even after getting bail?"

"That was just bail, sir," Lucky said, "I was still supposed to continue fighting the case till I got an acquittal."

"You could have done that while returning to the Agency."

"Easier said than done, sir. The case took strange twists and turns after almost each hearing. A small oversight and the case would have slipped out of my hand irreversibly."

"The Agency could have posted you close to Haldwani."

"That would have saved me the physical exertion, but what

about the mental aspect of it? Besides, I had seen enough in the last three years to know that the Agency did not care whether I won or lost the case. Even if it did, it certainly did not enjoy enough authority to influence the judgment of the court in case it was going to be ruled against me."

Manoj Mishra froze with a tactical glare. He was amazed at Lucky's temerity to lash out at the Agency without any efforts at caring to weigh words.

"Alright, Mr Bisht," Manoj Mishra said, "why didn't you report even after getting the acquittal. Why?"

"My weapons were in the custody of the police. I was waiting to have my weapons released before reporting to the Agency."

Lucky was trying to build alibis and that was the reason he had delayed collecting his weapons. The proceedings went on for a while along the same lines. Nine months later, when the trial was nearing its end and Lucky had put forth compelling arguments in his defense, Colonel Mishra went through Lucky's records in the files. But his record only showed him as one of the distinguished Agency personnel who was the recipient of numerous recognition and accolades by the Agency as well as the government.

Finally, the allegations were lifted and the Agency restored to him all the honour and accreditation he had earned in the 15 years of his long career. He again expressed his desire to meet the brigadier to ask for a voluntary retirement and quit the Agency. No Agency personnel can ask for a voluntary retirement before he has completed 10 years and 55 days of service in the Agency. Lucky had exceeded that term by nearly five years, that too with an impressive track record. The Agency was finding it difficult in getting him to drop the idea of quitting.

He spent his time in Manipur keeping off from work and constantly asking to be granted an early retirement. Colonel Mishra used to visit him from time to time to convince him to get the idea of resignation out of his mind and serve the Agency and the nation for as long as he could. The Agency did not want to lose a commando of his caliber and they did everything in their power to try and retain him. But try as they might, an embittered Lucky just wasn't in a mood to make any reconciliation.

The Agency had to give in at last. On 23rd February 2019, keeping in mind his impeccable track record, the Agency decided to serve him a "compulsory retirement of service" letter as there were no grounds on which they could justify his termination and serve him a permanent suspension. The serving of such a retirement meant that he could rejoin the Agency if he wished to do so at any time in the future and he will be paid the entire salary of the interim period as soon as he rejoined.

But it also had a downside as the person served with compulsory retirement of service was not eligible to receive pension. Lucky did not mind losing the pension as he was keen on walking out. He consented, fulfilled the necessary formalities and resigned from the Agency at last. The separation of Lucky from the organization he had served was on a partially good note as the Agency kept inviting him to their regimental parties. Getting back to his town, he made a general announcement that if anyone faced any kind of harassment, demand for extortion or land grabbing under his name then such a person should register a complaint against the offender in the local police station. He reminded his people that he was a commando, not a gangster.

In one such party in the later years, Lucky was seated with his former colleagues, each clad in splendid partywear. It had been a few years since his resignation. Lucky was chilling with his colleagues and seniors when he felt a hand on his shoulder. He turned around to see that it was Colonel Manoj Mishra.

"So, Lucky," he said, "the Agency has identified the location of a high-value target. We are launching an operation soon." He paused in anticipation of getting a certain reaction but he wasn't getting one. Lucky stood there swirling the drink in his glass nonchalantly while appearing to listen with due diligence.

"But you want to be a civilian for the rest of your life, yes?" the colonel said.

"Yes sir," Lucky said. "But once a soldier, always a soldier."

Colonel Mishra put his arm around Lucky. After all the hell he had been through, only time would tell if the commando was ready to execute a top-secret mission for the Agency. Right now, Laxman Bisht aka Lucky was only smiling in the knowledge of something that few except him knew.

—THE END—

Acknowledgements

Pursuing a story comes naturally to someone who has been an investigative journalist for more than two-and-a-half decades of his professional career. I have investigated and written about terror attacks, crime syndicates and mafia bosses, where breaking barriers and digging information is a daunting task. But seldom has a story pursued me with such doggedness, with all its complications and questions and nuances. The story of Laxman Singh Bisht is such, and posed many challenges before leaving an indelible mark on my imagination.

This was a totally unfamiliar thread of a narrative and a peep into the psyche of a man who is cold-blooded as a robot, whose physical skills were at par with the world's best commandos, whose survival instincts cannot be described by a layperson like me. And then, this patriot was accused of murder, he was jailed and he even gained the notoriety of a don, a bahubali in the hilly regions of Uttarakhand.

The seeds of this book were sown in the most interesting manner. Since the time I stopped reporting in the print media, I thought I should narrate different kinds of stories on my YouTube channel. For one of those videos, I wanted to interview Laxman Singh Bisht alias Lucky whom I had known for more than two years. He was introduced to me through one of his associates. Amongst all the people that I have met, Lucky did not even get a fraction of attention from me. So whenever I was told about the exploits of Lucky Commando, I thought his friends were talking about someone else who was not present in the same room.

But after a few meetings, I was told that he's the guy, the R&AW agent, he's Lucky commando. I sized him up from top to bottom. Really? He's the guy? *Are they taking me for a ride?*

I thought maybe I could interview him for my YouTube channel and listen to his story. I interviewed him for 45 minutes and found that he had a fantastic, fascinating and gripping story, which kept me riveted throughout.

For me, Lucky was just one of those stories that I've done for the YouTube channel. But Lucky overstepped. He spoke to a couple of journalists and gave them a perception that I am doing a book on his story which was totally unimaginable for me. At that time, I was very upset with Lucky that he should not have planted those stories. It was very unethical of him to try and convert one interview into a book. But then I started getting calls from some journalists and some director friends and also a producer friend who said that he is interested in buying the rights of the book. That was the moment of epiphany for me.

I had never thought highly of Lucky until that time. For me, it was an interesting story but I didn't know that Bollywood or my audience, always looking for fresh content, would really latch on to this interview. The viewership of my YouTube channel and of this particular story was growing by leaps and bounds. Since then, Lucky's video on my channel has racked more than one million views.

Perhaps, people wanted to experience a different story like Lucky's. So I started writing but had no publisher locked for this book. I started pitching the story to various publishers. Simon and Schuster was the keenest amongst all and they were also eager to publish the book. I must thank my publishers at Simon and

Schuster India; and Sayantan Ghosh for being such an encouraging editor. This book has been one of most expeditiously written in the three decades of my writing career. Sayantan was rock solid and showed incredible patience with me.

This story would not have been as interesting and gripping if Lucky would not have spent hours narrating it with the kind of skill and devotion which I'm sure he must have exhibited when he was practicing in Israel for his commando training. Lucky's passion and dedication towards his work was clearly manifested.

I must reserve a mountain of gratitude and an ocean of thankfulness for all my colleagues who worked on this book. Without their cooperation and indefatigable diligence, this book wouldn't have been completed and finished as per the schedule.

The efforts of Kashif Mashaikh stand out extraordinarily. He has been a fabulous editor and totally indispensable on this project. Had he not been there, I would not have seen the completion of this story and the publication of the book under a tight deadline. We debated on several aspects. Kashif also behaved like my alter ego. At times, there was disagreement, dissent and even reservation on several issues which I would say was extremely valuable for the book. Through our discussions and debates, we figured out the best solutions in the interest of the story.

I would extend my gratitude and my thanks to others who were equally helpful on this project. I discovered Zaid Khan during this journey. He had worked with Kashif on some earlier projects. During this project, Zaid was immensely dedicated. I found him to be a promising young man. I also realized that the man can do much better. Perhaps, he had never come across a good trainer or someone who could encourage him to become a better writer. Kashif did plenty of hand-holding with Zaid and he has grown professionally while working on this project.

After finishing the first draft of the manuscript and looking at the research work accomplished till then, I realized there were some gaps and blanks that needed to be filled and a trip to Haldwani was inevitable. I turned to my most dependable researcher Yesha Kotak for the challenge. Yesha is a young and superbly resourceful reporter who I have seen growing from print to television and becoming seasoned in her legwork. She has been a part of the team since my *Byculla to Bangkok* days. For the many risky assignments she has done for me, I feel that she's almost bulletproof. She has interviewed so many dangerous gangsters, like Ashwin Naik, and returned unharmed and unhurt. So once again, I assigned the task to Yesha.

She is now a journalist with CNN-News18 and she traveled to Haldwani and interviewed scores of people in a span of two days. Some of them were cops, some of them were very suspicious people but she came back and filled all the gaps in the narrative. It was because of her accurate reporting skills that we managed to verify many facts and add authenticity to the story.

Nevertheless, the task of capturing the essence of the book is left to a designer who can encapsulate it through his imaginative skills on the cover. Mohsin Rizvi has relocated to London and has been a successful entrepreneur par excellence. Despite all his preoccupations, I asked him to design the cover as I felt that he is the one who can do justice to the task. Mohsin got down to creating a marvel that you now hold in your hand with the magnificent cover. Thanks, Beta.

I would end this note with my extreme thankfulness to Mr Neeraj Kumar, the former Commissioner of Police, New Delhi. He has been a friend, colleague, philosopher and my thinking pad. Neeraj Kumar has been a treasure of wisdom, insights and those unknown nuggets of intelligence which not many people would be aware of. Mr Kumar was someone who, as a police officer, put rationale, balance and intellectual equilibrium into the story with his insights. I have loved his analysis though he had questioned Lucky's credibility at a few places. Without taking any offense, his foreword is a part of the book so that the readers can see a top cop's perspective of this story.

I have managed to gather documentary and photographic evidence to be convinced of the story of Laxman Singh Bisht. But at the end of the day, I am a journalist, a reporter who is only reporting the facts without being judgmental. There might be people who are not very convinced by Lucky's story and they might think that perhaps he is exaggerating some details. I think the judgment is their own.

In the end, for all the accuracies in the story, I would credit Lucky Singh Bisht, Kashif Mashaikh, Zaid Khan and Yesha Kotak. If there are any oversights, those will be totally mine for which I take full responsibility.

Finally, I am profoundly and immensely grateful to my wife Velly Thevar. My journey of journalism began with her. She has been my fiercest critic and strongest ally, but most importantly, she has always remained by my side.